UNTIL
Thanksgiving

Michael Rupured

To Janet,
Lord only knows the stories we'd tell now if we'd run around together in our late teens and twenties. That we didn't is probably for the best! Thanks for all your encouragement and support with this writing gig, and for being my friend.
Love,
Michael Rupured
12/28/2012

Dreamspinner Press

Published by
Dreamspinner Press
5032 Capital Circle SW
Ste 2, PMB# 279
Tallahassee, FL 32305-7886
USA
http://www.dreamspinnerpress.com/

Until Thanksgiving

Cover Art by Brian R. Williams
brianrwilliams.com

ISBN: 978-1-62380-240-0

Printed in the United States of America
First Edition
December 2012

eBook edition available
eBook ISBN: 978-1-62380-241-7

Dedicated to Aunt Toodles and The Robot Unicorn Cult

• ACKNOWLEDGMENTS •

MY FIRST novel would not have been possible without the encouragement and support of a great many people. Thanks to my parents for not messing me up too much and to my sister, my many aunts, uncles, and cousins for loving me just the way I am and teaching me the value of a sense of humor. Thanks, especially, to my Aunt Toodles, who made me promise on her deathbed that I would write a book. This isn't the book she wanted me to write, but I know she'd still be tickled pink. My father passed away two weeks before Dreamspinner Press offered me a contract for this book. I hope he would be proud. My mother is very proud and horrified that I'm using my real name—a fact that won't change when she finally gets a chance to read it.

A special thanks to Andy Davis for being my rock for the past twelve years and for his selfless support of my writing career no matter how much it cut into our time together.

Thanks to many, many excellent teachers over the years, including Maxine Littrell, the elementary school librarian who inspired my love of reading; Pat Scully, my junior high English teacher who was the first to suggest that maybe I had a gift for writing; and Judy Downey, Janice Highland, Susan Stiles, and Helen Cooke—all high school English teachers who made a big impression on me and my writing style.

I never would have tried to write a book without the encouragement and support of my good friends Terri Clark, Pam Blevins, and Susan Comisky. I'm especially grateful for the education I received about how to write a novel from the Athens Writers Group (aka the Robot Unicorn Cult): Amy Severson, Ed Wyrick, Sam Barnum, Misty Hawkins, Adrienne Wilder, Kaitlin Bevis, and Stephen Morgan. And of course, thanks to the folks at Dreamspinner Press for making my dream of becoming a published author come true.

• 1 •

JOSH FREEMAN left the Bar Complex well before last call. Except for the hustlers that prowled the streets behind Lexington's one and only gay bar, nobody noticed him leaving. A rough-looking kid in a tank top and jeans sized him up and walked toward him.

"Looking for some company?"

"No, thanks." Josh kept walking. The gravel crunching under his Justin Ropers didn't cover the laughter the boy got from the other hustlers. Josh wasn't hard up enough to pay for sex. Yet. The cold shoulders at the bar had been bad enough.

He unlocked his red Toyota Celica. Gay life in Lexington, Kentucky, had changed. The bar crowd that evening was nothing like the good old days, when the place overflowed with good-looking, readily available men—before AIDS and the siren call of gay meccas like Atlanta, San Francisco, and New York. That school was out for the summer didn't help. The class of '97 had moved on, and the class of 2001 hadn't yet come to town.

Going to the Bar had been a mistake. Josh hadn't talked to anyone and nobody had talked to him. He wasn't surprised. Unless he needed help crossing the street or had fallen and couldn't get up, the college boys shaking their stuff on the dance floor had no cause to talk to him.

He started the car and headed to Jerry's Restaurant for a late-night snack, smoking the rest of the joint he'd left in the ashtray. Smoking pot kept him from feeling so lonely. These days, he smoked so much he didn't really feel anything.

"Table for one?" asked the waitress, chomping her gum and tugging on a severely strained bra strap.

"Table for one" sounded like a life sentence. Absent enough money to justify the sugar daddy label, he had slim to no chance of finding another lover.

"Here ya go, darlin'." The waitress plunked down a food-stained menu and a glass of water. "Can I get ya some coffee or something to drink?"

"Water is fine, thanks."

"Ready to order or do ya need a few minutes?"

"I can order. I'd like a J-Boy plate."

"Sure. I'll be right back out with that for ya, darlin'."

A tiny spark of hope still glimmered, enough to get Josh off the couch earlier that evening and into the shower. By ten o'clock, he'd whipped his hair into a look, fingered through some gel, squeezed into his best jeans, and donned a Polo golf shirt for a solo night out on the town.

The waitress returned with his food, interrupting his thoughts. She set the burger, coleslaw, and mountain of crinkle-cut fries down in front of him. "Ya gonna save some room for hot fudge cake?"

Josh was tempted to say yes. He could eat whatever he wanted now. What difference would it make if he got big as a house?

"No, thanks. I'll be doing good to eat this."

"Well, just let me know if ya change your mind." She left the check on the table and headed to the hostess stand to seat a group of punk rockers that had just arrived.

Josh glanced at his watch and noticed it was after one o'clock. The bars had closed, and a line waiting for tables had formed just inside the door. He wolfed down the rest of the burger, finished off the slaw, and made a noticeable dent in the mountain of fries. After leaving two bucks on the table for the waitress, he picked up the check, settled with the cashier, and returned to his car.

The J-Boy plate had filled him up, but left him feeling just as empty as before. Instead of going home where he belonged, Josh headed for the bookstore.

He parked under the trees at the very back of the parking lot, smoking a cigarette and watching guys coming and going through the bookstore's rear entrance. A steady stream of cars cruised slowly through the parking lot. Now and then the cars paired up, driver's side to driver's side, for quick conversations. If the drivers connected, a two-car convoy headed to a secret rendezvous for a hookup. More often, both cars returned to the parade circling the bookstore in search of a hot encounter.

After seventeen years with Ben Dixon, Josh was single. It wasn't his fault. He'd done everything right. The idea of cheating never even occurred to him. As far as Josh was concerned, once you decided to move in together, death was the only way out.

He thought Ben agreed. In a way, he did. Ben didn't want the relationship to end, either. Not the relationship with Josh or the relationship Ben had on the side with his coworker, twenty-five-year-old David Hicks. That Josh considered David to be a good friend added insult to injury. In one fell swoop, he'd lost two of the most important people in his life.

Oh well, Ben is history. No more lies. No more worrying about what's going on behind my back.

But the absence of gnawing paranoia was a small comfort in the face of reality. Josh knew his best chance for finding the love of his life was now behind him. Downhill was the only direction left for a single, middle-aged gay man.

He locked his car and made for the rear door of the bookstore. When he crossed the threshold, the scent of Pine-Sol punched him in the nose. There wasn't enough cleanser in the world to cover the smell of all the sex that went on in the cubicles making up the dim back half of the store. The brightly lit front of the establishment featured dirty magazines, an eclectic collection of pornographic videos for sale or rent, and a wall of dongs, dildos, and other sex-related paraphernalia.

A dozen small cubicles with coin-operated video players featured an assortment of porn. Scattered throughout the dark maze connecting all the cubicles lurked maybe a dozen horned-up men. Some were married and popped into the booths for the blowjobs their wives refused to deliver. Most of the rest were there to oblige. The way they leered made Josh uncomfortable.

Never a lurker, Josh stepped into a cubicle and dropped some quarters in the slot to watch some gay porn. On the screen, an obviously bored African-American plowed the ass of a homely white dude who tried to act like it hurt. Neither performer was likely to win any acting awards. Josh pushed the button and the scene changed to a blond frat-boy type blowing a hairy, muscular white guy.

Fearing what he might sit in, Josh ignored the wooden bench seat and remained standing. The black plywood walls of the booth were riddled with holes of various sizes, none part of the original construction. Smaller holes allowed for spying on the action in the neighboring cubicle. Larger openings served more illicit purposes. Every few years, the police raided the place and the owner would board up all the holes. New holes reappeared in days.

Watching the action on the little screen gave Josh a hard-on. When a finger appeared through a baseball-sized opening on the right side of the booth, beckoning, he figured what the heck. Getting off was getting off. He went over, lowered his pants to his knees, and stuck his cock through the hole into the warm, wet mouth waiting on the other side.

Josh concentrated on the video, imagining the frat boy sucking his dick instead of one of the leering men he'd seen outside the cubicle. He dropped more quarters in the slot, then focused on the video and the mouth milking him through the glory hole. Soon Josh was pounding the wall with his hips. The sound attracted bystanders to the holes in surrounding cubicles to see what the noise was all about.

Josh felt the beginning of his climax tingling in his balls and groaned. The hot mouth working urgently on his throbbing cock quickly produced the desired result. On still trembling legs, Josh zipped up his pants and headed home to his empty bed.

• 2 •

THE doorbell's steady ding, ding, ding woke Josh from a sound sleep. He stumbled out of bed and tripped over an assortment of pizza boxes, dirty clothes, old newspapers, and empty cans on his way to the front door. He saw his friend Linda Delgado through the peephole and opened the door.

"I've been ringing your doorbell forever. You up?"

"Does it look like I'm up?" Squinting from the bright sunlight, Josh looked at his arm and then remembered his watch still sat on his bedside table. "What the hell time is it, anyway?"

"Way past time for your sorry ass to still be in bed. You were supposed to meet me at the pool two hours ago."

He rubbed his eyes. "You could have called."

Linda put her hands on her hips and glared. "I did. Three times."

Josh looked over and saw the red blinking light on his answering machine. "Oh. Sorry." He ran his hands up over his eyes and through his hair, pulling the bangs back, then letting go and shaking his head. "Guess I was sleeping pretty heavy. I went downtown last night and was a little late getting home."

"Late getting home? Did you get lucky? Is he still here?"

Josh decided not to mention the anonymous blowjob to his one and only friend. Women really didn't understand about casual, anonymous sex. "No, I didn't get lucky. Nobody even looked at me twice, much less talked to me."

"Poor Joshy. Everyone probably thought you were too busy enjoying your little pity party to bother with anyone else."

Josh shook his head. "Linda, sometimes you're a real bitch."

"As your best friend, it's my job. If I don't tell your hunky ass the truth, who will?" She looked past him. "Are we just going to stand here on the porch all day and talk?"

Josh yawned and stepped back, opening the door wider so Linda could come in. "Sorry. I'm still about half asleep."

Linda pushed her way past Josh into the condo. She took three steps, then turned back to Josh. "Jesus Christ! What the hell is that smell?"

Josh sniffed the air. "What smell? I don't smell anything."

"It smells like a crack house in here, or maybe a dumpster." She covered her mouth and nose with her hand and talked between her fingers. "Damn, Josh! When was the last time you took out the trash?"

"Uh. I dunno. Sometime before Ben moved out."

"That was more than three weeks ago. Can't you smell it?"

Josh sniffed again and shrugged. "Not really. Maybe a little when I first come in. You get used to it."

Pinching her nose and holding her hand over her mouth as she kicked through trash and clutter, Linda made her way into the living room. On the coffee table, empty cans and glasses surrounded an ashtray overflowing with cigarette butts and the tail ends of an uncountable number of joints. Linda kicked a bunch of dirty clothes and old newspapers off the sofa and onto the floor to clear a place to sit.

She looked slowly around the living room, her eyes jumping from mess to bigger mess as she took it all in. "So this is what three weeks of wallowing in self-pity looks like."

Josh cleared himself a spot on the sofa, knocking over a half empty glass of what might have been milk as he sat down. "I guess so." He picked a small pipe from the table. "You mind if I catch a little buzz before we hit the pool?"

Linda sighed. "Sure. Why not?" She glanced around the room again. "I may even have to join you."

He was more than a little surprised. Since divorcing a guy with a deep affection for cocaine who everyone thought could easily have passed for Josh's brother, Linda rarely got high. Josh retrieved the jewelry chest his mother had given him for his twelfth birthday, and after knocking a bunch of cans to the floor, cleared a spot for it on the coffee table. He opened the chest and took out a nearly empty bag of pot to replenish his pipe.

"Guess I've been smoking a lot since Ben left."

Linda glanced around at the filthy, cluttered condo. "No shit. Too bad getting high doesn't inspire you to go on a cleaning binge."

"Ben usually did all the cleaning." Josh filled the pipe and offered it to Linda.

Linda hesitated. "When in a frat house, do as the frat boys do." She took the pipe, fired it up, inhaled deeply, and held her breath before returning it to Josh. "Are you going to tell me about your night downtown?"

Josh took a big hit and then exhaled. "There's really nothing to tell. I had a couple of drinks, took in the drag show for a while, then watched a bunch of people I don't care to know dancing to music I'd never heard before. It was a good time."

He looked at Linda. Two years younger than Josh, she was still beautiful, with short raven hair, olive skin that quickly tanned a dark brown, and dazzling blue eyes. Their mothers had been best friends. They'd grown up together, and Josh could tell she knew there was more to his story. She looked at him and cocked her head. "Did you run into Benjie and David?"

Josh shook his head. "No. They weren't there." He relit the bowl and took another hit.

"That's good." She reached across and pulled his chin around so she could see his eyes. "You know you're going to run into them sooner or later, don't you?"

Josh returned his attention to the pipe. "Not if I can help it. David knows Ben has trouble keeping it zipped. The Bar is the last place they'd be."

He loaded the bowl again and handed it to Linda. Having outgrown the youthful crowd of regulars, he and Ben had long ago quit going to the Bar Complex. In truth, the decision to avoid the place had been less about the young crowd than Ben's wandering eye.

Linda snorted. "If David was that smart, you and Ben would still be together."

"Yeah, and if I was smart, we would never have hooked up." In hindsight, Josh should have seen it coming. Ben had left his previous lover to be with Josh. If they'd do it *for* you, it was only a matter of time before they'd do it *to* you.

"Do you miss him?"

Josh looked at her. "I don't know, maybe. Part of me is glad he's gone. It's like a big weight has been lifted from my shoulders." He shrugged and looked at the floor. "Maybe I should become a monk. Then I could put all this celibacy to good use."

Linda laughed. "You're not really the celibate type." When he didn't laugh, she slid closer to him and wrapped an arm around his waist. "Thought any more about that job offer?"

Josh draped his arm across her shoulder and rested his chin on her head. "Not really."

Walker, Cochran, and Lowe, the law firm where he worked, had offered him a promotion to national director of communications. The catch was he'd have to transfer to the Washington, DC, branch of the firm. Ben had been opposed to the move, but what he thought didn't matter anymore.

Linda leaned her head into his neck. "Why not go? It's a great opportunity for you, and there's no better time than now to get the hell out of Dodge." She sat up, pushing him away. "You should go."

Josh looked into her eyes. He couldn't remember a time when she hadn't been part of his life, and he loved her like the sister he never had. More than her words, the concern for his well-being he saw on her face told him she was serious.

But he couldn't imagine life without her, especially now that his love life was over. If he couldn't have a lover, at least he had Linda. Being single without her to keep him company was just unimaginable. He set the pipe in the ashtray and stood up.

"Come on. It's a beautiful day outside. Let's not waste it in here chitchatting about work."

Linda laughed and shook her head. "If you insist."

"I do. Let me jump into some trunks."

Josh returned a few minutes later in navy-blue swim trunks, a white T-shirt, and flip-flops. "Ready?"

"I was ready two hours ago," Linda smirked.

BRIGHT sun beamed down from a cloudless sky. Linda and Josh rubbed sunscreen onto each other's backs. With the sun behind him, Josh stood at the foot of his lounge chair, shifting it to the left until his shadow fell in the middle of the vinyl slats. Linda shifted her chair to line up with Josh's.

A group of high school kids played volleyball in the pool. The team in the shallow end had a definite advantage. After handily winning the game, they moved to the deep end for a rematch.

Josh enjoyed the smell of the chlorine and the sun's warmth on his skin. He closed his eyes and the volleyball game faded to white noise. He could taste salty perspiration when he licked his lips and felt cool splashes on his legs from the action in the pool.

His mind drifted, as always, to the breakup. Maybe he'd focused too much on work. The effort had certainly paid off, for both him and Ben. Walker, Cochran, and Lowe had promoted Josh several times, with pay increases allowing the two of them to do more or less whatever they wanted. Nice vacations every year, the newest electronic gadgets, a fancy condo with all the amenities—all possible because of Josh's steady rise from graphic designer to communications director.

Now Ben slept on a futon in David's studio apartment and ate peanut butter and jelly sandwiches for breakfast, lunch, and dinner. Josh smiled. Yes, Ben's reduced standard of living did somewhat soften the blow.

Josh sensed Linda looking at him, opened his eyes, and met her gaze. The intensity of her blue eyes never ceased to impress him, especially when she was this tan. "What's up, beautiful?"

"You really should go to DC."

"I'm lonely enough here, where I grew up and went to school. How lonely would I be hundreds of miles from here in a big city where

I don't know a soul?" He looked away and hoped she wouldn't see how upset and afraid he really was.

"Josh, you can do this. DC isn't Lexington. The change of scenery would be good for you. I won't bail on you like I did when you first came out and I couldn't stand the sight of you."

Josh remembered all too well. Before he had any inkling he was gay, he and his lifelong friend had been high school sweethearts. Josh had believed with all his heart that he and Linda would marry, have a passel of children, and live happily ever after. Having witnessed firsthand the impact of his father's infidelity, cheating was the farthest thing from Josh's mind. And yet, that was exactly what he had done on a drunken camping trip with the guys his junior year in college.

Linda had been hurt when he told her what he had done and discovered about himself. Her tears had ripped his heart in two. When her hurt finally turned to anger, he was grateful. For months she wouldn't have a thing to do with him, refusing to return his calls, ignoring letter after letter of apology.

Linda's voice broke through his thoughts. "We can talk every day, if you like."

The walls fell and Josh's fears escaped. "I don't know, Linda. What if I don't like it? What if I don't make new friends? What if I just sit in an apartment and wish I'd never left Lexington?"

Linda stood up, crossed her arms, and let go with her own fears. "What if you do like it? What if you make a hundred new friends and get too busy for your old pal here in Lexington?" She took his hand and waited for him to look her in the eye before continuing. "It's a risk for me too, but one I'm willing to take because I can't stand to see you this way."

He dropped her hand and looked at his feet. "What way is that?"

"Where do you want me to start? Staying stoned, eating junk food, trashing your condo, spending too much time by yourself. Need I go on?"

Josh shook his head. Struck by a sudden desire for something to do with his hands, he reached for his cigarettes and lighter.

She made him move over so she could sit next to him on the edge of the lounge chair. "Josh, you are an amazing man. You're not over the hill by any stretch of the imagination. If you were straight, every woman I know would love to have a crack at you. You're smart, kindhearted, compassionate, and drop-dead gorgeous."

He shook his head. "I'm gay and almost forty. That's the same as being sixty in the straight world. I *am* over the hill. Spent. Done."

"Do you hear yourself? You've been totally worthless ever since you kicked Ben out. Being single is not the end of the world. And even if it was, at least you were happy with Ben for a while. Do you know how long it's been since I've even been on a date?"

Josh felt like a heel. Despite her beauty and vivacious personality, Linda rarely if ever dated. After her short-lived marriage went south, she said she'd had enough of men and vowed to stay forever single. He never understood how she could be so content without someone special in her life. Josh could barely function.

He leaned over and put his head on her shoulder. "I'm sorry."

Linda pushed him away. "Oh, shut up with the sorry already. You are the neediest, most codependent person I know. I feel at least partially responsible. I was more of a security blanket for you than a lover. Half my anger when you told me about your little camping tryst was at myself for letting things go on as long as I did."

Josh didn't know what to say. He knew she was right. Though he hadn't been aware of it, he had always been gay.

Linda took his hand and looked into his eyes. "Josh, I love you and I always will. I know you love me too. That's not going to change whether you stay in Lexington, go to DC, or move halfway around the world.

"You've outgrown this town. It's time to move on. This isn't about us, it's about you. Give DC a chance—until Thanksgiving. If it doesn't work out, you can come back. You've got to do something because I can't stand to watch what you're doing to yourself now."

Neither of them noticed the volleyball game had ended and the boys had left the pool area. They were alone. The prolonged silence was deafening.

She was right. Except for Linda and her mother, there was nothing left for him in Lexington. Maybe it really was time to move on.

The more he thought about it, the more the idea appealed to him. He certainly didn't have anything to lose.

Josh felt a flock of butterflies in his stomach leap into flight as the idea of maybe moving became the decision to move. He turned to Linda, took a deep breath, and said, "Okay. I'll go, but you'll have to come and visit."

Linda nodded. "Say the word and I'll be there. Have Honda, will travel."

And with that, it was decided. Josh laughed, then stood up and leaped into the pool. Linda jumped in behind him and the pair engaged in a splashing battle reminiscent of the wars fought in the aboveground pool in Linda's backyard when they were still in grade school.

• 3 •

THAD PARKER stood with a small crowd waiting at Gate 13 for Delta Flight 3313 to arrive from Lexington, Kentucky. Thirteen had always been his lucky number. He had been born at 1300 hours on January 13, 1963, and considered his thirteenth year to have been among the best of his childhood. That was the year he'd realized he was more interested in boys than girls and had gone to spend the summer with his Uncle Philip.

The flight had landed. Thad watched for the Jetway door to open, and when it did, he held up the sign he'd printed off from his computer the day before: Josh Freeman. He knew Mr. Freeman was transferring from the Lexington branch of Walker, Cochran, and Lowe to be the new national communications director, but little else. As the sole employee of the relocation and travel division of the firm, it was Thad's job to help Mr. Freeman find housing in Washington, line up the movers, and otherwise help with his relocation from Lexington.

He watched the passengers coming off the flight, smiling benignly at the men, knowing one of them would be Josh Freeman. An obviously gay middle-aged man with gray hair and a faded pink golf shirt that almost covered his sizeable paunch looked at the sign Thad held and smiled. Thad smiled back and hoped he wouldn't be spending the rest of the afternoon fending off the man's advances. If so, he was in for a very long day.

"Hello. I'm Josh Freeman."

It took Thad several seconds to realize the voice had not come from the pink-shirted man. He turned toward the source of the voice and gasped. A tall, tan, ruggedly handsome man with thick brown hair smiled and offered his hand.

Thad looked at the hand for several seconds, then along the darkly tanned forearms to the athletic chest and the dazzling smile before he fell into an impressive pair of soulful puppy-dog brown eyes. He reached out slowly and shook hands with the man. A high voltage jolt traveled up his arm, then forked to send a tingling sensation rushing to his scalp, all ten toes, and the fingertips holding the sign bearing the man's name. He felt his knees go weak, and until he saw the group of girls walk past holding hands and singing, would have sworn he heard a choir of angels.

"Welcome to Washington, Mr. Freeman," he stammered. "I'm Thad Parker, your tour guide for the next twenty-four hours."

"Nice to meet you, Thad. Can you call me Josh? Mr. Freeman is my dad."

Normally Thad would have laughed. Instead, he mumbled, "Okay." He knew he was staring but couldn't look away. Something about Josh Freeman had knocked him for a loop. He realized too much time had passed. An awkward silence he was at a loss to fill stretched on because he couldn't think of a thing to say.

Josh broke the silence. "Any idea where I go to pick up my luggage?"

The question jarred Thad back into reality. "Yes, sir! Baggage claim is right this way." Thad talked as he walked. "Since it's too early to check into the hotel, we'll drop your luggage off at the office before we start checking out apartments. Will that be okay?"

Josh nodded. "You're the boss. Just tell me what to do."

Where do you want me to start? A barrage of erotic images flew through Thad's mind, surprising him. He'd met lots of men, including some real lookers. None, however, had ever pushed his lust button quite the way Josh had managed to do with just one look from his dreamy brown eyes.

Focus!

"I've found four apartments that seem to meet your criteria, all within walking distance of the Walker, Cochran, and Lowe office. Would you rather take a cab to the office or ride the Metro?"

Josh practically skipped down the terminal. "Let's take the Metro. We have cabs in Lexington, but I've never ridden on a subway."

"Then Metro it is." Thad smiled. Josh's obvious excitement reminded him of a kid preparing for his first ride on a roller coaster.

Josh retrieved his badly beaten Samsonite suitcase from the baggage carousel. Thad and everyone else in the airport couldn't help but notice the silver duct tape on all four corners of the olive-green bag.

"Sorry about the luggage. My ex got the good stuff."

Single. The absence of wheels and a pulling handle made Thad wish Josh had opted for the cab ride. Since he hadn't, Thad hoped any friends who saw him focused more on the handsome man he was with than the antique bag he carried.

Inside the station, he showed Josh the Metro map and the route they would follow to reach their destination. Thad thought the way Josh asked questions was cute, like he was preparing for a big test.

On the long ride up the escalator from the Dupont Circle Metro station, Thad instructed Josh to stand to the right like a true Washingtonian so people in a hurry could pass, rather than stand in the middle like a tourist. Never mind that anyone seeing Josh's shabby suitcase wouldn't be fooled for a minute.

At the top, Thad indicated the direction they needed to go. "We need to cross through Dupont Circle to get to the office."

As they walked, Thad explained that Dupont Circle was a park, a traffic circle, and a neighborhood. The popular park was anchored by an enormous, two-tiered marble fountain surrounded by benches and a well-landscaped grassy area in the center of the giant, four-lane roundabout that connected Massachusetts, Connecticut, and New Hampshire Avenues, P Street, and Nineteenth Street. The neighborhood included nearly two hundred acres and extended several blocks in every direction from the fountain that marked its center. As they crossed through one of several sidewalks that dissected the landscaping, Thad pointed out the sidewalk that ran along the perimeter of the park and the old men engaged in intense battles on concrete chessboards. The fountain roared in the background.

Thad gave Josh a tour of the Walker, Cochran, and Lowe headquarters that ended with his new office. Considering he wasn't an attorney, Josh's office was nice, with a big leather chair behind a large oak desk, a seating area with comfortable-looking upholstered furniture, and a window overlooking the Dupont Circle fountain. His tattered suitcase was oddly out of place in the luxurious setting.

Over the next few hours, Thad took Josh to see apartments in several properties in the Dupont Circle neighborhood. He listened as Josh peppered the property managers with a thousand questions they couldn't possibly answer, with a drawl heard more often in the mountains than on any plantation.

Having helped dozens of transfers and new hires relocate to DC, Thad had learned to start with the worst option. Most people came to Washington expecting accommodations similar to that available in the smaller cities they were leaving behind. Checking out two or three less desirable options first made getting them to like his first choice a lot easier. Cute as he was, Josh was no exception.

After Josh signed the lease and wrote the check for the deposit, Thad took him back to the office. He pointed out the CVS drugstore as a landmark for the intersection of Dupont Circle and P Street, two blocks from Josh's new apartment. Minutes later, they were back in Josh's office at Walker, Cochran, and Lowe to retrieve his luggage.

"Ready to go to your hotel?" Thad asked.

"Yes, I'm beat." Josh picked up his shabby suitcase. "I really appreciate you showing me around today. I was afraid I'd have to make another trip up to find a place before the move. The apartment is great."

Thad talked as they left the building, heading east around the traffic circle. "You're most welcome. The West Park is one of the best in the area." He didn't need to know Thad lived just a few blocks away. Not yet, anyway. "Tonight you're staying at the Carlyle Suites on New Hampshire Avenue. It's an old art-deco hotel with a fun atmosphere. I think you'll like it."

Thad gave Josh a rundown of his itinerary. "You're having dinner with the partners at Vidalia—one of my favorite restaurants in the city. They'll pick you up from the lobby of your hotel at seven o'clock."

Josh fought back a yawn. "Great. It's only four now, so I can squeeze in a nap before I get ready."

"Tomorrow morning, I've arranged for a limousine to pick you up from the hotel at eight o'clock to take you to the airport. Your flight leaves at nine thirty. You'll have plenty of time to get checked in and find your gate."

Josh smiled. "I'm sure I'll be fine."

Be fine? You are totally fine just the way you are. Thad paused for a minute to remember what he'd been talking about. *Oh, yeah.* "I've already lined up a moving company for you. The representative should be in touch with you next week to set up all the details." He reached into his shirt pocket and handed Josh a business card. "If there's anything else you need tonight or when you get back to Lexington, don't hesitate to call."

Finally they reached the entrance to the Carlyle. Thad fantasized about going in and showing Josh to his room.

Let me get you out of those clothes and tuck you in for that nap.

Focus!

"Well, this is it. You'll need to check in at the front desk. The reservation is in your name with all the charges direct-billed to the firm."

Josh took Thad's hand and shook it. "I really appreciate you showing me around today. You did a great job."

"Happy to help," Thad said, releasing Josh's hand as another jolt shot through his system. "I'm really looking forward to working with you over the next few weeks." And he meant it too.

• 4 •

EVEN with Ben doing most the work, moving across town to the condo seven years earlier had been a big job. Preparing to move more than five hundred miles away felt like Mission: Impossible. Between closing things out in Lexington and arranging for utilities and other things he needed in Washington, Josh barely had time to sleep.

The condo sold the first week it was on the market. Josh and Ben had completely renovated from end to end after they moved in. Considering how quickly it sold, despite mountains of trash and clutter he hadn't yet dragged to the dumpster, Josh figured his asking price was too low. He didn't care—a quick sale at a lower price beat having to find renters.

Linda came over after work every day to help him pack. They picked a spot and tackled the mess together. Random discoveries of mementos from better times with Ben often caused progress to come to a screeching halt.

"Josh, you don't want pictures of all your vacations with Ben."

"What am I supposed to do with them?" Josh refused to let the tears forming in the corner of his eyes fall.

Linda took the pictures out of his hands and hugged him. "Throw them away. You don't need them and I doubt Ben wants them."

Josh gulped and wiped his eyes to hide the tears. "But if I throw them away, they'll be gone forever."

Linda nodded in agreement. "Exactly. You'll never have to look at them again."

"But...." Josh fanned out the pictures he held for Linda to see. "These too?"

"No 'buts' about it." She took the pictures from him and threw them in a box. "In fact, let's just burn them. We'll take this box over to Mom's house and light a fire in her barbecue pit with the contents."

At first, the idea of burning evidence of his time with Ben rubbed Josh the wrong way. He resisted, which upset him that much more. But Linda persisted, and once he eventually came to see the wisdom of her suggestion, over the next few days they delegated enough memories to the fire to fill several boxes.

Linda's mother popped in now and then with food. Aside from Linda, Mrs. Delgado was the closest thing to family Josh had.

The first night, Mrs. Delgado came by with something from one of the many restaurant chains in the area. She glanced around at all the discarded pizza boxes and carryout containers that still littered the condo, and the next day, she brought food prepared with tender loving care from her kitchen. Mrs. Delgado apparently worried he might never eat home-cooked food again.

He was grateful to both women. Linda's near constant presence kept him focused on the long to-do list of things he needed to accomplish for the move. When she wasn't around, he tended to just get high and stare at some random item, recalling how he and Ben had come to add it to their worldly possessions.

Aside from worrying about his gastronomic future, Mrs. Delgado gushed about how exciting living in the nation's capital would be, and all the things she would do given the opportunity. She even picked up a couple of books about sightseeing in DC for him. Her enthusiasm was infectious.

By moving day, Josh was more excited than worried about what the future held. He wasn't running away from Lexington and Ben. He was anticipating the new and exciting opportunities the move presented. Moving forward felt better than running away from something bad.

Thanks to the attractive redhead in the expensive suit who had shown him around, the trip to DC to find an apartment had turned out better than Josh expected. He imagined he'd gone home to each apartment for a drink and hopefully breakfast with the handsome man, whose name he could not remember to save his life. He discovered his guide looked great in any setting. And all he had to do to see that handsome face and those startling green eyes again was to close his eyes. If only he could remember his name.

The minute he walked into the lobby of West Park apartments, he knew he'd found his new home. The apartment was more or less the same as the others he'd seen, but light and airy instead of dark and foreboding. Rather than the wall of the building next door, the windows and a small balcony overlooked busy P Street. A rooftop swimming pool with a view of the Washington Monument cinched the deal.

Josh didn't know which appealed to him more, his new big-city apartment or the idea of finding out that redhead's name and getting to know him better. Focusing on his new future was easier than thinking about the past he was leaving behind.

After the moving truck drove away with practically everything he owned, Josh stayed at Linda's condo for a couple of days. He could have gone on to DC, but didn't see the point in arriving days ahead of his possessions. Besides, it was a good excuse to spend his last days in Lexington with Linda. He had a feeling their relationship would never be the same.

The night before he was to leave for Washington, Mrs. Delgado insisted he come to her house for dinner. From Linda's Honda came four boxes full of photographs, letters, ticket stubs, and other mementos destined for the barbecue pit. They sat on the patio for hours, drinking wine and tossing additional items into the pit whenever the flames died down. Josh had to admit, purging his life with Ben through fire felt pretty damn good.

The next morning, Josh jumped into Linda's brand-new 1997 Honda Accord for the ride to Bluegrass Field. The handsome guy from the relocation office had told Josh that living in the Dupont Circle area made owning a vehicle more of a liability than an asset. So Josh sold his Celica and bought a one-way ticket to fly up to DC to meet the movers.

"Thanks for all your help." Josh hugged Linda and kissed her on the cheek. "I don't know how I would have managed without you and your mom."

"I didn't have anything else to do." Linda shrugged. "Besides, I was afraid you'd get overwhelmed and back out. You know how you are."

Josh couldn't disagree. He was more spoiled than helpless, but the end result was often the same. "Think I can make it without you?"

"Absolutely. Besides, you can call me anytime, and there's always e-mail. You'll hardly know the difference. Thanksgiving will be here before you know it."

"I'm glad you're coming. By Thanksgiving, I should know if living in DC is for me. I should also know my way around well enough to show you the sights."

"I'm counting on it. And if you don't, your new boyfriend will."

"Yeah, right."

"Yeah, right. The last three months is the longest you've been single since before we were an item back in high school."

"You keeping track or something?"

She laughed. "As a matter of fact I am. Mom and I have a pool going about how long it will take to find Ben's replacement. I'm putting my money on that little redhead you told me about."

Josh laughed. "You always were an optimist."

"And you've always had a thing for relationships."

She had a point. After the breakup with Linda, he'd rented a tiny studio apartment and slept with almost every guy he met. Each was Mr. Right. He'd gone through a dozen "serious" boyfriends in just a few months before finally settling down with Ben.

"Things are different now, Linda. It's not as easy to meet people as it was then."

"You'll do fine, trust me."

Linda found a space in the short-term parking lot, popped open the trunk, and stepped out into the hot August sun. Josh grabbed his backpack and the new suitcase Linda had given him as a going-away present before slamming the trunk closed.

Josh set the suitcase down on the pavement and extended the handle. "Don't come in with me, Linda. I don't want a big scene."

"I was hoping you'd say that. I don't want a big scene either. It's not like we'll never see each other again. Call me tonight after you get settled into your apartment."

"You know I will. Thanks a million for... um... taking me to the airport."

They stood in silence. Josh looked her over, memorizing every detail. They hugged each other tightly. Reluctant to let go, Josh kissed her on the forehead.

"I'll call you tonight. Be careful driving home."

Before she could respond, he turned and walked toward the Delta ticket counter. He didn't look back. Seeing her tears would make him cry.

• 5 •

JOSH retrieved his suitcase from the baggage carousel at Reagan National and walked toward the Metro station. He studied the map and decided he could get to his apartment without having to ask for help. He just needed to catch the Yellow Line train to the Gallery Place/Chinatown station, then switch to the Red Line to get off at Dupont Circle. He bought a twenty-dollar fare card since the Metro, walking, and cabs were now his only transportation options.

Less than forty minutes later, Josh ascended the giant escalator from the Dupont Circle station, emerging at Connecticut Avenue and Q Street. The traffic noise and oppressive heat were not so subtle reminders that he was no longer in Lexington. He was glad he only had to walk a couple of blocks.

He spotted the CVS drugstore, and remembering it was on P Street, headed in that direction. Along the way, he picked up a copy of the *Washington Blade*. When he arrived at the apartment building, he rang the doorbell. A middle-aged, African-American receptionist seated at a small desk just inside the entrance buzzed him in.

"Hi. I'm Josh Freeman."

Her smile lit up the lobby. "Hello, Mr. Freeman, I'm Vanessa Jackson. Welcome to West Park. We've been expecting you. Did you have a nice flight?"

"Yes, thanks, and I even managed to get here from the airport on the Metro without getting lost."

She laughed. "Good for you! The movers are still unloading your furniture. Here are your keys and a few more papers for you to sign."

"Thanks." Josh took the keys and the pen she offered and signed for the mailbox and apartment keys.

"The mailboxes are just around the corner to your right. Beyond the mailboxes are the elevators. The laundry room is in the basement, the pool is on the roof, and the trash chute is located on each floor behind the elevator. If you have any questions, please don't hesitate to call."

Josh thanked the receptionist again, then walked across to an open elevator and pushed the button for the fourth floor. Number 419 was just across the hall from the elevators. He didn't need his key—the door was open. As he entered the apartment, he noticed the redheaded guy from the relocation office checking a clipboard as the movers brought in boxes, each one carefully labeled by Linda with the room where it belonged. He wasn't wearing a nametag.

"Welcome to Washington, Mr. Freeman. Perfect timing! The last of your things just came off the truck."

Josh still couldn't remember his name. "Thanks. Good to finally be here."

The relocation guy continued to talk. "I unpacked your coffeemaker and made your bed for you. Nothing worse than having to make your bed after a long day of unpacking."

Josh smiled at his nervousness. "That was very thoughtful of you... er...."

"Thad... Thad Parker."

"I'm sorry. I'm horrible with names. Thanks, Thad, I really appreciate everything you've done."

"No problem. Glad I could help." Thad checked more boxes off the list on the clipboard he carried. "Do you want to move any of your furniture around?"

Josh looked around, pleased with the way Thad had arranged things. In truth, the apartment was so small his furniture more or less had to go the way Thad had placed it.

"No, thanks. You've done a great job. I wouldn't change a thing." He glanced around the apartment, then shifted his attention to Thad. "So, tell me, have you lived in Washington very long?"

Thad continued checking off boxes and then rearranged the papers before latching them securely into place on the clipboard. "I've lived in the area for practically my whole life, but only recently moved to the District. Where I could afford the rent, you wouldn't want to live."

Thad laughed, a sound Josh liked. In fact, he liked everything about Thad. He was handsome, with a beautiful smile and a calm, pleasant demeanor. Straight strawberry-blond hair reached the top of his black-framed glasses, highlighting his green eyes and giving him a bookish, naïve look that defied his self-confident manner. Instead of a suit, Thad had on faded jeans, a green golf shirt that matched his eyes, and penny loafers without socks. Josh couldn't believe how much cuter he was than he remembered.

"Is there anything else you need, Mr. Freeman? I'm about done here and don't want to keep you from your unpacking."

"Please, call me Josh. And thanks again, for all you've done. I really can't thank you enough."

Thad looked at Josh for a minute and cleared his throat. "I hope you won't mind. I've taken the liberty of inviting some friends over Monday evening for a little get-together to welcome you to town. Is that okay with you?"

Josh was pleasantly surprised. "That's very nice of you. I'd love to come. Other than you and the partners, I don't know a soul in town."

"I figured as much. It's hard making friends in the District, especially when most of your coworkers live in the 'burbs. But once you get to know a few people, you'll find DC isn't really that big."

Thad wrote his address and phone number on his business card and handed it to Josh. "I told everyone to come around seven. Does that work for you?"

Josh slid the card into his shirt pocket. "Perfect. Can I bring something?"

"No, just yourself. I'll take care of the rest."

The last of the movers had left. Thad headed toward the apartment door. "If there's anything you need, just give me a call."

"I'm sure that won't be necessary." Josh shook his hand. "Thanks again."

"No problem. And I mean it—call if you need anything— anything at all."

Was it just his imagination or was Thad flirting with him? He didn't even seem gay. "Thanks, Thad. I'm sure I'll be fine. I appreciate all you've done."

Thad left, closing the door behind him, leaving Josh alone in his new apartment, adrift in a sea of boxes. He walked over to the sliding glass door and stepped out onto the balcony. On the street below, dozens of people hurried along, intent on reaching their destinations. He saw Thad emerge from beneath the West Park portico and admired his athletic physique as he walked up P Street toward Dupont Circle.

Josh inhaled deeply. The very air vibrated with energy. He definitely wasn't in Lexington anymore, a fact that now excited him. He went back in to start unpacking. The sooner he got unpacked, the sooner his new Washington apartment would feel like home.

• 6 •

UNPACKING went much quicker than packing had. Linda would have been proud of him. Within a few hours, Josh had arranged all his clothes in either the walk-in closet or his dresser, unpacked the kitchen and bathroom, and carted all the empty boxes to the dumpster. The remaining half dozen or so boxes contained books and an eclectic assortment of odds and ends that could go anywhere.

With the unpacking nearly complete, Josh decided to call it a day. He opened a box marked "Living Room" and pulled out the wooden jewelry chest his mother had given him. The chest contained several ounces of pot, rolling papers, his pipe, pipe cleaners, and a zip-top bag full of extra screens for the pipe. He wrapped all but one of the ounces in a sheet of white butcher paper he'd packed expressly for this purpose, making it look like a big roast or something similar, and stashed it in the freezer. Josh could live without men or without pot, but not both.

He grabbed his copy of the *Washington Blade*, the remaining bag of pot, and a dinner plate, then settled down on the sofa. He pulled a fat bud from the bag, and as he broke it up on the plate, he scanned the front-page headlines. Most of the articles revolved around a series of recent murders in the area.

Lexington didn't have a gay newspaper. Josh didn't subscribe to any of the national gay news magazines, either, and was completely out of the gay-news loop. Until he saw all the rainbow flags throughout the neighborhood on his apartment-hunting visit to DC, he hadn't even known the Walker, Cochran, and Lowe building was in the gay part of Washington.

With the pot broken up and cleaned to his satisfaction, Josh pulled a paper from the package of JOB 1.5s and rolled a joint. The task required all his attention. Since he already had everything out, he went ahead and rolled up several more. His friends claimed his joint-rolling ability far exceeded that of anyone else they knew. Not a résumé-worthy skill, but practical.

Until he got to know his neighbors, Josh figured he'd smoke outside, where the pungent aroma would be harder to trace back to its source. He took the *Blade*, one of the joints, and a lighter out onto the balcony, along with a chair from his dining room table. He checked the balconies around him for occupants and, finding none, fired up the joint.

After a couple of hits, he let the joint go out, then picked up the *Blade* and scanned through the articles about the murders. Someone had bludgeoned three gay men in the area—two outside of gay bars and one in Rock Creek Park. The victims were all white males in their thirties, and judging from photos, attractive. The killer was still on the loose.

Josh looked down at the street, where the late-afternoon sun cast long shadows. He wondered if the killer was one of the men he saw coming and going from several gay bars in the area. A shiver ran down his spine. He shook it off and turned his attention back to the paper.

He definitely wasn't in Lexington anymore. Besides gay news and special-interest stories, the paper contained several pages of personals, ads for massage and escort services, and larger ads about specials and attractions at numerous area bars and restaurants that catered to gay clientele. Because he'd never seen any before, Josh browsed slowly through the ads for escorts. Most were obviously selling a lot more than company. Though several of the descriptions intrigued him, paying for sex simply did not appeal to him.

A massage, however, sounded great. Josh had worked hard, not just today but for weeks leading up to the move. He studied the massage ads more carefully. Most featured descriptions of the masseur that might have been ripped from the pages of an erotic romance novel. A few mentioned various massage techniques and certifications. None included a price.

Josh took the telephone out onto the balcony and dialed a number. Instead of a person, he got an answering machine. Rather than leave a message, he hung up. He called several more until finally he got a real person.

"Yes, I'm calling about your ad for massages in the *Washington Blade*."

"In call or out call?"

"I'm sorry. I haven't done this before. What's the difference?"

"You want to come to me or do you want me to come to you?"

Josh pondered the question. Since he didn't really know his way around, going out for the massage could get complicated. "You can come here."

"Okay, that will be two hundred dollars for the first hour and seventy-five dollars for each additional hour."

"Damn." Josh nearly dropped the phone. He'd had no idea a massage was so expensive. "How much if I come to you?"

"One hundred-fifty dollars for the first hour and sixty dollars for each additional hour."

"Uh… let me think about it. Thanks."

After hanging up, Josh returned to the ads. He tried more numbers, got answering machines, and hung up. Just when he was about to give up, he heard a live voice.

"Hello?"

"Yes, I'm calling about a massage. I saw your ad in the *Blade*."

"Oh, great! Is it okay to come to you? I don't really have a place to do a good massage here."

"How much do you charge?"

"Sixty dollars for just me, ninety dollars if you want my roommate to come too."

Josh thought getting a massage from two people at the same time would be awkward. "Just you would be fine."

"Great! Where do you live and when do you want me to come?"

He didn't sound like a serial killer. Josh gave him his address. "Do you have any time available this evening?"

"Sure. I can be there in forty-five minutes. Does that work for you?"

Josh looked at the clock. "Perfect. I live in apartment 419. Ring the bell next to my apartment number and I'll buzz you in."

"Cool! See you in forty-five minutes."

After he hung up the phone, Josh realized he didn't know the guy's name. Oh well. It wasn't like he expected other visitors. He relit the joint, and after taking a couple more hits, again let it go out in the ashtray. He went back inside, looked around, and decided the apartment was presentable enough. He stashed the pot and the half-smoked joint in the jewelry box and settled onto the sofa to channel surf until the masseur arrived.

Though Josh listened for it, the sound of the buzzer still startled him. He walked over to the intercom, and without asking who rang, pushed the button allowing entry to the building. For all he knew, he was about to meet a killer.

Josh heard a quick knock and looked through the peephole to see an average-looking guy in gym shorts and a tank top who appeared to be maybe thirty years old. He certainly wasn't threatening in any way. Josh opened the door.

"Hi, I'm Josh. Come in."

"Hi. Mitch. Nice to meet you."

Josh looked Mitch over more carefully as he came through the door. He had dirty-blond hair and was quite a bit shorter than Josh's six feet. Other than a fanny pack emblazoned with a rainbow triangle, Mitch didn't have anything with him. Josh had expected a massage table and maybe an assortment of oils and lotions.

Mitch looked around. "Nice apartment. You like living here?"

"Too soon to say. I just moved in today."

"Oh?" Mitch's eyes roamed over the boxes stacked against the living room wall. "Where from?"

"Kentucky… Lexington."

"Never been, but I hear it's nice there. Dupont Circle is a great area. I think you'll like it. We'd live here if we could afford the rent."

He paused and looked around the apartment. "Where do you want to do this?"

Ruling out the sofa and the floor, Josh asked, "Will the bed work?"

"Sure!"

They walked into Josh's bedroom. After an awkward silence, Josh said, "What do you want me to do?"

"No offense, man, but I'm going to need the money first."

Josh reached into his pocket, fished out the sixty dollars he'd placed there before hiding his wallet, and handed the money to Mitch. "Now what?"

Mitch put the money in his fanny pack, which Josh noticed also contained condoms. "Take off all your clothes and lay facedown on the bed."

Josh unbuttoned his shirt, stepped out of his shorts, and then stood awkwardly in white boxers.

"You can leave your underwear on if it makes you more comfortable."

Relieved, Josh laid down on the bed as directed. Mitch straddled his back and began to rub his shoulders, moving gradually to the top of his back and working slowly down his spine. The warm hands on his back felt good, but no better than amateur massages he'd received from Ben or Linda in the past.

"You like that?" Mitch asked.

"Yeah… feels nice." Not great, but better than Josh could have done by himself.

After a few minutes of aimless rubbing, Mitch told Josh to roll over. Josh complied, not caring that his slightly enlarged cock had escaped from his boxers. As a gay masseur in DC, surely Mitch had seen dicks before… lots of them.

"Nice," Mitch announced, taking the still limp cock in his hand and squeezing it.

Josh nearly jumped out of his skin. He hadn't expected a happy ending to come with the massage. Mitch relaxed his grip and traced the pulsing veins with his fingertip. He looked at Josh. "Want me to stop?"

Josh hesitated before answering. He thought about his options and made a decision. "Uh… no… that feels good." Then he closed his eyes and tried to think about the blond frat boy he'd seen in the bookstore porn flick. But Thad was the only man that came to mind.

Mitch bent over and traced the veins on Josh's now fully engorged dick with his tongue. Josh almost came off the bed but instead let out a low moan.

"You're the boss, man. Tell me what you want."

Josh suddenly realized what would have been obvious to anyone else long before now. The massage was just a cover for the real business at hand. He had just paid sixty dollars for sex, and now it was too late to back out. He looked at Mitch and said, "Suck me."

Mitch tugged on Josh's boxer shorts until Josh reared up enough for Mitch to slide them off. He dropped the boxers on the floor, grabbed Josh's cock around the base and squeezed up, then bent over slowly to lick the tip. Josh groaned and arched his back. Clearly Mitch was much better at sucking dick than giving massages.

Josh grabbed Mitch's head with both hands, and holding it in place, began to thrust into his mouth. Mitch groaned. Josh responded by thrusting harder and faster, convulsing several times, and then coming to a complete stop.

"That was hot," Mitch said, smiling from between Josh's legs. "Usually the guys who call me are trolls. You're one very hot man— like a leather daddy."

Josh laughed. "First time I've ever heard that."

"You're kidding, right?"

"Nope."

"Look at you! Your beard, dark hair, and eyes make you look kinda rough, and you have a great body. And that cock… damn. I think you're going to be very popular in this town, especially when word gets out about your dick."

Josh couldn't believe what he was hearing. He'd gained a lot of weight in the years he'd been with Ben, enough for Ben to harass him about being fat and frumpy. Obviously Mitch didn't think so.

"Next time you should let me bring my boyfriend."

Josh didn't know what to say, but he was dead certain there wouldn't be a next time. Retrieving his boxers from where they'd fallen on the floor, he stood up and slipped them on. "Thanks."

"Hell, you wouldn't even have to pay. That was hot. Really. Next time is on me."

Now fully dressed, Josh herded Mitch toward the door. "Thanks, Mitch. I'll give you a call."

"That would be great. You're sexy. I would love to feel that big cock in my ass."

Josh guided him out the door. "Thanks. You'll hear from me."

After Mitch left, Josh thought about what had happened. He couldn't believe he'd just paid for sex. Getting an anonymous blowjob in a bookstore was one thing. Paying for sex was an entirely different category. In truth, he hadn't really paid for sex. He'd paid for a massage—the blowjob was not part of the deal.

The rationalization was small consolation. Paying for sex still made Josh feel like some kind of degenerate. Too tired to analyze it, he climbed into bed. He'd think about it tomorrow.

• 7 •

THE stories in the *Washington Blade* about the murders upset him. No, he wasn't sorry about what he'd done. It was a dog-eat-dog world, and if he hadn't killed them, Caleb would surely have killed him.

It wasn't his fault. If they hadn't been cruising him, luring him with admiring looks and come-on smiles, they'd still be alive. Why couldn't they just be satisfied that he'd called them?

Just because I called didn't give you the right to star-sixty-nine. I didn't give you my number for a reason. Too risky. Calling me back was a foolish, foolish mistake. Stalking me was stupid too. You had to die because you just couldn't leave well enough alone. None of them could.

Until he saw the write-ups in the *Blade*, he didn't even remember their names. Reading about thirty-seven-year-old Scott Everson and the bright future he'd had with a liberal Washington think tank; the role thirty-five-year-old Brian Davis had played in launching an HIV education program; or the wonderful work Frank Goodloe, age forty, was doing with inner-city youth just pissed him off. Dumbasses would still be alive if they hadn't stalked him.

He dropped the *Blade* in the trash and kept walking. He liked to walk. Exercise made him feel good about himself. Six years in the Marines had put him in great shape, and he worked hard to stay that way. In fact, thanks to the injections and at least two hours at the gym every day, he was even bigger and stronger than he had been before his discharge.

Thinking about his discharge pissed him off all over again. *Fuckers. Put a bunch of aggressive, physically fit young men together in close quarters for months at a time, shit happens.* So what if he liked sucking dick? The men in his outfit didn't mind. Receiving a dishonorable discharge for providing a service that kept the guys happy was totally fucked up.

Hell yeah, he'd charged for it. On what planet did someone get quality blowjobs for free? The fact he enjoyed sucking dick didn't change anything. *Nothing in life is free. The goddamn government paid welfare queens more than servicemen. Had to do something to supplement that sorry paycheck. It was a win-win situation. The men in the unit got the best head money could buy, and I made a few hundred extra dollars a month for my trouble.*

He'd gone back home right after his discharge and taught some of his former classmates a few lessons too. He enjoyed pounding the faces of the kids who'd tormented him and called him a fag when he was younger and too small to defend himself. Making them pay had felt great. Yeah, they paid all right. Paid with blood and broken bones.

Scott, Brian, and Frank had paid too. Saying he would call after hooking up didn't mean he would. Straight guys did that to girls all the time. But girls had enough sense to shut up about it. Not Scott, Brian, or Frank. No, they had to go shooting off their fucking mouths.

The thought of Caleb finding out made him break out in a cold sweat.

He loved Caleb more than anyone he'd ever known. Feared him too. Thanks to a dozen years as a Navy SEAL, Caleb was the only man he'd ever met who could flat-out kick his ass. Except, of course, his father.

His relationship with Caleb reminded him a lot of his parents' marriage. As long as she didn't fuck up, his old man had been good to his mom. Fear kept her from leaving the old prick. Adam understood.

No, it wasn't his fault the men were dead. They died because they were stupid. How could they think someone like him was available, anyway?

He'd met Scott for a walk in Rock Creek Park. Dumbass thought they were going to have sex in the woods. Instead, he'd bashed Scott's head in with a rock that he then tossed into the creek.

Brian had followed him to his car one night after he left the Green Lantern and talked about how sex with him had made him see fireworks. Brian probably saw some stars after Adam cracked his skull open with the baseball bat he kept on the floorboard in the backseat of his car.

He thought about Frank, the last one. The stupid prick had walked right up to him at the Eagle. Said he was disappointed that his phone never rang. Lucky for him, Caleb had stayed home that night. Not so lucky for Frank, who had been eager to go with him out onto the patio, and even happier to slip through a nearly hidden gate to the street where Adam had parked. Frank thought they were going to get busy with some hot action in the car. Instead, he got the bat upside the head a couple dozen times.

Adam glanced at his watch and quickened his pace. Caleb would be home soon. If he got supper started and had the townhouse cleaned up, maybe Caleb would let him suck his dick. If not, well... he really didn't want to think about what might happen.

• 8 •

JOSH had never been to New York City, but if it was anything like DC, he could understand why they called it the city that never sleeps. Sirens screamed almost continuously. A boisterous crowd moved back and forth between several gay bars a stone's throw from his balcony, getting louder as late night turned to early morning. About the time the bar crowd cleared out, a deafening cacophony of trash trucks descended upon the neighborhood dumpsters. The noise finally died down around six o'clock, about the time he'd be getting up for work.

The sound of his phone ringing woke Josh from a sound sleep. "Shit!" He knew it was Linda. He also knew she was probably pissed he'd forgotten to call her the night before.

"Hello, Linda… sorry I didn't call. I fell asleep on the sofa, and when I woke up, it was too late to call."

"Good morning, Josh. No need to apologize. I figured as much, but hoped maybe you'd stumbled across a drunken orgy to celebrate your first night in the big city."

"Ha! You know I'm not that kind of guy." *No*, he thought, *I'm the kind of guy who pays for sex and then lies to his best friend about it.*

"Oh, you're that kind of guy, all right. You've just never had the opportunity. So how's life in the big city?"

"Noisy." As if to prove the point, a fire truck sped down P Street, siren blaring.

"Are you outside?"

Josh reached for his cigarettes and waited for the siren to pass. "Nope. Sitting in bed."

"Wow. That's going to take some getting used to. Maybe you should get one of those white-noise machines."

"Good idea. I'm going to have to do something—sleep is practically impossible. I can't imagine ever getting used to all the noise."

"So tell me all about your first night in DC. Did you get everything unpacked? You promised me you'd do a better job keeping things picked up than you did in the condo."

Josh glanced at the clothes he'd worn the day before, now strewn across the bedroom. "Just about. I have a few more boxes to go, but mostly I'm done. The cute relocation guy's name is Thad. He helped a lot. He arranged all the furniture, got the movers to put the boxes in the right rooms, and even made the bed for me."

"Did he now? And was he waiting in it when you arrived?"

"I wish. He's even cuter than I remembered. Looks like Ron Howard did on *Happy Days*, only with good hair. He's got a really nice smile, great eyes, and these adorable black-frame glasses that give him a bookish look. He didn't ping my gaydar, but at one point I thought he was flirting with me."

"Probably was. Your gaydar is defective—always has been. Hell, you didn't even know about yourself."

Josh laughed. "You've got a point."

"So did you two go out on the town?"

"Nope. He went home. I never even left the apartment."

Linda sighed. "I hope you intend to get out today."

"Yeah. I don't have to go to work until tomorrow, so I've got the whole day to explore the neighborhood. I need to find a grocery store."

"Met any of your neighbors yet?"

"Nope. I smoked a joint out on the balcony last night and didn't see a soul on any of the balconies on my side of the building." Another fire truck blared by.

"I can understand why, with all that racket. What's the rooftop pool like?"

"Haven't been yet. I'm hoping to spend a couple of hours up there today." Josh rubbed his cigarette along the edge of the ashtray to knock off excess ash before taking a long draw.

"Having a pool on the roof is too cool. Shame it won't be open in November when I come for a visit. I'm already getting excited about the trip—seeing you, meeting your new boyfriend, and checking out the sites."

Josh exhaled a big cloud of smoke and laughed. "You're such a nut. I'm looking forward to your visit too."

"Well, I didn't really want anything except to see how you're doing. Next time we talk, I want to hear about something other than the inside of your apartment, okay?"

"You will. I'm getting up now." Josh opened the blinds and looked out the window. "There's not a cloud in the sky, so I think I'll start my day with some laps and a little sun."

"Good idea. Maybe you'll make some new friends around the pool."

"Maybe so. Thanks for calling, Linda—sorry I didn't call you last night."

"I'll let it go this time—just don't let it happen again. I love you!"

After the call, Josh's growling stomach reminded him he hadn't eaten anything since the peanuts the stewardess provided on the flight from Lexington the day before. He remembered a bagel shop he'd seen from the balcony, slid on some shorts and a T-shirt, and after grabbing his wallet and keys, headed out for some breakfast.

Josh inhaled an egg and cheese bagel sandwich, a glazed donut, and a carton of orange juice at the bagel shop before visiting the grocery store, conveniently located on the ground floor of the West Park. The tiny grocery was maybe twice the size of his apartment, yet seemed to contain everything he could want. He picked up stuff for sandwiches and a few staples and then headed back to his apartment.

He changed into his swimming trunks, grabbed the book he'd been halfheartedly trying to read for months, and a towel before hopping the elevator upstairs to the pool. Despite the near perfect weather, the pool was deserted. Josh set his belongings on a lounge chair and dove in to swim a few laps. The water felt great.

He heaved himself out of the pool and walked over to the rail to look out over a large, tree-covered park to the Washington Monument. Being ten stories off the ground provided a nice breeze. Josh had always thought big cities were just buildings and concrete and was surprised by all the green space and the lush tree canopy visible in every direction.

He settled into his lounge chair, picked up his book, and started reading. Restless, he set the book aside and swam a few more laps. The idea of a quiet afternoon alone by the pool didn't appeal to him. He decided to give Thad a call to see if he wanted to join him.

Thad said he'd love to and would be over in thirty minutes. Josh smoked another joint on the balcony. He thought about waiting to smoke it with Thad, but because he was a coworker, decided against it. The less people at work knew about his private life, the better. When he saw Thad coming down P Street, he went inside to brush his teeth, and then waited for the intercom to buzz so he could let him in.

• 9 •

JOSH'S call caught Thad completely off guard. He expected a question about the nearest dry cleaner or something equally mundane—the kind of calls he routinely got from people he'd helped to relocate a few days after they arrived in DC. When Josh instead invited him over to hang out at the pool, Thad resisted the urge to scream like a teenaged girl at a Backstreet Boys concert. He took a deep breath to calm himself before saying he'd love to and would be there in thirty minutes.

Never mind that sunning himself around the pool was not something he normally did. With his fair complexion and red hair, the last thing he needed was sunburn. But the thought of spending an afternoon with handsome Josh Freeman overrode any objections he might normally have to spending a day by the pool. He tossed a bottle of SPF-15 sunscreen into a bag with his towel, then changed into swimming trunks and a T-shirt before heading out to Josh's.

As he walked, Thad decided he was glad to have completed his workout early. On the weekends, he usually didn't go to the gym until after noon. Fantasies about being with Josh had kept him awake for hours the night before and then haunted his dreams. He awoke with a morning hard-on from hell. His first waking thought was that he needed to get to the gym, pronto. He'd learned years earlier that working out was a good way to relieve sexual tension. Given his lack of interest in any of the men he knew, he'd been spending a lot of time at the gym the last few months.

His parents had instilled in him an appreciation for a healthy lifestyle. From a very early age, he had enjoyed a wide variety of physical, often strenuous, activities alongside either his mom or dad or both. His mother loved water sports and had involved him in competitive swimming and diving. His father enjoyed calisthenics and taught him how to play football, basketball, and baseball. Together, the family often hiked, played tennis, or water-skied.

Thad walked past the market and thought about how he avoided fried foods, limited his intake of red meat, and made sure to eat lots of fresh fruit and vegetables. He never smoked, rarely drank, and avoided drugs like the plague. In fact, many promising relationships had ended because of his unyielding opposition to substance abuse. Drugs were not only bad for you, but against the law. He couldn't imagine why anyone would risk everything for a temporary, distorted view of the world.

When a shirtless Josh opened the door to let him in, Thad took in his darkly tanned skin, the silky hair on his chest, and the happy trail that vanished into his swimming trunks, and then forced himself to keep his eyes focused on the handsome face. The beard, tousled hair, and sleepy eyes gave Josh a rough look that Thad found appealing. He resisted the overwhelming urge to drag Josh back to the bedroom.

"Thanks for inviting me over," Thad said as he stepped into the elevator. "I haven't gone swimming for years."

"Glad you could join me," Josh said as they got off the elevator and walked up the steps to the pool.

"I can't believe there's nobody up here on a beautiful day like today. I would have expected the pool to be packed," Thad said. He walked over to the corner closest to the Washington Monument. "Couldn't ask for a nicer view of the city and Rock Creek Park."

Josh pointed to the woods next to his apartment. "That's Rock Creek Park? Where one of those guys got killed?"

"Yeah, the grassy area along the creek just below your apartment is called P Street Beach. It's usually filled with sunbathers. I bet that's where the killer hooked up with his victim."

Thad glanced around and settled on two chairs overlooking the deep end of the pool. "Want to sit here?"

"Perfect." Josh tossed his towel on the recliner and lined it up for maximum exposure to the sun. Thad spread his towel across an adjacent recliner and lined it up with Josh's before kicking off his Birkenstocks and sliding his shirt over his head.

"Would you mind putting some sunscreen on my back?" Thad asked. "With my fair skin, I'll burn up without it."

"Sure." Josh squirted the lotion Thad gave him into his palm. Instead of slowly massaging the lotion into his back, he swiped it on with a few quick strokes. When he was finished, he dove facedown onto his lounge chair.

"Want me to do you too?" Thad asked.

"That would be great."

The firm warmth of Josh's skin beneath his hands undid what two hours at the gym had finally accomplished. He dove face-first into the lounger to hide a not so subtle reaction to the oddly intimate encounter. "So what do you think? Glad you moved to DC?"

Josh nodded. "DC is definitely a big change from Lexington. It's going to take some adjusting, but I think I'm going to like it."

"I can't imagine living anywhere else. Have you always lived in Lexington?"

"Yeah, pretty much in the same zip code. All four of my grandparents were born in the area too."

"You don't hear that in DC. Between the politicians and college students, there's a lot of coming and going. I don't think I know anyone who was born here. What do you think you'll miss most about Lexington?"

Josh didn't hesitate. "I'd have to say the horse farms. The city is almost completely surrounded by a band of them. No matter which way you head out of town, within a few minutes rolling pastures of bluegrass, miles of plank fencing, and stacked limestone walls surround you. I don't think there's any place else quite like it."

"Sounds beautiful."

"It is. DC is beautiful too, just in a different way. Without all the green space and trees here, I'd definitely miss Lexington more than I do."

Between long silences, Josh and Thad chatted all afternoon. Chatting with Josh was both pleasant and frustrating. Though at first he hadn't been so sure, he was now convinced Josh was gay. If he hadn't been a coworker, he might have taken the bull by the horns and said something. That they managed to spend three hours alone together without ever broaching the subject was frustrating and more than a little odd. Was Josh afraid? Or maybe he just wasn't interested.

Either way, Thad enjoyed spending time with Josh and was glad he'd invited him over. They did get to know each other better. Josh talked about Lexington and his time in school. Thad was surprised to learn Josh had a graduate degree in graphic arts. He didn't strike Thad as the graduate-school type.

"Once I got my bachelor's degree in communications," Josh said, "the only jobs I could find were more or less the same kind I could get before I got a degree. Graduate school had never been part of my plan, but I applied and ended up with an assistantship."

"That's great," Thad replied. "Once I finished my undergrad degree, I was ready for a break. My parents always expected me to go to graduate school. Maybe I will one day. Since I don't plan on having any children, I'm not on anyone's time schedule."

Thad was sure Josh would recognize his comment about not having children as code for being gay. He didn't. Short of drawing him a picture, he didn't know what else to do and decided to let it go. Surely he'd figure it out Monday when he saw that all the guests at the party he was throwing for him were gay. If not, Thad thought he'd be spending a lot more time at the gym.

• 10 •

JOSH had always known he was easy on the eyes. For as long as he could remember, people—mostly women—had commented on how pretty he was. Pretty, not handsome. Pretty was for girls, and maybe little boys.

No one had called him pretty for a long time; not since he'd put on thirty pounds. At just over six feet, he carried his weight well, but was far from ripped. As he dried off, Josh caught his reflection in the mirror. No, he definitely wasn't buff—not even close—but he wasn't fat either.

He thought about what Mitch, the call boy/masseur, had said about him. Josh never thought of himself as hot or particularly well hung. He stroked his cock. He'd certainly seen bigger—lots bigger. Thinking about Thad's sexy body quickly produced the desired result. He walked into his bedroom, pulled a tape measure from his desk drawer, placed the end at the base of his now throbbing member, and extended the tape across the top to the tip.

"Damn. Eight and a half inches."

He wrapped the tape measure around the thickest part of the shaft. Almost six inches. He'd never measured before. While he admired big dicks, he wasn't overly obsessed with them, and because Ben was huge, had long ago written off his own as merely average. The discovery of his actual size caused him to wonder how big Ben's cock must have been.

Returning to the bathroom, Josh thought about the leather-daddy label Ted had used, recalling Tom of Finland images of muscular, mustached men with dark hair and dark eyes, decked out in leather gear that he'd drooled over when he first came out. Given his lack of interest in working out, the big-daddy body probably wasn't going to happen. The idea of himself decked out in leather made him laugh.

The beard Josh now sported was the result of skipping the daily shave for more than a week. He lathered up his face, and except for a thick mustache extending beneath his nose to his jaw line, shaved off the beard. He wiped his face clean and stood back from the mirror to admire the result.

"Wow." He couldn't believe the difference. The new mustache made him look like something out of *Honcho* magazine. All he needed was a chest harness and some buttless chaps to complete the look—not that he'd ever resort to that. He considered the leather crowd to be about the same as the drag set. Dressing up was dressing up.

He slipped on some gym shorts and a T-shirt, then grabbed a joint from the jewelry box, and after dragging a chair from the dining room table, he took a seat outside. Except for several pots of dead plants on the balcony next door, the balconies around him were deserted. He watched people on the street coming and going, all in a hurry.

He stroked his new mustache, enjoying the feel of it on his face. He wondered what Ben would think. Then he knew. The realization hit him so suddenly that the joint fell from his mouth and nearly rolled off the edge of the balcony.

Ben wouldn't like it. In fact, Ben hadn't liked any of the changes in Josh. Ben's new and much younger lover, David, was reed thin— like Josh had been when he and Ben first met.

Despite Ben's constant comments about Josh's weight gain, he wasn't fat. He was just too big for twink-loving Ben. Josh wasn't his type anymore. Instead of the boy Ben had fallen in love with seventeen years ago, Josh had grown into a full-fledged man.

Josh headed out to explore the neighborhood. He walked up to Connecticut Avenue with a newfound spring in his step. He spent most his time browsing through Lambda Rising—the first gay bookstore he'd ever seen that didn't revolve around porn, peepshows, and sex toys. He bought *Tales of the City* by Armistead Maupin and *The Vampire Lestat*, the newest volume in Anne Rice's Vampire Chronicles. On the way back to the apartment, Josh counted sixteen different restaurants. He thought about stopping at one for dinner, but the idea of eating at a table for one didn't appeal to him. Instead, he stopped at the Burger King and picked up a Whopper meal to take home.

Back at the apartment, Josh started reading *Tales of the City*. After an hour of reading, he thought about taking a nap so he could check out some of the bars in the neighborhood later, but decided against it. He really didn't want to come in to his first day of work with a hangover.

Josh heard the sound of the growing bar crowd from the street below and smoked another joint. The people on the street were oblivious to his presence. Josh watched in horror as a homeless woman he'd seen panhandling in the area stepped into an alley across the street, dropped her sweat pants, and sprayed a thick stream of urine against the wall. He couldn't decide if he was more shocked by her ability to hose the wall or that she did so in public.

He went back inside and lay on the sofa for more reading. Now and then, he glanced at the clock. At some point he must have fallen asleep because the next thing he knew, the trash trucks were noisily emptying dumpsters.

• 11 •

JOSH was excited about his first day at the new office. Other than dodging the puke and puddles of pee left on the sidewalk the night before by drunks and homeless people, the walk to work was pleasant and quiet.

The morning at the office flew by. He knew most the staff, having worked with them for years via telephone and e-mail. Still, it was nice to have faces to go with the names—none of which matched his preconceived mental images.

To his surprise and delight, Thad stopped by his office right before lunch.

"Love your new mustache."

Josh beamed. "I'm surprised you noticed. First time I've ever had one, and I have to admit, I'm liking the change."

"It suits you. Got plans for lunch? I thought maybe I could introduce you to one of the local eateries."

Josh hadn't even thought about lunch. Eating with Thad sounded a lot more interesting than anything he would have come up with on his own. "I don't. Thanks for thinking about me."

Thad flashed pearly whites worthy of a toothpaste commercial. "Great. I'll stop by in about fifteen minutes. Do you like Italian? There's a great little place on P Street just up from your apartment I really like."

"Sounds great." Josh would have eaten dog food if it meant having lunch with Thad. Though not as sexy as in swimming trunks, he was much more handsome dressed in a coat and tie for work than he'd been in jeans and a golf shirt at the apartment.

Thad returned exactly fifteen minutes later. Josh knew because he'd been watching the clock. Thad's smile focused Josh's attention on his full, kissable lips.

"You ready?"

Josh rose from his desk. "Sure am. I really appreciate you thinking about me. Otherwise I would have enjoyed my second meal at Burger King since arriving in DC."

Thad frowned. "Eating fast food in a city like DC should be illegal. That stuff will kill you. There are dozens of really good restaurants in your neighborhood. Some are at least as cheap as Burger King, and most do a big carryout business."

Josh thought the way Thad's frown caused his nearly white eyebrows to vanish for a moment behind the thick black frames of his glasses was adorable.

"That's good to know."

"The Italian place we're going today doesn't do carryout. Al Tiramisu is more upscale than most, with some of the best Italian food in the city. I really think you'll like it."

Josh thought he'd happily eat anything Thad served.

Al Tiramisu was dark, quiet, and intimate with white tablecloths on small tables arranged for more privacy than one would expect from a restaurant so small. Josh liked the place immediately. The maître d' showed them to a table for two near the bar and handed them each a menu.

Josh looked over the specials written on a chalkboard over the bar. "What's good?"

"Everything. Whatever you get, be sure to leave room for dessert. The tiramisu is out of this world."

"Everything looks good." *Especially my lunch companion*, Josh thought. "I can't make up my mind."

"Want to share an appetizer? I absolutely love the grilled smoked mozzarella with pears and gorgonzola sauce." Thad closed the menu and set it on the table.

"Oh, that does sound good." Josh flipped the pages back and forth. Thad described several of his favorite dishes and convinced him to try the swordfish.

Thad picked up the wine list. "Want wine?"

"No, thanks. I don't drink much." Josh closed the menu and set it down in front of him. "Last thing I need is to come back after lunch on my first day with a buzz."

Thad dropped the wine list on the table and laughed. "I doubt anyone would notice, and you probably wouldn't be alone. Most people who commute from Virginia and Maryland go out for two-cocktail lunches. It's too much trouble to come back into the city after work or on weekends."

"You live outside the District?"

"No. I live on P Street, a few blocks from you—between Seventeenth and Eighteenth."

The waiter interrupted to take their order. Thad ordered for both of them, in Italian.

Josh looked at Thad, amazed. "I'm impressed! Where did you learn to speak Italian?"

"My parents both work for the State Department. Dad was the ambassador to Italy for a few years when I was a kid. Mostly I know how to read the menu with an Italian accent—I'd be lost in Italy."

Josh was still impressed. He'd taken a few years of French in high school but had never mastered the language or the accent. Hell, to folks who hadn't grown up in the south, he barely spoke English.

The food was every bit as good as Thad had promised. Josh liked being with Thad, enjoying both his company and the conversation. He found himself wishing the lunch would never end.

Over the much-anticipated tiramisu, Thad said, "Hope you haven't forgotten about the get-together tonight at my place."

"Nope. I remember. Looking forward to it too. Are you sure I can't bring anything?"

"No, just yourself. Dress is casual."

When the waiter dropped off the check, Josh picked it up over Thad's objections. "Really, it's the least I can do for all you've done for me."

"Well, if I'd known you were going to grab the check, I would have taken you someplace cheaper. Al Tiramisu is more than a little pricey."

"It's okay." Josh smiled. "They pay me well, and other than rent and Metro passes, I really don't have any expenses."

Thad laughed, a sound Josh found more and more pleasing to the ear. "Thanks. I really wasn't expecting you to pay. After all, I'm the one who asked you out to lunch."

"Really, I insist." He almost added he would take it out in trade, but decided against it. He hoped Thad was gay, and thought he probably was, but he still wasn't sure.

"Well, thank you." Thad moved the linen napkin from his lap to the empty plate in front of him. "I guess we need to head back to the office."

"Yeah. I can't be too late my first day on the job."

As they walked back to the office, Josh kept looking at Thad. Gay or straight, Thad was handsome, sweet-natured, and a lot of fun to be around. Surely tonight he'd find out one way or the other. Seven o'clock couldn't come soon enough.

• 12 •

JOSH changed clothes no fewer than fourteen times. He had no idea what to expect at Thad's little get-together. Casual dress covered a lot of territory. He finally settled on blue jeans, a Polo shirt, and a nice, but not too nice, pair of comfortable shoes.

After dragging the chair out onto the balcony, Josh smoked a joint and tried to focus on reading *Tales of the City*. He was enjoying the book, but couldn't concentrate tonight. His mind kept wandering, wondering what kind of party Thad had put together for him.

Finally it was time to head out. He brushed his teeth, spritzed on some Quorum cologne, and after checking himself out in the mirror for the hundredth time, decided he looked fine. He hoped Thad and his guests would agree, or at least not think he looked like Jethro Bodine from the *Beverly Hillbillies*.

Rather than apartments and restaurants, the block of P Street where Thad lived featured large homes in a variety of architectural styles with little flower gardens between the front porches and the sidewalk. Some of the buildings had been converted into apartments, but most, including the one Thad lived in, appeared to be single-family homes.

Before Josh could ring the bell, Thad opened the ornately carved door. "Welcome to Casa Philip. Come on in and meet our host."

Josh thought Thad was hosting the party. A little confused, he stepped into the stylish entryway. "Your place is beautiful!"

"Thanks. It's all Philip's. He can't wait to meet you. Come on back."

Josh followed Thad across inlaid hardwood floors, admiring the beautiful furniture and artwork scattered throughout the spacious rooms. Philip appeared to be doing quite well for himself.

They ended up in a sunroom larger than Josh's apartment, surrounded on three sides by floor-to-ceiling windows. Anchored by a small pool with a five-tiered fountain, the rose garden outside looked formal and well tended. Several guests milled in the center of the room around a large table mounded high with food. Still more guests stood before a handsome young man in a tuxedo shirt and bow tie serving drinks at a bar in the corner of the room. All the guests were men. The light came on for Josh. *Philip must be Thad's lover. Damn.*

A rotund man in his late fifties or early sixties walked toward Thad and Josh, a big smile lighting up his face. "You must be Josh, our guest of honor. I'm Philip Potter. Welcome!"

That Philip was clearly old enough to be Thad's father caught Josh off guard. "Uh… nice to meet you, Philip. Your house is beautiful."

"Thank you, Josh. Blame my addiction for pretty things. Speaking of which, step over here to Matthew and let's get you something to drink."

Philip took Josh by the arm and led him over to the bar. "Matthew, this is Josh, our guest of honor. He's surely parched from the walk. What would you like?"

Glancing at the well-appointed bar, Josh ordered. "I'll have a bourbon and Coke, please, with a wedge of lime if you've got it."

The handsome bartender scooped ice into a cocktail glass. "Nice to meet you. You want to taste the Coke or do you prefer something stronger?"

Josh laughed, "I definitely want to taste the Coke. Thanks for asking."

"I aim to please," Matthew said, handing him the drink with a smile and a wink.

Philip laughed. "Yes, you certainly do. Walk with me, Josh, and allow me to introduce you to our guests."

Philip escorted Josh around the room, introducing him to first one group, then another. Overwhelmed, Josh quit trying to remember names after the first few introductions. Everyone clearly adored Philip.

Thad reappeared as Philip was wrapping up introductions. "Thad, darling, you've really outdone yourself this time. I'm so glad you suggested this little soiree and I am delighted to be the one to introduce Josh to the rest of the gang. He's gorgeous and quite charming."

"Oh, Philip, you say that to all the guys," Thad said, laughing.

"Yes, I do, don't I? But that doesn't make it any less true. At my age, they're all gorgeous."

Thad laughed, and grabbing Josh by the elbow, herded him toward the food table.

"He likes you. I knew he would. Being a friend of Philip's opens a lot of doors in this town."

Josh wanted to ask about Thad's relationship with Philip but decided against it. "I can't thank you enough. When you said little get-together I had no idea…."

Thad took a plate and proceeded to make his selections from the sumptuous spread. "Philip doesn't do anything small. I would have warned you, but was afraid you might not come. He can be a bit much sometimes, but has a heart of gold."

Following Thad's lead, Josh picked up a plate. "With a smaller group, I might have remembered a name or two. In this crowd, the only names I remember are Philip, Matthew, and at least half a dozen Michaels."

Thad laughed. "Yeah. When you can't remember a gay man's name, Michael is a good guess."

Josh transferred several stuffed mushrooms to his nearly full plate. "I had no idea you were gay."

Thad topped off his plate with a rich-looking pastry. "Your gaydar is even worse than mine. I wasn't sure about you either, until I made your bed. Straight men don't have designer sheets, or at least, not any I've helped move."

Josh added a pastry to his plate and saw a waiter in a white coat emerge from the house who proceeded to refill the serving dishes on the table. *A catered party*, thought Josh. Philip had spared no expense. The food was excellent, well prepared, and obviously expensive.

Most of the guests either worked for the government or with a nonprofit. Josh felt very much out of his league. Politics and talk of the murders dominated the conversations around him. Josh decided this was, beyond a doubt, the most educated group of gay men he'd ever seen. Nobody talked about the bar scene, what others were wearing, or who was sleeping with whom. Preferring to let everyone think he was an idiot rather than open his mouth and prove it, Josh didn't talk much.

Philip, the life of the party, roamed from group to group, making witty remarks and teasing his guests in a way that suggested they'd been friends for a long time. Josh wondered how Thad and Philip had come to be lovers. He thought about Thad's comment about not wanting to live where he could afford the rent and hoped something more than Philip's obvious wealth was the reason they were together.

The welcome party lasted well into the evening. Around ten o'clock, the guests headed out in small groups to stop off at one of the nearby bars for another cocktail before heading home. Several invited Josh along, but he politely declined. He'd already had two drinks—his limit, especially for a work night.

Thad left him to mingle. As the crowd thinned out, Josh decided it was time to go. He looked around for Philip to say good-bye.

"Philip, I can't thank you enough for the party."

The older man hugged him warmly. "Think nothing of it. I'm always looking for a good excuse to surround myself with handsome men. It was my pleasure. I hope we'll see a lot of you around here."

"I hope so too."

"Did you happen to see this week's *Blade*?" Philip asked.

"Yeah. Shame about those guys getting killed. One of them got killed right across the street from my apartment."

"That's what Thad said. Hard to imagine what would make someone do something like that. Makes me glad I don't go out very much."

Thad reappeared as Josh extracted himself from Philip's bear hug.

"Leaving so soon?"

"Yeah, I'm a lightweight. So nice of you to arrange for all this. Y'all really know how to make a guy feel welcome."

"It was our pleasure. You'll find out soon enough, Philip jumps at any occasion to host a party."

Josh laughed. "So he says."

Thad gestured toward the front entrance. "Let me walk you to the door."

He led Josh back through the beautiful home to the heavy antique door. Again Josh admired the contrast of the dark mahogany against the light ash filigree in the floor. An awkward silence enveloped the two.

Josh extended his hand. "Thanks again, Thad. I'm really impressed with all your friends and look forward to getting to know them better."

Thad grasped it warmly. "Trust me," he said, "the feeling is more than mutual. You were quite a hit. Everyone asked if you were single. I told them you were, but to give you a chance to settle in before trying to sweep you off your feet."

Josh laughed halfheartedly. Thad pawning him off to the other guests confirmed his suspicions about him being in a relationship with Philip. None of the other guests had Thad's good looks, sweet disposition, and charming personality, but he wouldn't complain. At least he had more options here than in Lexington.

Thad broke the awkward silence. "See you tomorrow?"

"Yeah, I'll be there. Thanks again."

Josh headed home through dark streets and noticed that nobody else he saw was alone. Thoughts of the murders caused him to pick up his pace. Though disappointed about Thad being off the market, Josh decided to focus on the positive. Several of the other guests were interested in him. Linda was right: moving to DC had been exactly what the doctor ordered.

• 13 •

THAD leaned against the door and sighed. For a minute, he'd thought Josh might kiss him. That he had not was disappointing, but not terribly surprising. The man still didn't appear to have a clue about Thad's feelings for him.

The simple truth was he couldn't get Josh Freeman off his mind. Ever since they'd met at the airport, fantasies about the tall, handsome man had filled his waking hours and tormented his dreams. Thad hadn't been this interested in anyone since coming out of the closet, back when he was thirteen. He was obsessed.

Philip, his mother's only sibling, was likely the cause of Thad coming out at such a young age. Because of the steady stream of mostly attractive young men that came and went at Philip's house, Thad grew up knowing his uncle was gay, and until middle school, didn't know being gay was anything out of the ordinary. Unlike many of his friends, Thad's family hadn't freaked out when he came out. His parents said they were glad he'd found himself and sent him to spend the weekend with Uncle Philip.

Over the weekend, his uncle had impressed certain facts upon Thad. "Fact number one: God created gay people and, consequently, loves them just as much as he loves anyone else. Fact number two: being gay means some people will give you a hard time. Always remember it is his or her problem, not yours. Fact number three: being gay doesn't define who you are any more than having red hair or wearing glasses defines you."

These facts served Thad well over the years and had spared him much of the anguish coming out produced in some of his friends.

Thad returned to the sunroom. Philip was leaning against the bar, talking earnestly with Matthew, his new project. Philip was constantly taking on projects—handsome young men with families who didn't seem to understand being gay wasn't a choice. Thad worried one of those castaways would break his heart or worse, but Philip always managed to escape unscathed.

Most of the guests had already left. Thad navigated the room, picking up plates and glasses while the caterer cleared what was left of the food. As he tidied up, he thought about how fortunate he was to have an uncle like Philip.

Acceptance from his own family had spared Thad a lot of the struggles Philip's strays and most of Thad's gay friends experienced after they came out. Thanks to Philip and his own parents, Thad had never been desperate to find someone to love and accept him, and as a result, at the tender age of thirty-four had never been seriously involved with anyone. He'd dated some and fooled around a little, but had never had even so much as a serious crush.

Thad credited Philip with helping him dodge the messy entanglements he'd seen so many of his friends pursue. Avoiding bad relationships had spared him the heartbreak and nasty breakup scenes he'd witnessed so many times. Philip constantly encouraged him to wait for the right guy and assured Thad he would know him when he saw him.

Philip had been right. The moment Thad had laid eyes on him, he knew Josh Freeman was The One. It wasn't that Josh was tall, dark, and handsome—though the fact he was gorgeous certainly didn't hurt. Something about Josh touched Thad deep inside.

Finding out from a coworker at the Lexington branch how deeply wounded Josh had been by the end of his seventeen-year relationship helped. But it was more than that… a lot more. Thad couldn't say for sure what it was, but something about ruggedly handsome Josh Freeman had grabbed onto his heart and wouldn't let go.

Thad was glad Josh bought his story about always making the bed for people he helped relocate to DC. A fantasy about the two of them jumping into the sack had motivated Thad to check the box marked "bedroom linens" for sheets, pillows, and a bedspread. Only the presence of the movers along with the stern warning from Philip not to be too forward had prevented him from shedding his clothes and climbing into the bed to wait for his dream lover.

Yes, he had been a little hurt that Josh hadn't remembered his name after the hours they had spent together checking out apartments. Still, Thad didn't hold it against him. Moving more than five hundred miles away from family and friends had to be hard on someone like Josh. He had clearly been too preoccupied with the decisions he had to make to pay much attention to his tour guide. Besides, on moving day he'd warmed up considerably by the time Thad left and had even invited him over to the pool.

Popping into the office on Josh's first day at work wasn't standard operating procedure, either. Josh's invitation to join him at the pool had encouraged him, but taking Josh to lunch had been Philip's idea. The welcome party tonight had been Philip's idea too. Thad wasn't worried about Josh making a good impression on his uncle, but that he had was a relief.

After dropping off an armful of dishes, Thad returned from the kitchen to an empty sunroom. He could hear Philip laughing in the entryway, bidding farewell to the last of their guests. Matthew and the caterer were nowhere in sight and had apparently already been paid and sent home. Thad collected the last of the dishes from around the sunroom.

When he returned, Philip was behind the bar. "Join me for a nightcap, nephew?"

Thad smiled. "You know I hate to see you drink alone. Sure, I'll take a light one."

After the drinks were made, Philip took a seat in a comfortable chair overlooking the garden, now illuminated by the lights around the fountain. Thad took the cocktail from his uncle and sat in a matching chair beside him.

"That went well, don't you think?" Philip asked.

"Yeah. Thanks again for putting together such a nice party. What did you think of him?"

Philip took a drink and turned to Thad. "I liked him, and can see why you're so attracted to him. He's even better-looking than you said, and unlike many good-looking gay men, not at all full of himself. I approve."

Thad watched the water dropping from tier to tier on the fountain. "I'm glad you like him. The more I'm around him, the more I like him."

"I can understand why. He's very nice. I can tell he likes you too."

Thad sighed. "I hope so. When I was telling him good-bye, there was a moment I thought he might kiss me. It was hard letting him leave without kissing him good-bye when what I really wanted was to drag him upstairs to my bedroom."

Philip sipped his cocktail. "I think maybe Josh is a little overwhelmed by our fair city. Coming from a college town like Lexington, he's bound to feel a bit like a kid in a candy store."

Thad frowned. "Yeah, and I'm black licorice in a room full of chocolate candy bars."

"I'd chastise you for being melodramatic, but it touches my heart that you're at least a little like me." Philip smiled. "Be patient. Good things come to he who waits."

"I sure hope you're right. I can be patient, but I worry about him falling for someone else."

• 14 •

THE rest of the week flew by. Josh's in-box overflowed with projects waiting for his input, enough to make him take work at home to keep from falling behind. He didn't mind; it wasn't like he had anything else to do.

He looked forward to Friday. Greg Tucker, whom he'd met at Philip's get-together, had called, inviting Josh to join him and some other guys for cocktails after work at the Fireplace, a bar across the street from the West Park. Josh couldn't remember Greg and hoped he'd recognize the face when they met up.

After work on Friday, Josh rushed home. He wanted to change clothes, and because drinking really wasn't his thing, smoke a joint. He was doing just that on the balcony when he recognized Greg and a couple of the other guys from the party going into the Fireplace. He stubbed out the joint, returned it to his stash, and brushed his teeth before heading out.

Bare picture windows on two walls did little to light the interior. It took him a moment to adjust to the smoky dark bar. Music videos played on televisions mounted near the ceiling on either end of the room. A lone bartender was encircled by a bar, surrounded by patrons he seemed to know. Josh found Greg and his friends at a window table overlooking Twenty-Second Street.

Greg—thin, pale, and topped with a curly mop of mousy brown hair—stood to greet him. "Hey! Glad you could make it. I'm sure you remember Ed and Michael from Philip's party."

Josh shook Greg's hand. "Of course! Good to see you guys again. Thanks so much for asking me to come along."

"Good to see you again, Josh. I'm Ed Pierson." Ed was tall and very tan with a mustache that more than compensated for the lack of hair on his head.

"Nice to meet you." Josh shook his hand and noticed an expensive-looking watch and several equally pricey rings.

Michael was the looker of the three—short, with an ethnic look. Italian, or maybe Greek. Josh could barely keep from staring.

"S'up? Michael DeLuca here. What can I get you to drink?"

"Uh… make mine bourbon and Coke," Josh stammered. Figuring Michael had enough to remember, he didn't mention the chunk of lime he normally enjoyed with his cocktail of choice.

Josh took a seat next to Greg and across from Ed. Michael returned, set four drinks down on the table, and then went back to the bar. He returned moments later with four shots of something chartreuse. Sitting next to Josh, he grabbed one of the shot glasses and raised it in a toast.

"To new friends!"

Greg and Ed grabbed a shot, clinked glasses, and waited for Josh to lift the fourth. Josh picked up the last remaining shot, clinked glasses with the three men, then sniffed the chartreuse concoction gingerly before tossing it down.

Josh made a face and shook his head. "Whoa! Not sure I've ever had a green drink before."

"Lightweight! It's called a Green Eye," Michael proclaimed. "Getting you drunk is going to be easier than I thought."

Josh laughed, "Yeah, I'm not much of a drinker."

Ed switched the shot glass for the cocktail he was drinking. "We'll fix that! Michael, Greg, and I are seasoned vets. We'll show you the ropes."

Josh sipped on his bourbon and Coke and listened to the three friends talk. Michael was the ringleader. Easy-going Greg went along with whatever Michael and Ed wanted. Ed was harder to read, and seemed to be looking at him whenever Josh looked his way.

Several drinks later, Greg excused himself, only to return with yet another round of drinks for everyone and four more shots. This time the shot glasses contained something red.

"Time for a Red-Headed Slut," Greg said, raising one of the shots.

Josh had barely made a dent in his first cocktail. The shot had gone straight to his head. He took the second shot, and after clinking glasses, surreptitiously dumped it into one of the nearly empty glasses on the table. Then he promptly handed the glass and several others to the barback collecting unused glasses, empty bottles, and full ashtrays.

The three friends were clearly just warming up. Josh excused himself to go to the bathroom. Announcing he had the same need, Ed got up to follow.

They stood side by side, relieving themselves in a trough large enough to accommodate half a dozen men. Josh finished first, zipped up, and then stepped over to the sink to wash his hands. Ed soon followed suit.

As they stepped out of the bathroom into a dark hallway, Ed said, "Wait!"

Had he seen Josh dump the shot out? Uncertain about what was going on, Josh turned. Ed looped his arms over Josh's shoulders. Holding Josh firmly in his grip, Ed kissed him hard, thrusting with his tongue, trying to entice a similar response. Shocked, Josh clamped his mouth shut and tried to break away.

After an unsuccessful attempt, Ed broke off the kiss. "You are so fucking hot. I've wanted to kiss you ever since I saw you at Philip's."

Josh didn't know what to say. What came out was, "And now you have." Completely freaked out by Ed's pass, Josh turned toward the bar. "Come on, let's get back before Greg and Michael wonder what's happened and come looking for us."

Ed grabbed his arm, preventing Josh's departure. "Don't you like me?"

Josh could tell his rejection had hurt Ed's feelings. "Yeah, I like you fine. I don't mean to be rude, but I don't want to be rude to our friends, either."

Ed kissed him again, this time reaching down to caress Josh's cock through his jeans.

Josh pushed him away. "Come on, man, not now."

Ed struck a defiant pose. "What's the matter? Aren't I good enough for you?"

"Ed, let's not do this, okay? I'm just out having a good time with friends."

Ed closed the distance between them. "Yeah, I'll show you a good time. I'd love to get inside those jeans."

Exasperated, Josh backed away from Ed's groping hands. "Ed, stop. You're making an ass of yourself. Let's go back to the table."

Ed turned belligerent. "Who you calling an ass, you self-righteous little prick?"

Josh pushed Ed away and practically sprinted back to the table, where Michael and Greg were enjoying yet another shot—this one a deep blue. Two more of the blue concoctions stood waiting for Ed and Josh, along with yet another round of cocktails.

"Everything okay?" asked Greg.

Josh took his seat. "Not really."

"Ed being an asshole?" asked Michael.

Josh took a big swig from the new bourbon and Coke in front of him. "You could say that."

Michael laughed. "Don't take it personally. He gets a little obnoxious after a few drinks."

Greg nodded. "Yeah, Michael's right—and he's a bit of an asshole even before he drinks. Let me go talk to him."

Josh appreciated Greg's intervention. The last thing he wanted was a big scene during his first outing with new friends. He turned to Michael. "That was awkward."

"Not if you know Ed as well as we do." Michael scooted his chair over closer to Josh and placed a hand on his leg. "I'm glad the two of us have a minute to talk. I was hoping maybe you'd join me after this little drinkfest breaks up to hit some of the other bars around here."

Josh thought about grabbing the hand on his leg and dragging Michael across the street and up to his apartment. Instead, he said, "I... uh... I really don't know what to say. Greg is the one who invited me along. Leaving with you wouldn't be cool."

The look Michael gave him made Josh blush. "Greg invited you along at my request. He rarely goes anywhere without Ed. They've been friends for a long time."

The hottest man he'd ever seen was hitting on him. Josh felt his cheeks flush. "Oh... I see."

Greg returned with an embarrassed-looking Ed. "I think we'll be heading home now. Sorry to bust the party up early. You mind?"

"Not at all," said Michael, winking at Josh before tossing back the rest of his gin and tonic.

Concerned about breaking up the party, Josh looked at Greg. "I hope I haven't caused any problems."

"Not at all. Ed's sorry." Greg turned to Ed. "He'll apologize when he's pulled his head out of his ass."

Ed smiled sheepishly. "Sorry, Josh. I have a weakness for hot men."

"No harm done. Apology accepted."

Greg started toward the door, dragging Ed behind him. "See you, Josh. Thanks for coming out with us. We'll have to do it again."

"Sure. I'd like that."

Josh was relieved they were gone but wondered what he'd gotten himself into. Michael's smile caused a stirring in Josh's jeans.

Michael slid his hand farther up Josh's thigh. "Problem solved. Ready for another drink?"

Josh looked at Michael in disbelief. "Are you kidding? I don't think I've had this much to drink in ten years."

Michael teased, "You really are a lightweight. Don't they have bars back in Kentucky?"

Josh shook his head. "Only one gay bar, mostly for college students. I've been maybe five times in the last five years."

Michael nodded in agreement. "Yeah, that would get old. College kids think the whole world revolves around them. With one or two exceptions, the DC bars definitely cater to an older crowd."

Josh took another sip from his drink and turned to Michael. "I thought gay men over thirty turned straight or something. You sure don't see many of them in Lexington."

Michael laughed and patted Josh on the leg. "Older gay men are either happily partnered and avoid the bar scene altogether, or they move to big cities like DC, Philadelphia, and New York where they can act like they're still twenty-two."

Josh felt the heat of Michael's hand through his jeans. He took another sip of his drink, now diluted with melted ice, and peered into Michael's bedroom eyes. "What do you do when you're not hanging out at bars, acting like you're twenty-two?"

Michael held his gaze. "I run a small bed-and-breakfast up in Maryland. I've known the owners since I was a kid. They retired to a cabin in the West Virginia mountains a few years ago and left me in charge."

Josh slid his gaze down Michael's handsome face to the tuft of fur sprouting from the collar of his shirt, then continued to his muscular forearms. "Not what I expected. Given your tan and your build, I thought maybe you worked outside."

"Nope. I just go to the gym and tanning beds a lot. Things are pretty competitive in the big city, and I need all the help I can get."

Josh didn't think Michael needed any help at all. Even without the killer body he would turn heads.

The way Michael looked him over made Josh blush. He watched the Sylvester video playing on the television over the bar for a moment to collect his thoughts and took another drink.

Michael looked at Josh's near-empty glass. "You ready to go? Let me show you around to some of the other bars in the neighborhood."

An image of Thad at the pool popped into his head.

Would he rather it was Thad who wanted to show him around? Absolutely. But Thad had a lover. Besides, Michael was even sexier than Thad, though definitely not as easy to be with. If he was going to move on, there was no time like the present. He'd follow Michael wherever he wanted to go.

Josh stood up and the room swayed. One more cocktail and the world would start spinning, he'd barf, and this would be the kind of first date that usually did not lead to a second. He grabbed the back of the chair to steady himself. "Whoa... maybe I'd better not. One more drink and you'll have to carry me home."

Michael stood and looked at him with concern. "Are you okay?"

Josh nodded, let go of the chair, and was pleasantly surprised when he didn't fall to the floor. "Yeah, but I think maybe I should call it a night."

The warm, smoke-filled room closed in on Josh. The crowded bar suddenly grew noisy. Michael stepped closer, his mouth nearly against Josh's ear. "Let me walk you home. Where do you live?"

Michael's warm breath across his ear sent shock waves tingling through his body. When the tingling reached his loins, Josh felt the hair on his neck rise. His throat closed up as he stammered, "Right across the street. Step outside and you can see my apartment."

Michael held onto Josh's elbow and led him through the crowd to the door and out into the street. A blast of fresh air at least fifteen degrees cooler than the stifling bar hit his face. He was glad the smell of pizza and French fries coming from the deli didn't make him sick. Looking across the street to the West Park, Josh pointed as he counted over one from the corner and up three. "That's my apartment, next to the balcony with the dead plants on it."

Michael looked to where Josh pointed. "Great location. I've always wanted to see an apartment in that place."

Josh knew Michael wanted to see more than his apartment and couldn't believe it. Reinvigorated by the thought of what was about to happen as much as by the cool, fresh air, Josh smiled. "No time like the present. I'd be happy to show you around."

• 15 •

JOSH pushed the elevator button for the fourth floor. As the doors closed, Michael covered the distance between them in two steps. Before Josh knew what was happening, Michael smothered his lips with a kiss Josh felt all the way down to his toes. He returned the embrace, softly thrusting his tongue into Michael's open mouth.

Michael groaned and pulled Josh closer to him. Josh ran his hands over Michael's firm ass. He felt the results of Michael's time at the gym and sensed lust building inside of him equal to his own. When the elevator door opened on the fourth floor, Josh broke the embrace and fumbled in his pocket for his keys. Once he found them, he struggled to unlock the door until Michael finally took the keys from his shaking hands to complete the task.

Inside, the pair came together again. Josh untucked the T-shirt from Michael's jeans, pulled it over his head, and ran his hands over the hairy, muscular chest he had uncovered. Michael yanked Josh's shirt off, then kissed him thoroughly as he explored Josh's naked chest with hands that felt like warm velvet on his skin.

They made out like teenagers at a drive-in movie. Josh caressed the muscular arms from strong, slender wrists to rock-hard shoulders before tracing his fingers down Michael's spine to the furry patch just above the ass crack hidden by his jeans. As they kissed, Josh felt Michael's thigh pushing against him, insinuating. Pulling away, Josh took Michael by the hand and led him through the apartment to the bed.

Michael pulled Josh to him again and kissed him deeply. Josh tasted gin as he explored his mouth with bold thrusts, gently pinching the nipples that poked through the mass of hair on Michael's firm chest. He savored the kiss, the feel of the fleshy nipples between his thumb and forefinger, and the brush of chest hair against his palm as Michael unbuckled his belt, unfastened his pants, and pulled down the zipper to his jeans. Michael probed deeper into Josh's mouth with his tongue, and Josh dropped his hands from the solid chest to Michael's belt. He fumbled for a moment with Michael's jeans, until finally the two of them stood naked beside the bed.

Josh stared in awe, taking in every detail of the most beautiful body he'd ever seen. The furry barrel chest nipped down to a tiny waist, accented by a happy trail that expanded rapidly to a diamond-shaped bush that then melted into solid, muscular thighs. In the center of the diamond, Michael's impressive cock jutted at an angle above low-hanging, fur-covered balls.

"Damn, Michael, you are one hot man."

"Shut up and kiss me."

Michael took charge. Josh had never been so completely dominated and found the experience to be much more satisfying than he'd ever expected. He'd never been pinned on his back and ridden like that before. Now the two of them lay together, spent. Michael broke loose and rolled onto his back beside him in the bed. "Which way to the bathroom?"

Josh pointed him in the right direction and thought about how gorgeous Michael looked as he padded naked on bare feet to the bathroom. They had barely touched the tip of the iceberg as far as Josh was concerned. When Michael returned with a wet washcloth and a towel, Josh was thinking about all the things he still wanted to do with him in bed.

"Here ya go," Michael said, tossing the washcloth to Josh. "I thought you might need this."

While Josh cleaned himself up, Michael sorted through the clothes on the floor in search of his jeans. Josh watched him dress, admiring the muscular physique and wishing he wouldn't leave.

"You can stay if you want."

"I wish I could, but I have to open the B&B early tomorrow. Better get home."

Josh got up and slid into his jeans to walk Michael to the door. He was disappointed he had to leave but understood. Work came first.

Michael tucked his T-shirt into his jeans. "Thanks for asking me up. I had a nice time."

"You're more than welcome. I had a great time. Hope we can do it again… soon."

Michael smiled, kissed him on the cheek, and opened the door to the hall and the elevators. "You're sweet. That would be nice. Take care!"

He watched as Michael got on the elevator, then closed the door. On the way back to bed, he realized they hadn't exchanged phone numbers. Oh, well, Michael knew where he lived. He'd hear from him again.

• 16 •

JOSH slept soundly for the first time since moving to Washington. Whether from exhaustion, the alcohol, or the stellar sex with Michael, he didn't know. He sat up, stretched, reached for a cigarette, and then picked up the phone to call Linda.

Linda answered on the second ring. Before she could say hello, Josh chirped, "Good morning, sunshine! How's the most beautiful woman in the world this morning?"

Linda laughed. "Fine as frog hair and glad to hear from you. You sound awfully chipper."

Josh blew a smoke ring and smiled. "I actually got some sleep last night—first time since I got here."

"Glad to hear it. Did you get one of those white-noise machines?"

"No. Better. I got laid."

"Oh?"

"Yeah. Mr. Right."

"Dammit! I thought it would take another two weeks. Looks like Mom wins the mani-pedi. So who is he?"

"Remember Thad, the relocation guy I told you about?"

"Yeah. The handsome redhead with the black-framed glasses? At least I got that part right."

Josh shook his head, "No. He has a much older partner, Philip. They hosted a welcome-to-DC party for me."

"So you and Mr. Right met at the party?"

Josh blew another smoke ring. "Sorta, but I barely remember him. There must have been thirty guys there—too many for me to really keep up with. Greg, another guy at the party, called to invite me out with a couple of his friends for drinks yesterday after work."

"So Greg is Mr. Right?"

"No, if you'll just give me a minute, I'll tell you."

Warmed up, Josh blew a smoke ring, then tried to blow a second one through the middle of it, without success. "I think maybe Greg was with Ed—another guy in the group. Ed followed me to the bathroom and tried to make out with me."

"Geez, you gay men are something else. Sounds like the makings for a good soap opera. So who is Mr. Right?"

Josh stubbed the cigarette out in the ashtray. "Their friend. He runs a small bed-and-breakfast just outside the District in Maryland. A little cocky maybe, but I'd be cocky too if I looked like him. He's so hot. I can't wait to see him again."

"I can understand why. When is your next date?"

Josh stroked his mustache and stared at the ceiling. "We don't exactly have one."

"Oh. I see. Are you going to call him today?"

Josh paused to study a hairline crack in the ceiling. "I don't have his phone number."

"You don't? Well, maybe he'll call you."

Josh decided not to mention that Michael didn't have his phone number.

"We had a great time. I'm sure he will."

After talking with Linda, Josh lay back down on the bed and thought about what he was going to do with his weekend. It would be great to go out with Michael again. Maybe he could get his number from Thad. But something about calling him for Michael's number didn't feel right.

He needed to go shopping. Besides a white-noise machine and maybe some clothes more in line with his newly discovered look, he needed to pick up some condoms. The thought of using a condom had never entered his head the night before.

Engaging in unprotected sex with someone he barely knew was a problem. The last time he'd been single, nobody had even heard of HIV and AIDS. Because he and Ben were in an allegedly monogamous relationship, Josh ignored the safe-sex messages, thinking he had nothing to worry about. Things were very different now—he'd have to do better. He hoped having condoms on hand would help him to remember to use one instead of risking his life with more unprotected sex.

Josh couldn't get Michael out of his head. He was, hands-down, the sexiest man Josh had ever seen, naked or dressed. But that wasn't all. Michael's total control over him had been a real turn-on. Josh thought of a hundred things he wanted to do the next time they were naked together. Being inside Michael had been fantastic, but what he really wanted was to be taken by the muscular man.

He ignored the hard-on thoughts of Michael had produced and headed for the shower. As he dressed after, Thad's card fell out of his shirt pocket. Seeing it as an omen, Josh decided to give him a call—to thank him for the party.

Thad sounded really glad to hear from him. Josh said, "I need to do some shopping today and wondered if you could tell me where to go. I'm looking for a white-noise machine and some clothes."

"You definitely want to go to Crystal City. The Metro stops right at the mall. They have a Nordstrom, Macy's, and a ton of nice shops. If you like, I'd be happy to go with you—we could grab lunch while we're out, and this time I'm picking up the tab."

• 17 •

THAD was waiting for him at the top of the escalator. Josh couldn't help noticing how good he looked; it was something about the glasses he wore. The thick black frames stood in stark contrast to his reddish-blond hair and porcelain complexion.

A train pulled into the station just as they arrived at the platform. They stepped aboard and settled into seats next to each other. Though it was only his third time on the Metro, Josh felt like an old pro. He looked up at the map and saw they needed to change to a Yellow Line train at the Gallery Place/China Town station to get to Crystal City.

Once he was clear on where they were going, Josh turned to Thad, "Thanks again for the party. I really had a nice time. It was so kind of you to introduce me to all your friends."

"I'm glad you enjoyed it. In truth, most of the guys are Philip's friends. He knows everyone in DC. Have you heard from Greg Tucker? I gave him your number the other day—hope you don't mind."

Mind? Josh had been thrilled. "Yeah, he called and asked me to join him and some other friends from the party at the Fireplace for drinks after work yesterday."

"Let me guess… Ed Pierson and Michael DeLuca?"

"Yeah, how did you know?"

"The three of them like to hit the Fireplace for happy hour. I've gone along once or twice and had to get a taxi because I was too drunk to walk three blocks back to the house."

"I know what you mean. I didn't even try to keep up and could barely make it home—and I live just across the street."

Thad laughed. "Yeah, I really can't drink like that—especially the shots. One or two cocktails and I'm done."

After a couple of hours, Josh was shopped out. He had purchased several new shirts, a new pair of jeans, and a small white-noise machine that came highly recommended from the salesperson at the Sharper Image. Thad bought a shirt, and being much more in the know about such things, provided much-appreciated feedback about Josh's clothing purchases.

"You about ready to get something to eat?" Josh asked, shifting his bags around. "All this walking and shopping has made me hungry."

"Sure." Thad stopped and turned to Josh. "What are you in the mood for?"

Josh was glad to have Michael to think about. Philip or not, he could easily have fallen into Thad's green eyes, watching him through nearly white lashes beneath almost too long bangs. "I'm easy. You're buying, so why don't you pick?"

"You like Spanish food? There's a great tapas bar a couple of blocks away from your apartment."

Josh couldn't believe his ears. "Topless bar?"

Thad laughed. "No, tapas—small portions, like appetizers. They're made for sharing."

"Oh." Josh felt his face flush. "Sounds good."

Josh and Thad hopped the Metro, and after reaching Dupont Circle, they walked to an upscale eatery on the first floor of the Radisson Barcelo Hotel. Along the way, Thad pointed out several landmarks and commented on the quality of the various shops and restaurants they passed. Josh was glad he'd worn comfortable shoes. By the time they arrived at the tapas bar, he'd had worked up quite an appetite.

They didn't have any trouble getting a table. Josh looked at the menu and thought it might as well have been written in Greek. Even the descriptions of the dishes contained unfamiliar words. He had no idea what to order.

The waiter rattled off a number of specials, each even more unfamiliar than the items on the menu. Josh finally settled on a dish that Thad described as eggs and bacon with rice and tomatoes.

Thad looked over the wine list. "Are you going to have a cocktail?"

"No, thanks. If I did, I'd fall asleep."

"Yeah, me too. I don't see how Greg, Ed, and Michael do it."

"Me either." Josh chose his next words carefully and tried to act nonchalant. "So what do you know about them?"

"Greg is the nicest one in the bunch. He's worked with Philip at the Smithsonian for years and is now his administrative assistant. I think Philip is grooming him to step into his job as curator when he retires."

"He seems like a nice guy. I sort of got the impression maybe he had a thing for Ed."

Thad shook his head. "No, I don't think so. They've just been friends for a long time. Ed can be a bit of a jerk, especially if he's been drinking, but mostly he's a nice guy. He has a particular fondness for married guys who can afford to add to his jewelry collection. I'm not sure if he's seeing anyone now or not."

The waiter returned with their food. Josh was relieved to see the dish he ordered was more or less exactly what he'd expected. Not that it would have mattered—he was hungry enough to eat the tablecloth.

"Married guys? That's trashy. So what about Michael?"

Thad laughed. "Michael is a total jerk. He's had a lover for years, but you'd never know it by the way he acts."

Josh nearly choked on his bacon. "Really?"

"Yeah. His lover owns the bed-and-breakfast where Michael works. I think Michael would have left him years ago if it wasn't for the job. Watch out for that one…."

"I will. Thanks for the warning."

Josh felt like a fool. He hoped Thad couldn't see how crushed he was by the news and was glad he hadn't said anything to him about the night before or his crush on Michael. He was embarrassed enough as it was.

After Thad paid the check, they walked outside to P Street.

Josh gave Thad a hug. "Thanks for lunch and a great afternoon."

Thad returned the embrace and said, "You're welcome. Thanks for asking me to come along." He waved as he headed back up P Street toward home.

Josh watched him walk. The more he was around Thad, the more he liked him. Philip was a lucky man. Josh couldn't complain, though. Thad was turning out to be a great friend—almost as good as Linda. And a good friend was worth a thousand lovers.

· 18 ·

JOSH headed back to his apartment, thinking about how Michael had lied to him about the bed-and-breakfast and that he was guilty of being "the other man." He hoped Michael's lover wasn't the jealous type. Josh knew one thing for sure: he wouldn't be seeing Michael again, not even for drinks. He'd learned the hard way from Ben. Once a cheater, always a cheater.

Ed's thing for wealthy married guys troubled Josh too. He knew someone back in Lexington who preferred married men. They had talked about it one night, and Josh believed the preference was his way of avoiding serious attachments. Though not quite the same as cheating on a spouse or partner, Ed's preference struck Josh as pathetic more than anything else.

Josh decided to skip the pool. It was too late to get any sun anyway. Besides, he had the whole day tomorrow to relax around the pool with Mary Ann, Anna Madrigal, and Mouse from *Tales of the City*.

In the West Park lobby, one of the senior citizens he'd seen on the elevator a couple of times was engaged in a heated discussion about something with his favorite receptionist. After Josh buzzed himself in, the annoyed resident glared at him before stomping off to the elevator. As Josh walked by, Vanessa shook her head.

"What's up, Vanessa?" Josh asked.

"That lady is going to be the end of me. She sits up in her apartment day after day just waiting for something to happen that she can come down here and complain about."

Josh stopped and smiled. "She's probably just lonely."

"Yes, sir, you got that right. And she's gonna die lonely, too, sooner rather than later if she don't quit coming down here and getting all up in my face about some petty problem I can't do nothing about."

"That would be a mistake—no point messing up that fine-looking dress. Yellow is definitely your color."

Vanessa laughed. "You pretty talker, you. I don't know why somebody hasn't snatched you up. I'd come after you myself if I thought you'd give a tall, dark, and lovely lady like me a chance."

Josh laughed. "How do you know I wouldn't?"

"I see you going in and out of the Fireplace. Crying shame, that's what I say. Fine man like you needs a good woman to take care of you… someone like me." She batted her eyes at him in an exaggerated way and laughed again. "Thanks for checking on me. I'll be fine. The good Lord will see that old bat gets what's coming to her. I ain't gotta worry about it."

"I admire your faith," Josh said, and then he headed over to the open elevator door. He let himself into the apartment and noticed the message light blinking on his answering machine. He always checked for messages as he came through the door, even though entire months could pass without him ever seeing the little red light blink. He pushed the button and was surprised to find he had not one or two, but three messages.

The first message was an apology from Ed along with a request to join him for dinner. The second was from Greg, apologizing for leaving him at the Fireplace and asking if he had plans for dinner.

The last call was from Josh's father, wanting to know when Josh planned to tell him he'd moved away from Lexington.

Tom Freeman had taken up with his secretary shortly after Josh was born, and after the divorce had more or less disappeared. His mother never said anything bad about him. She didn't have to. By the time Josh started grade school, he'd already figured out his father made a lot more promises than he ever kept. After the divorce, he sent cards for maybe a third of Josh's birthdays, missed his high school and college graduations altogether, and when he found out Josh was gay, he blamed Josh's mother for being too soft on him. He hadn't even come to her funeral.

Linda must have given him the new number. She had a decent relationship with her father and thought Josh was too hard on his old man. Linda had witnessed the many times Josh had been hurt by promises his father failed to keep, yet somehow still seemed to believe he owed his father something. Josh begged to differ, but refused to argue with her on the subject.

He listened to all three messages again, this time with a pencil so he could write down the numbers. He decided he'd call his father next week. He'd already had his fill of cheating liars for the weekend.

Having two invitations to dinner was a first. He thought about suggesting the three of them go out together but decided against it. Together, Greg and Ed would probably drink him under the table.

He decided to call Greg first. He'd been the one to call Josh to set up the get-together the night before. Giving him first shot at dinner seemed like the right thing to do. Then he'd call Ed to let him know he had other plans tonight and to suggest getting together another night.

He dialed Greg's number, reached for his cigarettes, and took a seat on the couch.

"Hey, Greg. Josh returning your call."

"Glad you called. Got plans for dinner?"

"As a matter of fact, I don't. What did you have in mind?" Josh took a draw on his cigarette and kicked off his shoes.

"Do you like Chinese?"

"Sure do." Josh wondered if anyone in DC ever ate down-home comfort food, like meat loaf, fried chicken, or roast beef.

"Great. We can go to City Lights, up on Connecticut Avenue. What time do you want to go?"

"I had a late lunch with Thad. Would seven thirty be too late?"

"No, that's perfect. Where do you want to meet up?"

"Come by my place around seven. I live in apartment 419 in the building across P Street from the Fireplace. Just push the button next to my apartment number and I'll buzz you in."

"Sounds like a plan. See you at seven."

After Greg hung up, Josh got a dial tone and called Ed. The phone rang several times, making Josh think he'd maybe missed him. Just as he was about to hang up, Ed answered.

"How you doing, Josh?"

"I'm good, how about you?"

"Better, now that you've called—I was afraid you wouldn't. I feel so bad about the way I acted yesterday."

Josh thought Ed sounded sincere. "No harm done. In different circumstances, I wouldn't have minded at all."

"Well, how about we create some different circumstances tonight over dinner?"

Josh laughed. "I'd love to, but unfortunately, I already have plans. How about tomorrow?"

"Tomorrow works. Where do you want to go?"

"You're the local—surprise me."

"That sounds like a challenge."

Josh could almost see Ed leering. "Maybe it is. What time?"

"How about seven o'clock?"

"That works. Want to meet at the Fireplace? I live right across the street."

"Sure. See you tomorrow at seven."

Josh hadn't been on a real date for longer than he could remember. He and Ben had gone out for dinner now and then, mostly because neither of them felt like cooking, but it was never something they planned in advance. Before leaving Lexington, the anonymous encounter in the bookstore was the closest thing he'd had to a date since the breakup. He'd been in DC less than a month and had two dates lined up for the same weekend—three if he counted Michael.

No, Michael hadn't been a date. What had happened with Michael was a trick, barely one step above an anonymous bookstore blowjob. Never mind if he believed he'd found Mr. Right. He was doing the same thing he'd done between the relationships with Linda and Ben. Falling in love with everyone he had sex with might be expected from a twenty-year-old kid. But for a man pushing forty, it was just embarrassing.

Surely Michael wouldn't tell anyone. He was the one with the most to lose. Josh would just be embarrassed. If Michael talked, he could lose his lover and his job.

Glancing at the clock, Josh saw he had about two hours before Greg arrived. He rolled up a couple of joints, finished straightening up the apartment, and then headed for the shower to get cleaned up. For the first time in a very long time, Josh looked forward to the rest of his weekend.

· 19 ·

THAD let himself into the house. "Philip, you here?"

"I'm in the sunroom, darling. Come watch this lovely sunset with me."

Thad walked to the back of the house and found Philip ensconced in his favorite chair with a glass of wine in one hand and a book in the other.

"How'd your date with Josh go?" Philip asked.

"Same as all the others. Considering most gay guys move in after the second date, you could say we're taking things slow. I don't think he has a clue that I'm crazy about him."

"Based on my decades of experience, I'm inclined to believe in this case that ignorance is bliss. He's not entirely over his ex yet. If you're really serious about Josh, and I know you are, things will go much better later if you start off as friends."

"I'm sure you're right. He definitely seems to like me. We had a great time today—no awkward moments or uncomfortable silences."

"Be patient, darling nephew. He'll come around. Right now he's probably a little overwhelmed by all the attention he's getting from the Welcome Wagon. You know how they are whenever new meat comes to town, especially a cut as delicious as your friend Josh."

"But what if he settles down with one of them?"

"If he does, I doubt it will last long. Who has he been running around with?"

"Greg, Ed, and Michael."

Philip laughed. "I think you're safe. Greg is totally harmless and really isn't even in Josh's league. Michael has probably already tricked him into bed—he's not one to waste any time, especially with men as attractive as Josh. And with the exception of Ed, for reasons I'll never understand, Michael rarely returns for seconds. Ed could be a problem in the short term, but in all the years I've known him, he's never sustained a relationship for more than three months with anyone who didn't have a wife at home."

Thad knew his uncle was right on all three counts. He'd seen Josh blanch when he learned Michael had a lover. "So what do I do now?"

"Be his friend. Let him have his way around DC for a while. He'll get bored with the bar scene before too long, and when he does, you'll still be there. If it's meant to be, and I believe it is, he'll figure it out soon enough."

"I sure hope you're right."

"Have I ever steered you wrong?"

"No, you haven't."

"Then trust me. He'll come around."

Thad believed him. Besides, he wasn't in any hurry. As if he'd seen it in a crystal ball or some other seer's tool, Thad knew it was just a matter of time before they ended up together.

• 20 •

GREG arrived right on time. "Nice apartment. I've walked past this place a thousand times and always wondered what it looked like on the inside."

"Well, now you know." Josh stopped at the kitchen. "Can I get you something to drink? I've got water, Coke, or beer."

"Sure, I'd love a glass of water."

Josh led Greg into the living room area. "Make yourself comfortable while I get that for you."

After returning with two glasses of water, Josh handed one to Greg and took a seat beside him on the couch. A fire truck roared down the street, sirens screaming. Josh noticed Greg didn't even flinch, though he did wait for the truck to pass before speaking.

"How do you like living here?"

"Other than the noise, I like it a lot. I picked up a white-noise machine while Thad and I were at Crystal City today. I'm hoping it will make it easier to get some sleep."

"It will, once you get used to the white noise." Greg laughed. "Then you'll have a different problem. I can't sleep without mine and have to take it with me when I travel."

"I'll have to remember that; I'm sure I'll be the same way." Josh decided to take a chance. "Do you get high?"

Greg nodded. "I was going to ask you the same thing but was afraid maybe you'd be offended."

Josh laughed and reached into his jewelry box, then pulled out one of the joints he'd rolled earlier. "Little chance of that. Join me on the veranda and we'll burn one before we head out."

"Veranda?"

"Okay. It's just a balcony, but I've always wanted to ask someone to join me on the veranda."

Greg laughed. "Well, then, show me to the veranda."

"Grab a chair. My white wicker furniture hasn't been delivered yet."

The two men carried chairs onto the little balcony and took a seat. Josh checked the surrounding balconies before lighting the joint. After making sure it was lit, he handed the joint to Greg.

"I think I'm the only person in the building who actually uses my balcony."

"I've never noticed anyone on any of the balconies anywhere in DC." Greg handed the joint back to Josh. "Porches are more a rural or suburban thing. Here in the city, people are more likely to hit a sidewalk café or go to the park."

"Makes sense to me." Josh hit the joint, exhaled, and passed it back to Greg. "I like watching all the people come and go. I guess if you've lived here a while you get used to all the activity, but for me, it's new and exciting."

Greg took another hit off the joint. "Wow, this stuff is pretty good—a lot better than the swag I usually get."

"I brought it with me from Kentucky so I wouldn't get mugged or worse searching for a connection here in bad parts of town."

"Yeah, parts of DC are scary." Greg looked out over the balcony to the bar crowd wandering the street below. "Except for Rock Creek Park at night, it's pretty safe around here—I think thugs are afraid of all the homos."

Josh laughed. "Whatever works."

"Really, it's more about the heavy police presence because of all the tourists and foreign embassies. Even before the murders, some of the gay bars outside of this area were a little scary. I never go down around the Navy Yard or to Green Lantern or the Eagle." Greg took another big hit from the joint, inhaled deeply, and held it in for a few seconds before exhaling a cloud of smoke. "Did you read about them in the *Blade*?"

"Yeah. Scary stuff. Apparently one of them happened right over there." Josh pointed to Rock Creek Park.

"Probably some homophobic redneck. Or maybe a religious fanatic out killing queers for Christ." Greg handed the joint to Josh. "What did you and Michael end up doing after Ed and I left last night?"

Josh darted a glance at Greg, trying to decide if he already knew. "Nothing much. We were going to check out some bars, but I'd had too much to drink and didn't feel like going."

"At least you didn't have far to go to get home."

"Good thing." Josh let the joint go out in the ashtray. "Whose idea was last night, anyway?"

"Mine, I guess. The three of us hit the Fireplace for happy hour after work on Fridays every few weeks. I called Ed. He and Michael had already decided to go. I didn't want to be a third wheel and asked you to come along."

So Michael had withheld the fact he had a lover and lied about asking Greg to invite him along. "Third wheel? Are Ed and Michael dating?"

"Kinda sorta. Michael has a lover, but you'll never hear him say so. He and Ed are friends with benefits."

Josh couldn't believe his ears. "Sounds kind of sleazy."

Greg shrugged, stood up, and leaned back against the balcony railing. "Definitely not something I'd ever do, but it takes all kinds. You ready to go eat? I've got a serious case of the munchies."

They left the West Park and walked to City Lights of China on Connecticut Avenue, a block or so past the Lambda Rising bookstore. The hostess showed them to a table right away. Except for white tablecloths, everything in the place was a light teal color—the carpet on the floor, the paint on the walls, and the vinyl upholstery on the chairs. The hostess and all the waitstaff looked Chinese.

Josh was familiar with Chinese food, or at least the type served by a number of different carryout joints in Lexington. City Lights appeared to be a cut above any of those places. The long menu included lots of items he'd never heard of before along with more familiar offerings.

"People either love this place or hate it," Greg said as he browsed the menu. "They have the best Chinese food I've ever eaten. The service is so-so, but considering the prices and the quality of the food, I don't mind."

Josh ordered General Tso's Chicken. Greg ordered Pork Hot Pepper and steamed pot stickers to share for an appetizer. Josh saw the waitress write their order on the ticket with Chinese characters.

After eating and splitting the check, Josh and Greg walked back down Connecticut Avenue toward Dupont Circle. Most of the shops were closed. Even so, the sidewalk was full of people enjoying the cooler temperatures of a still warm September evening. After dessert at the Kramerbooks Café, the two men sat on one of the benches surrounding the fountain in the heart of Dupont Circle, people-watching and chatting.

Josh told Greg about dating Linda throughout high school and into college before finding out he was gay, meeting Ben, and then catching him in his bed with David Hicks seventeen years into the relationship.

"Seventeen years is a long time. Were you happy?"

Josh had to think about it. "If you'd asked me when we were still together, I would have said yes with no hesitation. But now that I've been away from him and on my own for a while, I'd say I was more comfortable than happy."

"What makes you say that?"

"We had a mutually beneficial arrangement. I paid for everything and Ben took care of things I didn't want to fool with, like shopping, keeping the house clean, and taking the cars in for service. We were good at living together but were never really friends."

Greg nodded. "That happens a lot. People rush into a relationship before they have a chance to really get to know each other. I've never been in a hurry to settle down. Drives anyone I've ever dated crazy because they're ready to move in after the third date."

Josh laughed. "Guilty as charged."

Greg stood up to leave. "I better get going. The trains stop running at midnight, and I don't want to get stranded. Thanks for coming out with me tonight. I really felt bad about asking you to come along yesterday and then leaving you with Michael."

Josh rose from the bench. "Thank you for asking. It was good to have the chance to get to know you better. We'll have to do it again."

"I'd like that."

Greg headed for the Metro station and Josh walked back to his apartment alone. On the way, he passed hundreds of gay men in groups of two or three, all headed for one of the bars near his building. Since he was already out, he decided to stop into Omega for a beer, just to check the place out.

• 21 •

OMEGA was located in the middle of the alley that connected P Street and O Street, between the West Park and the bagel shop. Josh noticed the place looked a lot bigger on the inside than it did from outside. The two levels were divided into several different rooms, each designed to appeal to a different crowd. There was a cigar bar, a room with a pool table, an upscale bar with multiple television screens playing music videos, and an upstairs bar for watching television.

After a quick walk-through, Josh bought a beer and leaned against a wall in the upstairs bar where everyone was watching *Saturday Night Live* on one of several televisions mounted on the wall near the ceiling. In a dark room to his left, several guys watched gay porn on similarly mounted screens. The crowd was definitely older than what he was used to seeing in Lexington.

He noticed an extremely well-built, good-looking guy around his age sitting at the bar. He wore a tan T-shirt, camo pants, and black boots. He looked military, but lots of people dressed up in various uniforms in gay bars. It was hard to know whether he was actually military or just trying to look that way.

Josh's eyes kept returning to Mr. Camo. It wasn't just his good looks. Josh wanted to run his hands over the man's huge biceps and find out what he looked like without the tight-fitting T-shirt. He thought about the way Michael had dominated him the night before, replacing the liar's image in his mind's eye with the muscular military man.

Mr. Camo looked right at Josh and nodded hello. With a start, Josh realized he must have been staring at the man. He felt his face flush and quickly looked away.

Josh turned up the longneck and dared to look back. Now Mr. Camo was staring at him. When he caught Josh's eye he nodded again, adding a smile. Josh nodded back, too stunned to smile. The man was cruising him.

Uncertain about what to do, Josh turned his attention to the television. Norm MacDonald was interviewing Will Ferrell on Weekend Update. Although he didn't have a clue what was going on, Josh laughed when everyone else laughed, pretending like he was focused on the show instead of Mr. Camo.

Josh darted another glance in his direction. Mr. Camo was staring at him, smiling broadly, nodding again as he caught Josh's eye. Instead of fainting, Josh nodded back, nonchalantly finished his beer, and returned his attention to the television.

Moments later, he felt a presence by his side. It was Mr. Camo. Josh smiled and tried to act like superhot men cruised him every day.

Mr. Camo handed Josh a beer. "You looked like you could use another beer, so I took the liberty of getting one for you."

"Uh... thanks. That was really nice of you."

"Adam, here. Adam Gordon."

"Josh Freeman. Nice to meet you."

Adam placed his palm on the wall above Josh's head, "You're not from around here. Where are you from?"

Trying not to stare at the muscular arm inches from his face, Josh wondered what had given him away. "What makes you so sure I'm not from around here?"

Adam smiled. "Your country accent."

"Country!" Josh had been teased about his accent before, but the teasing usually came with a positive comment about southern drawls. A southern accent was charming. A country accent was something altogether different.

Adam laughed. "No offense. I like it. Definitely fits your look."

Josh didn't know what to think. Apparently, he not only sounded country but looked the part as well. "Thanks... I think."

Adam laughed again. "Oh, it's definitely a compliment. So where are you from?"

"Lexington, Kentucky."

"Ahhhh… horse country. I bet you've ridden a few stallions."

Josh felt his face grow hot and took a swig from the beer Adam had brought him. "One or two."

Adam laughed again. "So what brings you to DC? You just visiting or here to stay for a while?"

Josh took another nervous sip from his beer. "New job. Looks like I'm here for a while."

Adam nodded his approval. "Good. I'd hate to think tonight was my only chance with you. I need to get back to my friends, but had to come over to say hello."

Josh attempted a confident smile. "I'm glad you did. Thanks for the beer."

"You're welcome. Now you owe me. There's no such thing as free."

Knowing he was off the hook for tonight, Josh relaxed. "Reckon we'll have to take it out in trade."

Adam roared a laugh that came from deep inside. "I reckon we will. You got a phone number?" He retrieved a pencil and a card designed just for such an occasion from a cup on the bar and handed them to Josh.

Josh wrote down his number and handed the card back to Adam. Without even glancing at it, Adam slid the card into his pocket.

"I've got to get back to my friends. You'll hear from me. Soon."

"I look forward to it," Josh said, and he meant it.

Josh couldn't believe what had just happened. The hottest man he'd ever seen anywhere—in expensive porn movies, on television, or even in Hollywood movies—had come on to him. He definitely wasn't in Lexington anymore.

Instead of leaving right away, Josh decided to enjoy the beer Adam had bought for him. That the beer had come from Adam somehow made it taste better. He wanted to savor every drop. He thought about taking the bottle home with him, like a souvenir to help him remember the night he met the man of his dreams.

As Josh enjoyed the best beer he'd ever tasted, one at a time, several guys wandered over to where he was standing and tried to get his attention. He ignored them, staring instead at meaningless images on the television screen over the bar, thinking about Adam, wondering when he would call, and where they would go for their first date.

Being lovers with someone built like Adam would mean some changes. Josh would have to start going to the gym. If he didn't, people would wonder why someone as hot as Adam stayed with someone as out of shape as Josh was. Even though the idea of going to the gym had absolutely no appeal for him, Josh decided he would. For Adam.

Josh wished Adam's sudden appearance at his side hadn't caused his brain to lock up. He wanted to know more about him. Where did he work? Where did he live? What kind of food did he like? What did he like to do for fun?

All he knew was that Adam looked like a movie star, was built like a brick shithouse, and thought Josh was country-come-to-town. Now that he had time to think about it, the idea of being country didn't bother him so much. Adam seemed to like it. And if it was good enough for Adam, it was definitely okay with Josh.

• 22 •

JOSH'S first waking thought the next morning was how to get out of his date with Ed. It wasn't about Ed sleeping with Michael and married men. Given how hot Michael was, Josh didn't blame Ed. Besides, sleeping with Michael didn't make Ed a cheater, though that and the fact he had a preference for married men certainly didn't enhance his image in Josh's mind.

The bigger issue was the chance he'd miss Adam's call. He'd promised to call soon. Soon meant in the next day or two, didn't it?

He thought about his options. He wanted to be as truthful as possible without coming right out and telling Ed the reason he wanted to stay home. Josh might withhold information but he rarely, if ever, outright lied. Though an admittedly fine line, it was a boundary he didn't like to cross.

Whatever excuse he came up with, he wanted to call Ed as early in the day as possible. At least that would give Ed the chance to make other plans. Josh picked up the phone and dialed Ed's number.

"Hey, Ed, it's Josh."

"I'm really glad you called. I was just getting ready to call you. Something has come up and I'm going to have to move our dinner date to another night. Do you mind?"

Josh couldn't believe his luck. "I was calling to ask for a rain check. Something has come up for me too."

Ed laughed. "That's a relief! I was afraid you'd be pissed and I'd have two strikes against me."

"Two strikes?"

"Yeah, one for trying to make out with you at the Fireplace and the second for canceling our date."

Josh laughed. "Until you reminded me, I'd forgotten all about our little encounter. I wouldn't call that a strike so much as a ball."

With an insinuating tone, Ed said, "Oh, I like balls."

"You're such a pig," Josh teased. "Is sex all you ever think about?"

"No. I spend at least as much time thinking about what I'm going to drink next time I go out."

Josh shook his head and laughed. "You're cracking me up. So, when do you want to get together for dinner?"

"Does tomorrow work for you?"

Josh thought about it. If Adam didn't call tonight, canceling the date tomorrow would be awkward in the extreme. Just to be safe, he'd give him Tuesday too. "No. How about Wednesday?"

"Wednesday would be great. We can go to Annie's."

"Annie's? What kind of place is that?"

"You've never been to Annie's? Oh my God! Annie's Paramount Steakhouse is an icon, and absolutely the gayest restaurant in DC."

"Well, that's definitely where we need to go. Now that I'm a local, I need to know about these things. Where do you want to meet?"

"We can still meet at the Fireplace, only we better make it six thirty instead of seven. Annie's is up on Seventeenth Street just a few blocks from there."

"Great. See you Wednesday night."

Josh hung up the phone, and if he could, would have done cartwheels around the apartment. Things were working out just fine. Surely Adam would call before Wednesday.

After a quick shower, Josh ran down to the grocery store to lay in supplies to get him through the next three days. The weather had turned rainy, making him feel better about having to skip an afternoon at the pool. With books to read and dozens of channels on television, Josh had plenty to do to occupy his time.

He really hoped Adam would call today, while he was off. Missing work simply wasn't an option. At least he could call home from work to check his messages.

Josh spent most the day finishing up *Tales of the City*. He couldn't wait to get back to the bookstore to pick up *More Tales of the City*, the next volume in the series. The thought of missing Adam's call kept him from going out and picking it up. So he started reading *The Vampire Lestat*. He smoked about half a dozen joints, unpacked the last few remaining boxes, and then fell asleep on the sofa for a couple of hours.

Instead of throwing something together from the few groceries he'd purchased, Josh ordered a pizza. He ate half and put the rest in the refrigerator. Thinking about the impact of half a pizza on his waistline and Adam's buff body, Josh did push-ups, sit-ups, and jumping jacks—the only exercises he could remember—for thirty minutes, for the first time since high school. He watched a few hours of television and then, disappointed but not disheartened, went to bed.

Monday he went to work. Even though he was busy, the hours dragged on. Every thirty minutes or so, he called home to check his answering machine for messages. Adam never called. After work, he finished off the pizza, halfheartedly repeated his exercise routine from the night before, read some more *Lestat*, smoked more pot, and watched still more mind-numbingly dull television before going to bed.

Still no word from Adam.

Tuesday passed much like Monday. After work, he remembered he needed to call his dad. Josh picked up the phone and dialed his dad's number. He wasn't home. Josh left a message on the answering machine to let his father know he'd called.

Josh lay in bed thinking about the word "soon." Soon meant today or tomorrow. If Adam had meant something else, he should have said "in a few days" or "early next week" or anything but "soon."

By Wednesday, Josh was downright depressed. Having camped out by the phone waiting for Adam's call for most of the previous three days, he decided not to cancel his date with Ed. Getting out would be good for him. Time to move on.

Still, he checked his answering machine from work about every thirty minutes. His heart leaped into his throat when the robotic voice informed him he had one new message. It was just his dad returning his call. Leave it to his dad to call when he was at work. Idiot.

After work, Josh got ready for his date with Ed. From his vantage point on the balcony, he smoked a joint and watched for Ed to show up at the Fireplace. When the phone rang, he jumped like a horse out of the starting gate to answer it.

"Hi, Josh. Thanks for calling me back. How's life in DC?"

Josh could barely hide his disappointment. "Pretty good, Dad. How have you been?"

"I'm doing great. Met me a pretty little girl about half my age that thinks your old man is the greatest thing since sliced bread. I was calling to invite you to the wedding. We're getting hitched in Vegas, and I thought maybe you would join us."

Yeah, right. "Congrats, Dad. What's this, number four? I've lost count."

"Number five, and I love this one more than all the others put together."

Josh rolled his eyes. "Glad to hear it. When's the big day?"

"We're going to spend Thanksgiving weekend in Vegas and get married that Saturday."

"Gee, Dad, sorry—Linda is coming up from Lexington to visit me here in DC. We've been planning it for weeks."

"Why don't y'all just meet up in Vegas instead? It'll be fun. Just like old times."

Josh wondered if maybe he was confusing him with someone else. Good times and his father didn't go together. "I don't think so, Dad. Linda has never been to DC before and is looking forward to seeing the sights. Sorry."

"I figured you wouldn't come, but had to ask. Sure would like it if you could. If you change your mind, let me know."

"I'll talk to Linda about it," Josh lied. He knew she'd be all for it, seeing it as an opportunity for him and the old man to reconnect or something.

"You do that, Josh. Good talking with you, but I gotta run. The little lady is waiting on me to take her to dinner."

"Good talking to you too, Dad."

As usual, the conversation was all about his father. He really didn't care why Josh had moved to DC, or what he was doing now that he was here. He just wanted to talk about himself—to brag about his new girlfriend. Insensitive bastard even said he loved his newest tramp more than he'd loved Josh's mother.

Josh looked at the clock. *Damn!* He'd missed Ed going into the Fireplace and now was going to be late.

• 23 •

JOSH walked into the Fireplace and scanned the happy-hour crowd that filled the place to near capacity. Ed was sitting at the bar with an empty shot glass and half a cocktail in front of him. He looked pissed.

"Ed, I'm so sorry. My father called right as I was walking out the door."

Ed brightened visibly. "I was afraid you weren't coming. Glad you could make it."

"Should we head on over to Annie's?"

Ed tossed back the rest of his drink. "Sure. We'll probably have to wait for a table. Are you hungry?"

"Yeah, but I can wait."

They left the Fireplace and walked up P Street through Dupont Circle to Seventeenth. The strip on Seventeenth between P Street and R Street overflowed with gay men walking on the sidewalk or sitting at tables outside the many restaurants. Josh had never seen so many gay men in one place in his entire life.

Halfway down the block was Annie's Paramount Steakhouse. The front appeared to have once been a porch that had long ago been converted into a large dining room with big windows on three sides. Behind the dining room, there were more tables across from a long bar, and further back, still more tables.

A guy in blue jeans and a green Annie's T-shirt stopped them just inside the door. "Table for two?"

Looking around at the crowd, Ed asked, "Yeah, any way we can get a table in the front?"

The host checked his list. "If you don't mind waiting an extra two hours."

"How long for a table in the back?"

"I'd say thirty minutes or less. What's the name?"

Ed turned to Josh. "You up for a two-hour wait?"

"No. I'm already hungry. The back is fine with me."

Ed turned back to the host. "Pierson. Can we wait at the bar?"

"Sure. I'll call your name when your table is ready."

The bar was standing room only. Ed ordered drinks for them, remembering Josh's preference for bourbon and Coke with a chunk of lime.

Josh took the drink from him and smiled. "I'm impressed. Considering how drunk you were, I'm surprised you remembered."

"Actually, I asked Matthew, the bartender at Philip's party. Knowing someone's drink is a great way to make an impression."

Much to Josh's surprise, Ed was the perfect date—attentive, polite, and easy to talk to. Josh relaxed, relieved he didn't have to fake having a good time.

Ed took a big drink from his vodka and tonic. "Sorry I was such a prick at the Fireplace last week."

"No need to apologize. Frankly, I was flattered. It was just awkward since Greg had invited me to come along."

Josh took a sip from his drink and nearly choked. Adam was at the door, with a date. The date was older than Adam, a little shorter, equally good-looking, and just as muscular. The two of them were heading toward the bar to wait for a table.

Ed touched Josh's shoulder. "Are you okay? You look like you just saw a ghost."

"In a way, I guess I did. See the guy coming this way, the muscular guy with the movie-star looks?"

Ed turned to look. "Yeah. The tall one or the shorter one?"

"The tall one."

"His name is Adam Gordon. The guy with him is his lover, Caleb Wilson. They've been together for about a hundred years. What about him?"

"He hit on me at Omega Saturday night. Got my number and said he was going to call me, but he never did."

Ed chuckled, "He won't, either. Collecting phone numbers is his hobby. I think he'd like to call but never does, because if he did, Caleb would kill him. You should see them at the DC Eagle with all their leather gear on. Hot."

"Yeah, I bet." Josh was pissed. As the two men approached, he stared at Adam. Unlike at Omega, the look he fired at Adam was anything but admiring.

Adam and Caleb stopped next to where Ed and Josh were standing. Josh turned to Ed and whispered, "Watch this," then turned to face the muscular duo.

"Hey, Adam. Good to see you again. Sorry I haven't been returning your calls. I've been busy since we hooked up."

Adam looked at Josh. The color drained from his face. "I don't know what you're talking about."

"Sure you do. Remember? We met at Omega one night and you couldn't wait to hook up."

Adam's face turned red. Caleb looked pissed. Josh smiled broadly. "Maybe we can get together again next week. Just give me a call."

"Pierson, your table is ready."

"That's us. See you next week!" Josh grabbed Ed's elbow and steered him toward the host.

The host directed them to a booth in the back. Josh sat where he could keep an eye on Adam and Caleb. Ed sat across from him and laughed. "Man, that was pretty gutsy. Weren't you afraid he'd hit you or something?"

"Hitting me would have made him look even more guilty. I hope Caleb is pissed. I'm tired of guys who are supposed to be in committed relationships playing games with me."

The waiter walked up to take their order. Josh ordered the seafood platter. Ed ordered a steak, well done. Both men ordered another cocktail.

"Michael told me what happened the other night after Greg and I left. I take it you know about his lover."

"Yeah, and now I feel like a fool. I never dreamed he'd tell anyone."

"You're not a fool, and certainly not his first victim. Michael has quite a reputation around here for hitting on tourists and new guys in town. I know I shouldn't, but we fool around now and then. He's so hot, I can't help myself."

"Until I found out he's a liar and a cheater, I thought he was hot too. Maybe I'm hypersensitive because of the way Ben cheated on me, but I have no interest in being 'the other man' for anyone."

"Good for you. You deserve better."

Josh was on a roll. "I thought my life was over after Ben and I split up. Before moving here, I thought the only sex I'd ever have without paying for it was anonymous glory-hole blowjobs. I thought I was too old to ever find love again."

"Man. Your ex really did a number on you, didn't he?"

Josh nodded, "He had me convinced I was overweight, over the hill, and lucky to have him."

"And you believed him?"

"Of course I believed him. It's not like I was hearing anything different from anyone else. The last time I went to the gay bar in Lexington, nobody even talked to me. Why would I think anything else?"

"Josh, everyone at Philip's party talked about how good-looking you are. They also thought you were more than a little intimidating. You're a big guy, and until you smile, you look like you eat chains and small animals for breakfast. Especially if they were all college kids, I'd say nobody talked to you because they were afraid of you."

Josh was shocked. "Afraid of me? You've got to be kidding!"

"Now that I've met you, except for when you're trying to humiliate some asshole who played you, I know you're a sweet guy. It's just the way you look."

The waiter delivered their food as Adam and Caleb were seated at a table in the front section.

"Check it out. The muscle boys got a table right by the window."

Ed turned to look. "Damn, that's my favorite table too. The host put them there for advertising, since everyone who walks by will see them. They sure didn't have to wait any two hours."

"Guess that means the door guy doesn't think we're A-list gays."

Josh focused on cleaning his plate. Trying not to think about Ben or Michael or Adam was like being told not to blink. He couldn't help it. His thoughts kept returning to the three men and the way he'd let them walk all over him. Hell, he hadn't just let them; he'd practically sent engraved invitations asking them to treat him like dirt.

The waiter returned with the check. Ed snatched it up. "My treat."

"You really don't need to do that. Can I at least get the tip?"

"Nope. I invited you out. Next time it's your turn."

After Ed got his credit card back from the waiter, they left Annie's. Outside, Josh paused in front of the window to wave at Adam, giving him a big wink when he was sure Caleb was watching. Adam glared at him in return.

Ed laughed. "Remind me not to get on your bad side. You can be a little evil."

"Only when provoked. I'd love to be a fly on the wall to hear what they're talking about. My ears have been burning ever since our little exchange."

"I'd say Caleb is drilling him about who you are and how you know him."

"Good. Maybe he'll think twice before he asks for some other guy's number."

• 24 •

ADAM barely touched his food. Anger radiated from Caleb like a searing heat as he attacked his steak. When the guy stopped and winked at him from the other side of the window, Adam thought Caleb would explode. His face turned nearly purple. The veins in his neck and temple pulsed and his nostrils flared. He glared at Adam, too furious to talk.

When the waiter dropped off the check, Adam knew better than to stall. He was safe in the restaurant, but any attempt at delaying their departure would only make things worse when they got home. The thought of what waited for him knotted his stomach.

Caleb slapped three twenties on the check and stood up. "Let's go."

"Yes, sir," Adam whispered. As he got up from his chair, he noticed his hands were shaking. He tried to put aside the growing fear he felt.

Caleb strode angrily toward R Street, where the car was parked. Adam followed two steps behind, trying hard not to do anything more to piss Caleb off. When they reached the Jeep, Caleb unlocked the passenger door and flung it open.

"Get in."

Adam slid in and reached across to unlock the driver's side. Caleb started the car. Tires squealed as he pulled out and headed toward home.

"I've warned you about cheating on me." Caleb's tone was menacing. His hands gripped the wheel, knuckles white. "You know I don't share. What's mine is mine, and you—you stupid little bitch—are mine."

"Yes, sir." Adam's voice quavered. He shoved his shaking hands under his legs, hoping Caleb wouldn't notice how scared he was.

"I told you what would happen if I ever caught you cheating again."

"Please, sir, I didn't cheat on you. I would never cheat on you. You're my everything."

"Shut the fuck up!" Caleb pounded his hands on the steering wheel with each word. "Did I give you permission to talk?"

"No, sir. I'm sorry, sir."

"Not as sorry as you're going to be."

Adam thought about running away. His height gave him an edge. He thought he could outrun Caleb. But then what? He'd have to face him sooner or later. And he knew from experience that time merely intensified Caleb's anger.

No, the sooner he received his punishment, the better.

Caleb pulled into a parking space on the street a few doors down from their townhouse. "Inside. Now."

"Yes, sir." Adam got out of the car and headed toward the condo. Caleb walked behind him. In the few minutes it took them to get to the condo, Caleb kicked him in the ass half a dozen times with his steel-toed boots. Adam flinched but knew better than to cry out.

Caleb unlocked the door to the condo and stepped aside so Adam could enter. "Downstairs."

"Yes, sir." Adam headed for the basement and the punishment waiting for him. Caleb walked behind him, smacking him in the head every few steps until they reached their destination: a windowless room they had converted to a dungeon.

Inside, Caleb closed the door and locked it. He turned to face Adam. Without saying a word, he hit him. Three quick punches, one to the throat and two to his kidneys. Adam collapsed on the floor in pain and fought back the urge to cry out. He lost track of the number of times Caleb kicked him. As always, the blows were concentrated on his back and chest, where no one could see the bruises.

Caleb vented his anger through more kicks and punches. Now and then he stopped. "Why do you make me do this to you? Why can't you just do what you're told? You know this hurts me more than it hurts you."

Adam knew better than to respond. He didn't groan or cry out or acknowledge the beating he was getting in any way. He just took it, concentrating on staying quiet and avoiding any action that might reignite Caleb's fading anger.

Finally it was over. Caleb kicked him one last time and then left the dungeon, turning out the lights and locking the door behind him. Adam curled up in a ball on the cold concrete floor. Everything hurt, but it wasn't the worst beating he'd received from Caleb. At least this time it didn't feel like anything was broken, and as far as he could tell, he wasn't bleeding anywhere.

He knew from years of experience that Caleb would come back in a few hours. And when he did, he'd be sorry. He'd apologize for hurting him, promise he'd never do it again, and tell Adam he was the love of his life. He'd hold Adam and tend to his injuries, just like he always did.

Adam knew something else too. The beating he had just received was nothing compared to what he intended to do to that asshole they'd run into at Annie's. Adam would run into him sooner or later. And when he did, he'd kill him. Just like the three before him.

• 25 •

JOSH and Ed walked down the crowded sidewalk toward P Street. Groups, mostly men, sat drinking and eating at sidewalk tables under awnings. Occasional outbursts of laughter thundered above the steady rain of a hundred conversations.

The noise level plummeted after the two men turned onto the residential section of P Street. Except for passing cars, the only sound was the crunch of Josh's heels against the sidewalk. As they passed Thad's house, Josh noticed the lights were out.

Ed cleared his throat. "Josh, do you know what would be good for you?"

"Not usually. Got any suggestions?"

Ed laughed. "As a matter of fact, I do. I think we need to go barhopping, and I don't mean to the Fireplace or Omega."

"Oh? What did you have in mind?"

"Let's go to the Eagle."

Josh stopped to light a cigarette. "I don't know, Ed. I've never been to a leather bar before."

"Yeah, that's what I figured, and that's exactly why we should go."

Josh exhaled a big cloud of smoke and resumed walking. "Isn't that where a guy got killed?"

Ed nodded. "Yeah, and one of them got killed right outside your apartment. We'll be careful."

"If you say so. Am I dressed okay?"

"You're dressed fine. It's just a bar. Some people will be decked out in leather, but most will be in jeans and T-shirts."

"Where is it? Can we walk? Greg said it's in a scary part of town."

"We could, it's only about two miles from here, over on New York Avenue. But I'd rather drive. Greg's right. Even without a couple of murders, the neighborhood is more than a little rough."

"Where did you park?"

"Behind those apartments across the street from the Fireplace."

"I live in those apartments. If you get high, we could stop by and smoke a joint."

Ed laughed. "I thought you'd never ask. Greg said you have some killer weed."

Josh dropped his cigarette, rubbing it into the sidewalk with his boot. "I'd rather smoke pot than drink. Getting high takes the edge off. Getting drunk makes me stupid."

"All things in moderation. Or, at least, that's what they tell me. Lord knows I wouldn't know. I'd rather drink than eat."

"I wouldn't know either. I'd stay high all the time if I could get away with it."

When they arrived at the West Park, Josh punched in his pass code and headed toward the elevator. Ed stayed two steps behind him. When the elevator doors opened, the smell of Bounce dryer sheets greeted them. The old lady who'd been giving the receptionist grief looked annoyed as she rearranged baskets full of neatly folded laundry to make room for them. They exited the elevator on the fourth floor. As the doors closed behind them, Ed said, "Wonder who pissed in her Wheaties?"

Josh unlocked the apartment door and smiled. "I think she buys them that way."

Ed came inside the apartment, and stepping closer, backed Josh into the now closed door to the public hallway. "Is being alone together in your apartment better circumstances than outside the bathroom at the Fireplace?"

Josh looked into Ed's eyes. "Definitely."

"Glad to hear it. Does that mean I can kiss you?"

"I'm thinking you mean 'may'. I already know you're able."

Ed laughed and pressed closer. Josh felt hands on his hips, pulling him forward until Ed rubbed his thigh gently against his crotch. Josh opened his mouth, allowing Ed's tongue to enter. Placing a hand on Ed's shoulders, Josh returned the kiss, sucking softly on Ed's tongue and lower lip.

Josh broke the kiss. "I thought we were going to the Eagle."

"We will. It's still early." Ed reached an arm around Josh's head and brought his mouth back to his. "Now shut up and kiss me some more."

Josh complied with the command. The two men leaned against the door, kissing. A hand had replaced Ed's thigh. Josh felt Ed undo his belt, then struggle with his zipper to free his fully erect cock from its confinement. He groaned as Ed wrapped his hand around the now exposed member, masturbating him slowly.

"Damn, you've got a nice cock."

Josh applied pressure to Ed's shoulders, pushing him down. Ed dropped to his knees, still masturbating Josh's rock-hard shaft. He licked the tip, eliciting a strangled moan from Josh. Then he took the head into his mouth and slowly moved forward until his nose was buried in Josh's pubic hair.

Closing his eyes, Josh put a hand on each of Ed's ears to slow the bobbing head to exactly the right speed. He could feel Ed's groans on his cock and the slight tingle that signaled the beginning of the end. Josh pulled Ed's head forward, increasing the speed as the tingling engulfed his cock. Right before his climax, Josh moved his hands to the back of Ed's head, holding him in place as his knees turned to rubber.

"Damn. That was hot." Ed said, standing up and wiping his mouth with the back of his hand to clear the drool from his chin.

Josh kissed him on the lips. "I'll say. Now that we've got that out of the way, want to come in?"

Laughing, Ed pulled up his pants. "Sure. I couldn't wait any longer. If you hadn't stopped me, the same thing would have happened at the Fireplace."

"That might have attracted a crowd."

"I don't care. I'm a little bit of an exhibitionist anyway."

Josh took Ed by the hand and led him into the living room. "Can I get you something to drink? I've got water, Coke, or beer."

"No, thanks. I was thirsty when I got here but not anymore."

Josh laughed. "You really are a pig. Still want to smoke that joint?"

"Yeah, that would be great."

Josh retrieved a joint from the jewelry chest. "I have no idea if my neighbors are cool or not, so we'll have to go out on the balcony. Grab a chair and follow me."

"I'm right behind you."

Josh lit the joint, settled back into his chair, and put both feet up on the rail. He passed it to Ed, who took the joint from him before lifting his feet to the rail. "You have a great view of the Fireplace."

"Don't forget the bagel shop," Josh said, pointing.

"That place cracks me up. The way they call back orders is like an Asian version of that Greek burger place on *Saturday Night Live*."

Josh laughed. "I hadn't thought about it, but now that you mention it, you're right."

"Greg wasn't kidding. This is great pot." Ed exhaled. "Michael was right too."

"Oh, really? And what did Michael have to say?"

"He said you have a really big dick. He also said he'd love to see you again. Guess I should tell him that ain't gonna happen."

"Yeah, he's blown it with me. Even if he and his lover split up, I wouldn't be interested. If he'll cheat for me, he wouldn't have any qualms about cheating on me."

"Guess not."

Josh roached what was left of the joint. He glanced at the clock and saw that it was nearly eleven. "Do you still want to go to the Eagle? It's kinda late and I have to work tomorrow."

"We can go Friday night if you want. There's usually a better crowd on the weekends, anyway. It'll be a lot more fun."

Josh stood up. "Friday would be better for me. Thanks again for dinner—next time it's on me."

Ed dragged his chair back inside. "Glad we finally got together. I really enjoyed it. Thanks for the buzz and a fun night out."

Josh kissed him good night. "See you Friday."

Ed walked out into the hallway and pushed the button for the elevator. "I'm already looking forward to it."

• 26 •

THURSDAY, on the walk home from work, Josh got his hair cut, stopped at the drugstore for condoms, deodorant, and cigarettes, and picked up his dry cleaning. Thad had been right: he didn't miss his car a bit. Parking was in short supply and expensive. Everything he needed was available from one of the shops between his apartment and work.

Living in the city meant he had more free time. The walk to and from work ate up half as much time as his commute back in Lexington. Keeping his apartment neat and tidy took a minimum of effort. He missed his little postage-stamp yard and flower garden, but not the time required to keep it looking nice. He almost never cooked, which also meant he didn't spend much time at the grocery store. With all the machines in the laundry room, even washing and drying his clothes took less time.

Seeing he had his hands full, Vanessa buzzed him into the West Park lobby. Josh thanked her, picked up a couple of bills and an L.L.Bean catalog from his mailbox, and then punched the button for the elevator. The doors opened, expelling the old lady from the ninth floor, still in the same housedress he and Ed had seen her wearing the night before.

Josh held the doors open and waited for her to exit the elevator. She nodded curtly and headed for the receptionist. He wondered what she was pissed about this time. After stepping inside the elevator, Josh used the corner of the L.L.Bean catalog to push the button to the fourth floor.

What was he doing with the extra time? Not seeing the sights. Since his arrival in DC, aside from a few walks in the Dupont Circle area and the trip with Thad to the mall, he hadn't checked out any of the places people come to DC to see.

Before the move, Josh had worried about how he would react to living within a stone's throw of so many gay bars. He feared the temptation might be too much and he'd revert to the six-nights-a-week barhopping routine he had before settling down with Ben. That he now had little or no interest in hitting the bars around his apartment surprised him.

He needed to get out more to see the sights. He'd call Thad later to see if he'd join him for some sightseeing on Saturday. Philip would probably be more than happy to show them around the Smithsonian. If not, well, he'd go on his own.

As he came through the door to his apartment, the blinking red light on the answering machine caught his eye. The electronic voice announced, "You have... two... new messages."

The first message was a request from his father to "give your old man a call when you get a chance." Josh groaned. No doubt he was going to try again to talk Josh into coming to Vegas for wedding number five.

The second message was from Linda. "Hey, Josh, give me a call. I've got some news!"

Curious, Josh picked up the phone and dialed Linda's number. Her answering machine picked up on the second ring, meaning she already had at least one message. The beep sounded. "Hey, Linda. Just returning your call. I'm in for the evening, so call me back when you get home."

Now he was really curious. Except for work and a weekly visit to see her mother on Saturday or Sunday, Linda never went anywhere. Nor did she ever get any calls. Mrs. Delgado refused to leave messages, insisting it would be a cold day in hell before she talked to a machine. Something was definitely going on.

Josh changed out of his work clothes, tucked *More Tales of the City* under his arm, grabbed a joint from the jewelry chest, and dragged a chair out onto the balcony. The angle of the sun had changed with the coming of fall. The absence of shade on the balcony might have been unpleasant if the temperature hadn't also dropped a few degrees.

He wished the swimming pool hadn't already closed for the season. Keeping the pool open from Memorial Day to Labor Day might make sense farther north, but in DC, closing after the first weekend in September was at least a month too soon. Dozens of sunbathers, mostly men in Speedos, relaxed in the grassy area across the street known as P Street Beach over in Rock Creek Park. Josh thought about joining them, but feared he'd miss Linda's call.

An hour later, Linda still hadn't called. Josh was hungry. Tempted to call her back, he picked up the phone, but instead of dialing her number, he set the handset down next to the cradle. With the phone off the hook, Linda would get a busy signal if she called. He grabbed his wallet and ran across the street to pick up a Reuben sandwich, a bag of chips, and a cup of broccoli soup from the deli next door to the Fireplace.

Back in his apartment, Josh returned the loudly beeping handset to the cradle, grabbed a beer from the refrigerator, turned on the television, and, after spreading his dinner on the coffee table, sat on the sofa to watch the evening news. Most the local news coverage revolved around the murders. Still no leads.

Josh tossed the remnants of dinner in the trash, grabbed another beer, and then switched the channel to Alex Trebek and *Jeopardy!* before lighting an after-dinner cigarette. Halfway through Double Jeopardy, the phone rang. Josh leaped from the couch, knocking over his beer in the process. "Shit! Hello?"

"Hi, Josh. It's Linda. What are you cussing about?"

He stretched the phone cord into the kitchen, grabbed a towel, and threw it over the foaming puddle of beer on the floor. "Oh, I knocked over a beer. I thought you'd never call. What's up?"

"Are you sitting down?"

As he bent over to wipe up the mess, Josh replied, "No, but I'm not far from the floor. Did you win the lottery?"

"In a way. I've met someone… special."

Josh couldn't believe his ears. Since swearing off men after her divorce more than ten years ago, Linda had rarely dated. Ignoring the mess, he sat down on the sofa and reached for his cigarettes.

"Josh? Are you there?"

"Yeah, sorry. Anyone I know?"

"I don't think so. He moved to Lexington about a month ago. His name is Rafael Maccado. His family is from Cuba, but he grew up in the Miami area."

"I've always wanted a Latin lover."

"I thought you were into Italians these days…."

Josh laughed. "Not so much. We'll get to that later. I'm still waiting to find out how you met this man."

"You know that overpriced condo across from the pool that's been on the market forever?"

"Yeah. I think the asking price for it was a big factor in mine selling so fast."

"Rafael bought it. He moved in a few days after you moved to DC."

Josh stopped to think. That would have been nearly two months ago. "Did he pay full price?"

"Probably. He told me the same kind of place back in Miami would have cost twice as much."

"Wow. What does Rafael do?"

"He's the stallion manager for Winding Brook Farm out on Paris Pike. His father works at Hialeah. Rafael has worked around horses on a big farm in the Miami area since he was a kid."

Josh was impressed. Winding Brook had fielded several Kentucky Derby winners and was one of the larger thoroughbred horse farms in Lexington. "Guess you better start shopping for your Derby hat."

Linda laughed. "He's a very sweet man. I can't wait for you to meet him."

"Me either. But you still haven't said how you met."

"Hanging out around the pool. We started talking, went to lunch together a few times, and have spent most our free time together ever since. Mom is crazy about him."

Josh felt a little like he'd been kicked in the stomach. "He sounds like a great guy."

"He really is. I'm sure you're going to like him. So what's up with you and the hot Italian?"

Josh sighed. "Turns out, he already has a lover. I haven't heard from him again."

"I'm sorry, Josh. At least you found out before things went too far."

Josh thought things had gone pretty far, but didn't correct her. "I guess you're right."

"Have you been running around with any of the guys you met at that party?"

"Now and then. Thad and I talk every day and get together for lunch once a week or so. He's turning out to be a great friend. Next to you, he's the best friend I've ever had. Did I tell you his lover is old enough to be his father? I was shocked."

"Thad sounds like quite a guy. Are you sure they're lovers?"

"Positive. It's obvious how much they love each other. You can see it in the way they look at each other." Josh stubbed out his cigarette and turned his attention to the mess he'd made on the floor. "Other than that, I've gone out to dinner a few times."

"You're getting out and about a lot more than you would have if you'd stayed here in Lexington."

Josh finished cleaning up the spilled beer. "True. Coming here was definitely a good idea. Living in the big city agrees with me."

"Glad to hear it. If you were miserable, I'm sure you'd never let me forget moving was my idea."

Josh could hear the smile in her voice. "Except for missing you, I'm glad I came. I'm really looking forward to your visit. Thanksgiving will be here before you know it."

"I know. I still think you'll have a boyfriend by then. Mom will be sorry to hear she didn't win the pool. Don't worry. We haven't given up on you. We'll start another one."

Josh laughed. "I'm glad you're both so sure. There are definitely more possibilities here than in Lexington, but I'm not holding my breath. I've got a date tomorrow with Ed, the guy who tried to make out with me in the bar when I met the hot Italian."

"Ed sounds like a real catch." Sarcasm dripped from her voice through the phone line.

"He's not so bad. We went out to dinner last night and had a great time."

"Two dates in three days? I know how you gay boys work. One more and one of you will be renting a U-Haul."

Josh laughed. "Given your whirlwind romance with Rafael, you're one to talk."

"Ha! I guess you're right. And speaking of Rafael, I really need to go. He'll be here in a few minutes to pick me up. We have an eight o'clock reservation for dinner at the Merrick Inn."

"Yum. Get some fried grouper fingers for me. Glad to hear you've met someone—he's a lucky guy."

"Thanks, Josh. I'll give you a call next week. I love you!"

"Love you too, Linda. Tell your mother I said hello."

He hung up the phone and reached for his jewelry chest. Linda's news had come as quite a shock. He'd felt the same way in sixth grade, when his mother started working and was no longer at his beck and call. Josh had assumed Linda would stay single forever and be there whenever he needed her. Now Rafael would come first.

Having broken through the walls Linda put up after her divorce, Josh figured Rafael had to have a lot going for him. He was happy for her and glad she'd have someone to share her life with.

Alone on the balcony with just his thoughts and the marijuana pipe, Josh reflected on all the recent changes in his own life. Thanksgiving was still weeks away, but he already knew. Beyond any doubt, the move had been good for him. He had a great job, several promising new friendships, and a completely different perspective about himself and the breakup with Ben.

Before coming to DC, Josh had fervently believed the breakup was his fault; he'd let himself go, devoted too much time and attention to work, and in the process neglected Ben, forcing him to find love elsewhere. Now he knew better. He had grown up. Ben hadn't and probably never would. Josh was better off without him.

On the downside, his current love life left a lot to be desired. But at least he knew he had options other than anonymous bookstore blowjobs and hustlers.

Meeting Thad and getting to know him better was the highlight of his time in DC. He was a great guy, the kind Josh would love to find for himself. Finding out Thad already had a lover had been a huge disappointment, but okay in the end because of the great friendship they had developed.

Michael hitting on him and ending up in bed with him had been a real high, until he'd found out about Michael's lover. Ditto the anticipation and excitement he'd felt waiting for Adam to call, and the devastating kick to the gut Josh had felt when he saw Adam with Caleb. Throw in his encounter with Mitch, and Josh was batting a thousand.

Watching the people come and go from the bars four stories below made Josh feel lonely. Maybe things would work out with Ed. Yeah, his dalliances with married men were troubling, but he was good-looking and fun to be around. They'd had a surprisingly good time at Annie's—better than Josh had expected. He'd have a better idea about Ed's potential after their date tomorrow.

• 27 •

JOSH rolled out of bed Friday morning, hit the off button on his white-noise machine, and nearly jumped out of his skin when a thunderclap crashed close enough to make the windows tremble in their frames. He pulled up the blinds in time to catch a lightning flash, followed a millisecond later by another boom. Rain fell in sheets, washing the street and sidewalk below clean of grime, litter, and assorted body fluids.

The power flickered but stayed on while Josh showered. The bedroom and living room contained the only windows in the apartment. If the power went out, he'd need something more than his Bic lighter to ever find anything in the kitchen or bathroom. As he finished dressing, Josh made a mental note to pick up a flashlight and some candles, just in case. He searched through the apartment and realized he needed an umbrella too.

He dug through his closet and found a rain slicker he'd worn maybe once since Ben bought it for him. Josh had wanted to add the bright yellow coat to the pile of clothing destined for the Salvation Army, but Linda had suggested he keep it. Today he was glad she had insisted he hang on to it.

By the time he stepped out of the West Park lobby, a wall of rain fell from the portico. Josh realized that even with the waterproof jacket, unless he wanted to get soaked to the skin, walking two blocks to work was simply not an option. He raised his arm and flagged down a cab.

"Walker, Cochran and Lowe up on Dupont Circle please."

The cab driver grunted, clearly disappointed by Josh's destination. He veered back into traffic, and two minutes later, pulled up to the entrance. "That will be two dollars and forty cents."

Feeling guilty for bothering him with such a short trip, Josh handed the driver a five-dollar bill. "Keep the change."

The hooded jacket kept Josh's hair and shirt dry, but not his pants or shoes. He entered the office looking like he'd waded to work through thigh-high water. As he walked past her desk, the perky blonde receptionist said, "Nice jacket," and giggled.

Josh felt his face flush. He walked past her without comment to the coat rack, where nearly every peg contained a black or khaki London Fog trench coat. He hung up his bright yellow slicker on an empty peg and added "new raincoat" to his mental shopping list. As he walked to his office, he cursed Linda's practicality and Ben's lack of taste.

Safe in his comfortable chair behind the fortress of his desk, Josh attacked an in-box filled with job orders, incoming mail, and a stack of interoffice memos. The attorneys he worked for laid waste to entire forests every month with some deep-seated need to put everything in writing. Memos fell steadily into his in-box, like autumn leaves on a windy day.

He was halfway through the most recent stack of memos when the intercom buzzed. "Mr. Thad Parker is calling for you on line three, sir."

Josh thought about asking her to keep an eye on his one-of-a-kind raincoat but instead said, "Thanks," and then he pushed the button for line three. "Hi, Thad. What's up?"

"Want to meet for lunch?"

Josh tossed the unread memos into the recycling bin under his desk. "I'd love to! Where do you want to go?"

"I'm in the mood for a greasy burger. Have you been to Mr. Henry's?"

"Nope, but I've never met a burger I didn't like."

Thad's laugh was music to his ears. "Well, then, you'll love Mr. Henry's. It's over on Pennsylvania Avenue near Capitol Hill. Meet me out front at eleven thirty and we'll take a cab."

"Sounds great. I'll look forward to it."

Thad's call lifted Josh's spirits. The rest of the morning flew by. Josh opened all his mail, returned several calls, and after a conference call about a new website for the firm with the communication directors from all the Walker, Cochran and Lowe offices, he managed to knock out a couple of job orders. At 11:25, he left his office, grabbed the yellow rain slicker from the peg, and headed down the stairs to meet Thad.

Thad was waiting for him at the front door. Upon seeing Josh, he said, "Where are the boots?"

Puzzled, Josh looked down at his still damp shoes. "What boots?"

"The boots that match that lovely yellow jacket." Thad grinned.

"Are you embarrassed to be seen with me?" Josh spun around like a model on a New York City runway during fashion week. "Our receptionist laughed when she saw me this morning."

"Embarrassed?" Thad shook his head. "Heck no. London Fog trench coats are the uniform in this town. Nice to see someone else break from the pack."

Josh admired Thad's jacket: an expensive-looking, tight-fitting light-blue number from Woolrich. "I hardly think you're in the same league as me."

"You're right." Thad performed an award-winning dramatic sigh. "I guess I can handle you getting all the attention. Since you're so much easier to see, why don't you hail us a cab?"

Josh stepped out of the building into the pouring rain and raised his arm. A cab swerved across two lanes of traffic, splashing water on his shoes as it skidded to a stop at the curb in front of them. Josh opened the door and motioned for Thad to slide across.

"Where to?" the driver asked over the Middle Eastern music blaring from his tape player.

Thad said, "Mr. Henry's, please, on Pennsylvania Avenue."

"Got it." The turbaned driver darted back out into traffic, causing Josh's still open door to barely miss closing on his ankle as it slammed shut. Josh fastened his seat belt and held on as the driver wove through traffic. An anxious ten minutes later, they reached their destination.

Thad selected an empty table with a view of the deserted, rain-soaked patio. A waiter dropped off menus and glasses of water, promising to return "in a jiffy" to take their orders.

Thad hung his jacket on the back of a nearby empty chair. "Mr. Henry's is a local institution. Before she was famous, Roberta Flack played piano and sang here. The food is pretty good for what it is."

Josh hung his rain slicker on the other empty chair at the table and then took a seat. "I love Roberta Flack almost as much as a good burger."

"Same here. And the onion rings are really good too."

Josh looked over the menu. "I should order a veggie burger, or maybe just a salad."

"Yeah, me too," Thad agreed.

When the waiter returned, they both ordered bacon cheeseburgers, onion rings, and large Cokes. He jotted down their order, retrieved the menus, and before heading back to the kitchen, said the burgers would be ready "in a jiffy."

Josh looked at Thad. "What the hell is a 'jiffy'?"

Thad laughed. "Damned if I know. Should we time him?"

Josh removed his watch and set it on the table. "Sure, why not?"

"You got big plans for the weekend?" Thad asked.

"I've got plans for tonight with Ed, but nothing for the weekend. I've been in DC for weeks now and still haven't done any sightseeing. I was hoping you'd be interested in showing me around a bit tomorrow or Sunday."

"I'd love to give you a tour. Philip and I are going to see my parents Sunday, but tomorrow works. Where do you want to go?"

Josh shrugged. "I have no idea. There's so much to do here. What would you suggest for a newbie?"

Thad thought for a moment. "Let's knock out the memorials and monuments and see if maybe we have enough energy left to hit the Smithsonian when we're done. Want to meet me at the Metro station at, say, ten o'clock?"

"Can we make it eleven? Ed's taking me to the Eagle tonight and I'm guessing we'll be late getting home." Was it just Josh's imagination or had Thad winced?

"Sure. Wear comfy shoes. We'll be doing a lot of walking. If it's raining, we'll skip the memorials and hit the Smithsonian first."

Josh decided he had imagined the wince. "Sounds like a plan."

A jiffy turned out to be a bit more than ten minutes. Barely visible beneath a mountain of onion rings, the half-pound burgers nearly filled the plates the waiter plopped in front of them.

Josh's eyes widened his eyes as he inhaled the aroma of fried goodness. "I'm so glad I didn't get a salad."

• 28 •

THE phone started ringing as Josh unlocked the door to his apartment. He had three more rings before the answering machine picked up, so there was no need to rush. He heard the answering machine click after the second ring and, realizing someone must have left a message for him earlier in the day, dove for the phone to answer before the caller hung up.

"It's Ed. We still on for tonight?"

"Yep. I'm looking forward to it."

"Want to grab dinner before we hit the Eagle?"

Still belching onion rings from lunch, Josh asked, "What did you have in mind?"

"I'm hoping for more of what I had the other night."

"Steak?"

"No. I'm talking about what I had for dessert, back in your apartment."

Josh laughed. "I should have known. You're such a pig."

"Oink, oink. It's not like you didn't know. Back to dinner. Do you like Thai?"

"Can't say I've ever had it, but I'm willing to give it a try." Josh looked at his watch and saw it was nearly five thirty. "What time?"

"How about I pick you up out in front of your apartment building at eight?"

"Perfect." Josh figured two and a half hours was plenty of time to work up an appetite. "I'll be there with bells on."

"Uh, unless they're on a collar, I don't think bells are appropriate for the Eagle."

Josh laughed. "Darn it. Reckon I'll have to find something else to wear, then."

"Reckon you will. I'd like to see you in a big harness and assless chaps."

"Sorry. My chaps are at the cleaners and I don't have time to clean the rust off my harness. What are you wearing?"

"Right now I'm not wearing a thing. Standing here buck naked with the big hard-on I got imagining you decked out in leather."

Knowing it only encouraged him, Josh tried not to laugh. "Not now—tonight. What are you wearing tonight?"

"Oh. Tonight I'm wearing jeans, boots, and a T-shirt. Unless you go in leather drag, it's the uniform."

"Gotcha. Okay, see you at eight."

Josh hung up the phone. The blinking red light on his answering machine reminded him he still had a message. He pushed play.

"Josh, it's your dad. Please call me as soon as you get this message. It's important."

Josh pushed erase. What was this about? His dad never called this often. His call about his wedding plans had been surprise enough. Since then, he'd called twice in two days.

Josh slid the pointer on the list finder his father had given him as a graduation gift after college to "F" and pushed the button. The top sprang open to the page where he'd recently added Tom Freeman's phone number, just below Friendly Cleaners and Fazoli's Restaurant, both back in Lexington. He dialed the number.

"Hi, Dad. Sorry I couldn't call you back yesterday. What's up?"

"It's the wedding."

Just as he suspected—his father was going to try to talk him into coming to Vegas. "What about the wedding?"

Even the background noise ceased. Had he been disconnected?

"Dad, are you there?" The background noise returned, but his father still hadn't answered.

"It's off."

"Oh?" *Interesting.* "What happened?" Josh waited through an awkward pause for his father to respond. When his father finally answered, his voice sounded weak, thin... defeated.

"I really don't know." He paused, like the question had only just occurred to him. "I think maybe she met someone else."

"Gee, Dad." Josh really did feel sorry for him. "I don't know what to say. I'm sorry things didn't work out."

Josh thought he heard his father sob but wasn't sure. He wondered if he'd been drinking. He heard ice clinking and then Tom Freeman's despondent voice. "I hate being alone, Josh. Mindy acted like she was crazy about me. I thought things would work out."

Josh could relate but didn't think saying so would help. He racked his brain for something to say. "Better that you found out now instead of after you got married." He instantly wished he'd said something else.

"I guess so." Josh heard ice knocking the side of a glass. "I was hoping maybe I could come to Washington for Thanksgiving. I know I haven't been the best father in the world and that you really don't owe me a thing. But you're the only family I have, and it would really mean a lot if I could come."

Josh was stunned. How much had the old man had to drink? He had no idea his father felt so strongly about him. "Sure, Dad. If it means that much to you, I'd love for you to visit."

"Thanks, son. I'm sorry to impose on you like this. Knowing I'll be spending Thanksgiving with you and Linda makes me feel better already."

The emotion he heard in his dad's voice touched him. Despite the alcohol, he knew the emotions were real. "It's not an imposition, Dad. I don't have room in my apartment, so I'll have to arrange for a hotel. I'll call you back as soon as I've worked things out."

Josh called Linda. After four rings, her answering machine picked up. "Hey, Linda. It's Josh. Looks like Dad is joining us for Thanksgiving. Give me a call when you get a chance."

Still in his yellow rain slicker, Josh rolled a joint and stepped out onto the balcony. Rain continued to fall. Gusts of wind blew enough drops onto the balcony to moisten the black grime that covered everything, turning it into an inky paste that would be difficult to remove even with a pressure washer. He leaned back against the sliding glass door, cupping the joint in his hand to keep it dry.

The conversation with his father had been a shock. He didn't know what to think. Was his dad just drunk? Or could it be that rather than the fun-loving partier he'd always imagined, Josh's dad was a lonely man? He smoked the joint down far enough to burn his fingers. Instead of roaching the tiny remnant, he tossed it over the balcony rail and watched it fall to the rain-soaked street below.

He lit a cigarette. No, he didn't have much in the way of fond memories with his father. Mostly he remembered all the times he'd been disappointed because his father hadn't followed through on promises he made. Time after time, he'd promised to make it up to Josh. The sad part was that Josh always believed him, setting himself up for yet more disappointment. Was he setting himself up all over again?

Maybe his father was not the man Josh believed him to be. Surely the man hadn't intended to break Josh's heart over and over again. Maybe his dad's failure to follow through wasn't about Josh at all. He had the best of intentions, but for unknown reasons, always fell short on following through. Would this time be any different? Josh didn't know, but decided to give the old man another chance.

• 29 •

JOSH stood outside the West Park waiting for Ed to pick him up. The rain had stopped and a nice breeze cooled the air. His thoughts kept returning to the phone conversation with his dad and the countless times he'd been disappointed by him in the past. He barely noticed the maroon Oldsmobile Cutlass that pulled up to the curb. The passenger side window came down and he heard Ed's voice.

"You're nuts if you think I'm going to run around and open the door for you."

Josh opened the door and slid in. "Sorry, Ed. I wasn't paying attention."

The second Josh closed the door, Ed hit the gas, honked his horn, and lurched back into traffic. "No problem. The way you were looking right at me, I was sure you'd seen me."

"Sorry. No, I was thinking about my dad. He called today to tell me his fiancée ditched him and he wants to come to DC for Thanksgiving."

"Fuck!" Ed honked his horn and flipped the bird at a taxi that had cut him off. "Sorry to hear that. Are you two close?"

Josh sighed. "If you'd asked me two weeks ago, I would have said not at all. After the conversation we had today, I think maybe he cares for me a lot more than I ever thought. He means well—he's just bad about following through on stuff and always has been."

"He and your mom get along?"

"No. They divorced when I was in grade school. Mom died of cancer a few years after I graduated from college. Dad didn't even come to her funeral."

"Ouch." Ed slammed on the brakes, barely missing the back of a stopped Metro bus.

"I can take you to pick him up at the airport if you like." Ed swerved across three lanes of traffic to make a turn, eliciting raised middle fingers from three taxi drivers and a soccer mom driving a minivan full of small children.

Josh tightened his seat belt and clutched the edge of his seat. "Uh, that's nice of you, but I can take the Metro."

"You sure? I don't mind," Ed said, hitting the gas to clear the intersection as the light turned from yellow to red.

"Yeah, I'm sure." Josh wondered if his face was as white as the knuckles clenching the armrest. "The Metro station is just a couple of blocks away. I'll be fine."

"If you change your mind, just let me know. Hold on!" Ed yanked the steering wheel hard to the left, whipping a U-turn across three lanes of traffic and another forest of raised middle fingers. Horns blared when he stopped suddenly before backing into an empty space at the curb. "We're here!"

Josh relaxed his grip on the armrest and waited for his pulse to slow back down to something closer to normal before unfastening his seat belt and exiting the car. "Thanks, Ed. You're too kind."

They walked half a block up U Street to the entrance of Sala Thai. The aroma of ginger and garlic greeted them at the door, followed by an elegant hostess dressed in a royal-blue silk, floor-length dress covered with an ornate gold print.

"Pierson's the name. I have a reservation for two at eight fifteen."

The hostess smiled and consulted her reservation book before inviting them to follow her to a linen-clothed table.

Josh took a seat and looked around. "Wow. This place is a lot fancier than the Chinese restaurants where I've eaten."

Ed settled into his seat and picked up the menu. "It's a lot fancier than most Thai places too. I wouldn't take you to a dump for our second date, especially since you're paying."

"How thoughtful of you." Josh gave Ed a teasing look.

Ed looked over the menu. "Any idea what you want to eat?"

Josh picked up his menu and scanned across the listings. Nothing was even vaguely familiar to him. He latched onto the one dish he'd heard of before. "I think I'll try the pad Thai."

The waitress materialized by the table, pen in hand. She was nearly as elegant as the hostess and wore a red silk dress, nodding and smiling as she wrote down his order.

Ed closed his menu. "That's as good a choice as any. I always get the Pad Prik Khing. I have no idea what it is but love the name."

Josh laughed. "At least you're consistent."

The waitress, still smiling and nodding, but apparently oblivious to the joke, wrote down Ed's order, backed away from the table, and headed toward the kitchen.

"So how's Thad?" Ed asked.

"Same as ever. He's such a nice guy. Philip is a lucky man."

Ed shrugged. "I've always thought Thad was the lucky one."

Josh was taken aback by the comment. Was Ed kidding? Thad was at least half Philip's age, with great looks and an even better personality. Sure, Philip was nice and obviously had a lot of money, but of the two, Thad could have about anyone he wanted. "Why do you say that?"

"I can only imagine the difference having a gay uncle would have made when I came out. My father kicked me out when he found out about me."

"You're kidding!" Josh exclaimed. *Thad is Philip's nephew?* His mind raced, trying to recall if either of them had ever said anything to suggest they were relatives rather than lovers.

"Nope. Told me he wasn't about to share his house with a faggot."

Josh didn't have the heart to clarify that his shock stemmed more from the relationship between Thad and Philip than from Ed's father kicking him out. "I'm sorry. How old were you?"

"Sixteen—still in high school."

"Oh my God! What did you do?"

Ed sighed. "I was homeless for a while. Sold my ass on the street to get enough money to buy food."

Josh was speechless. His own coming-out experience and all the drama with Linda and with his parents had been a walk in the park compared to Ed's experience. "I'm sorry. That's horrible. How did you survive?"

"Philip," Ed said. "He picked me up one night and brought me back to his place. I thought he was just another dirty old man, but unless you count hugs, he never touched me."

The waitress arrived with their food. Josh barely tasted what he was eating as Ed continued with his story.

"Philip took me under his wing and let me live with him. He got me back in school, pulled some strings so I could graduate, and even paid for me to go to the University of Maryland. I stayed with him until I finished college and could afford my own place. I don't know where I'd be without him. He's the most generous man I've ever known. A lot of gay men in this town could tell you stories about how he helped them turn their lives around. "

Now Josh understood why Ed thought Thad was the lucky one. He wondered how many of the other party guests were Philip's protégés. No wonder everyone loved him so much.

"I thought Thad and Philip were lovers."

Ed laughed. "No, Thad's mother and Philip are brother and sister. Thad's parents are great, and as far as Philip is concerned, Thad's as much his child as theirs."

Josh couldn't stop thinking about Thad. "How long have you known Thad?"

"Since he was thirteen. He came out to his parents while I was living with Philip and spent a lot of time at the house. Thad was always a sweet kid. Philip adores him. Everyone does, but as far as I know, he's never had a lover."

"Why not?" Josh asked.

"I don't know. My personal theory is that it has something to do with the unconditional love Philip and his parents rain down on him. In a lot of ways he's been sheltered—maybe even a little spoiled. He's never really needed anybody else to make him feel loved. Lots of guys have tried to land him, but nobody has ever succeeded."

"He's never even dated?"

"Oh, yeah. He's gone out with lots of guys and probably even slept with a few of them. But he's never been seriously involved with anyone. They'd have to get by Philip first, and so far, that hasn't happened."

Josh thought back to the party and Thad's excitement about Philip liking him. "What do you mean?"

"Philip is very protective of Thad. He's not manipulative or controlling. He just tells it the way it is. He never misses a chance to ride me about sleeping with Michael. He's not obnoxious about it, but he definitely lets me know how he feels. Thad trusts him without question. Everyone does, but few follow his advice the way Thad does."

Josh had finished eating but couldn't remember what anything tasted like. He saw his interactions with Thad through new eyes and realized that from the start, Thad had seemed more than a little interested in him. Why hadn't he asked about the relationship with Philip? Had he blown it?

• 30 •

AFTER Josh paid the check, they left the restaurant and headed back to Ed's car. Ed looked at his watch. "It's almost eleven o'clock. Ready for the Eagle?"

Josh thought about saying no and asking Ed to take him home. He wanted to call Thad. He imagined how the two of them would laugh about Josh thinking he was Philip's lover and that Thad would want him to come over right away. Then he imagined Philip picking up the phone and chastising him for calling at such a late hour. He decided to stick with the plan. "Sure. I have no idea what to expect and am more than a little curious."

Ed laughed as he started the car. "Fags are fags. They come in a bunch of different sizes, flavors, and colors, but in the end, they are regular guys like you and me."

The drive to the Eagle was less traumatic than the trip to the restaurant had been, but only because of less traffic. They passed a number of streetwalkers, shouting come-ons to cars as they drove by. Most were African-American men in outlandish hooker drag. He was glad they drove instead of walking.

They finally arrived at the Eagle. Dozens of motorcycles were parked in a line out front. Ed drove around the block until he found a well-lit spot on a side street to park the car.

Except for a scruffy-looking bartender with a long beard and a bandana around his head, the downstairs bar was deserted. Ed led the way to steps leading up to the main bar. Josh could feel the throbbing bass before he heard the music.

The first thing Josh saw was a long bar with television screens mounted above an island of liquor bottles in the center of the cavernous room. The glow of the porn playing on the televisions shed little light on the scene below. Along the edges of the room, he could make out dark masculine shapes, but not what they were wearing or looked like.

"What do you want to drink?" Ed asked.

"I better go with a beer—something in a bottle." Josh could barely hear Ed placing their order above the booming techno blasting from several five-foot-tall speakers placed around the room.

As his eyes adjusted to the dimness, he noticed a big man in a dark T-shirt with "Security" in white letters on the back interrupting a guy in a nearby corner, who was masturbating as a small group stood around him and watched. Further down the bar, a shirtless man in a harness wore leather chaps, a black trooper hat with a visor, and dark sunglasses. Two guys on leashes in skimpy leather shorts sat at his feet.

Ed handed him a beer. "Want to walk around?"

Josh couldn't imagine what else he might see. "Yeah, let's."

Ed strode confidently across the room to an area on the other side of the bar that was better lit than the rest of the room. "The freaks hang out in the darkest corners."

Josh followed behind, taking in all the sights. He had to admit, some of the guys in leather looked hot—especially the guys who obviously spent a lot of time at the gym. Ed pointed to a group Josh had been admiring. "They're all hairdressers at an upscale shop in Chevy Chase where the clientele are all little blue-haired ladies."

Josh laughed. "How do you know?"

"See the big guy on the left, with the hairy chest and big nipple rings?"

Josh looked. "Yeah. He's really hot."

"He's done my mother's hair for years. He can suck his own dick. Want to see?"

"Are you kidding?"

"Nope. His name is Don, but everyone calls him Donkey. You'll see why in a minute."

"This I've got to see."

Josh and Ed walked up to the group. "Hey, guys. I'd like you to meet my friend, Josh. He just moved here from Kentucky."

An enormous man standing next to Donkey walked over. Josh put out his hand, but instead of shaking it, the guy grabbed him by the shoulders, picked him up, and licked his cheek. "You've got the cutest damn dimples I've ever seen. They call me Bull."

After Bull returned him to the ground, Josh wiped his face with his hand. "Hi, Bull. Nice to meet you."

"Hey, Donkey," Ed said. "Show Josh your little trick."

Donkey whipped out the biggest dick Josh had ever seen, leaned over, and put the head in his mouth.

"Damn." Josh was impressed.

"Grab hold of it for him," Bull said. "Stroke it a couple of times and it'll get hard enough to where he can take more than just the head in his mouth."

"Uh. That's okay. I believe you."

Ed reached over, grasped the giant cock at the base and proceeded to move his hand slowly up and down. Sure enough, the cock started to thicken and grow longer. Donkey continued sucking himself.

The guy in the security T-shirt, an even bigger man than Bull, walked over. "Donkey, I've told you to keep that thing in your pants. If I see it again tonight, I'm going to throw you out. If the undercover vice cops in here every weekend see you, they'll shut us down."

Donkey stuffed the partially engorged dick back into his pants. "Sorry, Mike. I was just showing Ed's guest my parlor trick."

Josh felt his cheeks turn hot. Mike looked at him. "If you want to see Donkey perform, take him home with you. This is a bar, not some kind of carnival freak show."

"Yes, sir. I'm sorry. I had no idea…," Josh stammered.

As Mike walked away, Ed gave him the finger. "Prick. We were just having a little fun."

Mike kept walking but yelled back, "I saw that, Pierson. In your dreams."

"Pay no attention to him," Ed said. "It's his job to keep the rest of us from having any fun."

Josh took a drink from his beer and looked around the room. Not able to believe his eyes, he poked Ed in the ribs. "Is that who I think it is?"

"Where?"

Josh pointed. "Over by that door."

Ed looked where Josh had pointed and whistled. "Yep. Sure is. Adam in full leather drag. Damn, he looks hot."

Adam wore a black leather baseball cap, leather shorts that showed off his muscular thighs, a chain-link harness that barely contained his massive chest, and heavy, metal-toed boots. Leather gauntlets covered each arm from wrist to elbow. Both nipples sported thick rings. The way his muscles were pumped up, Josh thought he must have worked out for hours before hitting the Eagle.

Josh and everyone else in the place watched as Adam paraded across the room. He was an impressive and intimidating sight. The crowd opened before him as he walked through the bar toward Josh, Ed, Donkey, Bull, and the other hairdressers.

Donkey saw him coming too. "Did you hear what happened to him?"

Before Josh could respond, Bull said, "Yeah. Caleb beat the hell out of him for fucking around on him. He used to be a Navy SEAL, so I'm guessing he put a powerful hurt on Adam."

Josh felt the blood draining from his face. He didn't know for sure, but assumed he was the reason for the beating Adam took from Caleb.

Adam saw Josh and visibly bristled. He curled his lip into a snarl and hit his open palm with his fist. Ed saw it too. "Uh-oh," he said.

Josh thought about making a quick exit but decided to stand his ground. He hadn't done anything wrong. Besides, if things got out of control, he was with friends. He watched as Adam approached and stopped in front of him. Adam glared at Josh and said, "Motherfucker, I've been looking for you."

"You talking to me?" Josh asked.

Adam glared at him. "Who else would I be talking to, bitch? Your big mouth got me in a lot of trouble."

Now that Adam was practically in his face, Josh could see bruises on his neck and chest. "My mouth? Seems to me you asked for it. You wouldn't have gotten in any trouble at all if you hadn't bought me a beer and asked for my phone number."

Ed interrupted. "Come on, Josh. Let's just go."

Adam pushed Ed out of the way. "You trying to pin this on me? Fucking asshole. I was just being nice, and you turned it all around and made Caleb think we'd hooked up."

Angry that Adam was being such a jerk, Josh didn't back down. "That's between you and Caleb. It's not my fault he took the word of someone he's never met over yours. It's your fault if he doesn't trust you."

A now seething Adam took a step closer. "There you go again, poking your fucking nose where it doesn't belong. Sounds like you need a lesson about minding your own business."

"Don't blame me for your problems." Josh pushed him in the chest. "Back off."

"What's going on here?" Mike asked. He stepped between them, placing a hand firmly on each man's chest.

"Nothing I can't handle," Adam answered.

Josh interrupted. "This crazy guy wants to kick my ass because it's somehow my fault his lover doesn't trust him."

Mike looked at Josh. "Man, you're really attracting a lot of attention for a first-time visitor. I'm thinking maybe you should finish that beer and head on out." Then he turned to Adam. "Dude, you need to cool your jets or I'll put your ass out too. Let's you and me step out here on the patio and chat while these boys say their good-byes."

Adam said, "You better watch your back."

Mike grabbed Adam by the elbow and steered him outside. Josh watched the two men talking and saw Adam gesturing toward him angrily. Ed stepped in front of him, blocking his view. "Josh, I think maybe it's time for us to go."

"Not until I finish my beer. You heard Mike. He said I could."

"Yeah, and he also said to say your good-byes. We don't need any trouble."

Bull nodded. "If you ask me, Caleb should have kicked his ass a long time ago."

Donkey nodded. "The pair of them is bad news. Adam is blaming you for trouble between him and Caleb that started long before you got to town. Man is more than a little hotheaded. If I were you, I'd be heading out the door."

Josh turned up his beer. "I'm not looking for trouble, but I'm not going to let some hotheaded lump of muscle push me around."

Ed grabbed Josh by the shoulders. "Josh, you're really not making good sense. Adam was in the Marines."

"So?"

"He knows a hundred different ways to kill you with a paper clip. Let it go."

"I'm not afraid of him. Don't forget, I work for a bunch of attorneys. If he touches me, I'll keep him tied up in court for years."

Ed laughed. "Come on. Let's call it a night."

Josh reluctantly agreed. He hated getting kicked out of the Eagle. Oh well, at least he'd have a good story to tell Thad.

• 31 •

JOSH and Ed walked out of the Eagle a little after midnight. Josh looked up and saw a broken streetlight, but no sign of the moon or stars in the inky black sky. Ed's car was parked behind the Eagle, more than a block away. Once they turned the corner, the streetlights and the well-lit signs over the entrance to the bar offered no illumination. Josh couldn't help thinking about the recent murder near the Eagle. Despite the balmy evening, his skin prickled with goose bumps.

A siren wailed in the distance. Josh smelled garbage as they walked past a dumpster and jumped when a rat scurried across their path.

Ed laughed. "He's as afraid of us as we are of him."

"I doubt it. Rats give me the creeps." Josh shivered.

"I got used to them when I lived on the street. That doesn't mean I like them, but they don't scare me anymore."

When they turned the next corner, Josh could see Ed's car off in the distance, brightly lit by the streetlight he'd parked under. Just half a block more and they'd be home free.

A noise in front of them and off to the right got his attention. It sounded like a car door closing. Josh walked a little faster.

Maybe fifteen cars, parallel-parked along the curb, stood between them and Ed's car. Hoping it would calm his nerves, Josh stopped to light a cigarette. It took several flicks of his nearly empty Bic to generate a big enough flame. By the time he got it lit, Ed was several car lengths in front of him.

"Hurry up, Josh. People get killed around here!"

Josh picked up the pace. When he reached the car, the engine was running. Josh opened the door and slid in. Ed executed a U-turn and headed back toward Dupont Circle. Josh didn't give a second thought to the Jeep pulling away from the curb behind them.

ED DROVE up and down P Street looking for a place to park. After fifteen minutes, he expanded his search before finally finding a space on New Hampshire Avenue. On the walk through Dupont Circle back to Josh's apartment, they stopped at the fountain.

"Sorry about the way things turned out tonight," Ed said as he took a seat on one of the many wooden benches circling the fountain.

Josh sat down beside him. "It wasn't your fault. Who knew Adam was such an asshole?"

"Well, I kinda did, but you pissed him off before I could tell you. Want some coffee? I'm hoping we'll be up all night."

Josh laughed. "Sure, why not? Mind if I stay here and smoke a cigarette?"

"Not at all. What do you want?"

"I'd love a caramel macchiato."

"Yum, that sounds good, I think I'll have one too. I'll be right back." Ed headed toward the Starbucks.

The roar of the brightly lit fountain extinguished the sound of the traffic that circled the park. Josh pulled out a cigarette. When his lighter wouldn't work, he looked around to see who he could get a light from. Except for the homeless people sleeping under newspapers on several benches, the park was deserted. He walked over to a tree to create a wind-free zone between the palm of his hand and the trunk. He vigorously shook the Bic and tried again. A small flame appeared, lasting just long enough for him to light the tip of his cigarette. He turned and headed back to the bench to wait for Ed.

A hulking figure emerged from the shadows ten feet in front of him. Josh stopped in his tracks and thought about the recent murders in the area. He felt his bowels clench and his heart jumped into his throat.

The menacing presence stepped closer. Josh was about to turn and run when he realized it was Adam. He breathed a sigh of relief. He might get beat up, but at least Adam wouldn't kill him.

Then he saw the baseball bat.

His gut reaction was to run. But Josh knew if he ran now, Adam would continue to stalk him. He'd learned back in middle school there was only one way to deal with a bully: stand up to him.

He scanned the grass around him for something to defend himself with, but found nothing.

Adam walked slowly toward him, smiling as he closed the distance between them. "You ready for that lesson in minding your own business I was talking about?"

Josh stood his ground. The roaring fountain would drown out any cry for help.

"Do you really want to do this? Is it worth going to jail?"

"I don't know what you're talking about, asshole. Nobody knows I have it out for you but you, me, and Caleb."

"Ed knows, and so do Mike, Donkey, and Bull. You'll get caught."

"No, I won't. They don't even know I'm here. Nobody does but you."

Adam had chosen a dark area hidden from the street for his ambush. If Ed was on his way back from Starbucks, Josh couldn't be sure that he could see what was happening.

"You're twice my size, Adam. If you're going to kick my ass, why don't you lose that bat and fight me fair and square?

Adam smiled. "Because I'm not interested in kicking your ass. I'm going to kill you."

Josh again thought of running, but it was too late. Like it was in slow motion, he watched Adam swing the bat. He saw the bat coming for his face and noticed it was a Louisville Slugger. He turned his head, but was unable to move fast enough to dodge it. He saw stars, then felt an explosion of pain and cool wet grass against his cheek before everything went dark.

• 32 •

"THAD, wake up."

Philip sat on the edge of Thad's bed, shaking Thad's shoulder to wake him up. Thad figured they were going on another outing together, and that Philip had, as usual, waited until everything was packed and ready to go before waking him.

"Wake up, Thad. We're needed at the hospital."

Thad sat up. "Are Mom and Dad okay?"

"Your parents are fine. Ed just called. He was blubbering so much I had a hard time following him, but apparently, someone beat Josh up last night in Dupont Circle."

Thad leaped from the bed and grabbed the jeans folded neatly on the back of his desk chair. "Oh, my God! I thought they were going to the Eagle. Are they okay?"

"Ed is fine. I'm not sure about Josh."

Thad fought back a thousand questions as he dressed. He slipped into loafers and ran down the stairs.

Philip unlocked the passenger door and motioned for Thad to take a seat. Normally Thad would have driven. Philip started the car and headed for the hospital at breakneck speed.

Neither man talked. Nervous energy powered Thad's knee up and down in a steady, staccato rhythm. Philip reached over and placed his hand on Thad's knee. He stopped bouncing and placed his hand over his uncle's, grateful for the touch and the silence. His thoughts were full of regret. *If only I'd told Josh how I felt about him, then he wouldn't have been out with Ed. Things would have turned out differently.*

He pushed his bangs away from his glasses.

Who am I kidding? I have no reason to think Josh feels anything for me at all. Telling Josh how I feel probably wouldn't have changed anything. He sniffed and squeezed his eyes shut to keep any tears from falling.

Thinking about what he might have done differently kept him from imagining the extent of Josh's injuries. Both trains of thought upset him. He squeezed Philip's hand and tried to focus on the road.

When Philip pulled into the hospital parking lot, Thad opened the door and nearly leaped from the moving car. "Let me out here. I'll meet you inside."

"No," Philip said. "We'll go in together. Another two minutes isn't going to change anything."

Reluctantly, Thad agreed. He waited as Philip maneuvered the Lexus into a parking place. His uncle's presence would make a difference, especially for Ed, who was closer to Philip than he was to his own family.

The doors parted as they hurried through the emergency room entrance. The smell of blood, antiseptic, and unwashed bodies permeated the air. Thad saw Ed across the waiting room, talking to a police officer. Pulling Philip behind him, Thad headed toward them. The officer wrote on a clipboard, looking up now and then to ask another question.

When Ed saw them, he said something to the officer, then ran straight to Philip. He threw his arms around Philip, burying his face in the ample neck, sobbing. Philip whispered in Ed's ear and patted his back.

Seeing Ed cry was too much for Thad. The dam broke. Tears streamed down his cheeks. Philip saw him and raised an arm. Thad slid in, burying his face in Philip's neck. Philip hugged him close as he and Ed cried.

Eventually, Philip released his grip. "Ed, where's Josh?"

Ed stepped back from Philip and wiped his eyes with the back of his hand. "I'm not sure. Last I heard they were taking him over for X-rays."

Philip nodded and offered Ed a handkerchief. "I see. The police officer is waiting for you. Answer the rest of his questions and then we'll talk."

Ed wiped his face, pocketed the handkerchief, and returned to the police officer. Philip steered Thad to a group of chairs in a quiet corner of the waiting room. "Wait here while I see if I can find out anything about Josh."

Thad looked at the clock. The second hand ticked slowly toward 4:00 a.m. Tick. Tick. Tick.

After the officer had finished with him, Ed sat down beside Thad. He looked tired... exhausted. He leaned his head back and massaged the area around his eyes. Thad waited for Ed to say something, but he just kept rubbing his temple. Finally, Thad spoke up.

"Is Josh going to be okay? What happened?"

Ed dropped his hands to his knees and looked at Thad. "He's hurt pretty bad. I don't know if he'll be okay or not. It's all my fault. I never should have taken him to the Eagle or left him alone in the park."

Thad wanted to slap him and had to bite his tongue to keep from telling Ed to shut up about himself. "What happened, Ed?"

"Adam Gordon jumped him and beat him up pretty bad."

Thad's throat clinched. "Adam Gordon? Oh my God! Why?"

"He hit on Josh at Omega one night, said he would call, but never did. We ran into Adam and Caleb at Annie's the other night. Josh was pissed about Adam having a lover and hitting on him, so he said something in front of Caleb, implying they had hooked up. Caleb must have believed him because rumor has it he kicked Adam's ass."

Thad was too shocked to speak. Adam and Caleb were bad news. Getting between them was asking for trouble.

"Adam was alone at the Eagle. He and Josh got into a little shoving match, but security broke it up before things got out of hand. We left, and since it was fairly early, decided to sit and talk on one of the benches in Dupont Circle before going back to his apartment."

Ed sat silent as big tears rolled steadily down his cheeks. Thad tried to be patient. "Then what happened?"

Ed sniffed and wiped his face with Philip's handkerchief. "I went to Starbucks to get us some coffee. Adam must have followed us from the Eagle. I got back just in time to see him hit Josh in the head with a baseball bat."

Thad gasped. "Jesus!"

"I called 911 on my cell phone and took off running to help. Josh was down on the ground. Adam was kicking the shit out of him."

Thad fought back a wave of nausea. The idea of Josh helpless on the ground while Adam kicked him made him sick and more than a little angry.

"Adam didn't see me coming. I grabbed the bat and wrested it away from him. He turned back to Josh and I whacked his back. Got in a couple of good hits, but it didn't seem to faze him.

"Josh wasn't moving. There was a big puddle of blood around his head. I thought he was dead. When Adam turned and looked at me, I just knew killing me was next on his to-do list. The sirens must have scared him because he took off running. I chased him but he left me in the dust. By the time I got back to Josh, the police had arrived and the EMTs were working on him."

Thad hadn't seen Philip walking up behind him and jumped when he spoke. "Josh is in pretty serious condition, but it looks like he's going to live."

Thad breathed a sigh of relief. "That's good news. Can I see him?"

"No. He's in surgery right now and will be for the next few hours. The blow to his head resulted in a subdural hematoma. They're doing surgery to relieve the pressure on his brain. It's too soon to say if he'll fully recover from the head injury. He's also got several broken ribs and a collapsed lung."

Ed started blubbering. "It's all my fault."

Philip placed his hands on Ed's shoulders and looked him in the eye. "The doctor said Josh probably would have died if he hadn't received medical attention when he did. You can stop beating yourself up. You saved his life."

Ed sniveled. "But—"

Thad said, "You also kept Adam from hurting him more than he did. It's a good thing you were with him, Ed."

"Adam Gordon?" Philip asked.

"Yes." Thad quickly filled his uncle in on the whole story.

"I knew that one was bad news," Philip said. "Those body-obsessed types have more issues than *TV Guide*."

• 33 •

THAD found a table in the dimly lit cafeteria. He dumped a creamer and two sugar packets into his coffee, then reached for a donut. "Thanks, Philip. I'm not sure which I need worse—the coffee or the donut."

"I'm sure we'll need more of both before this night is over," Philip said, taking small sips from a steaming cup of black coffee. "Do either of you have any idea who we should call back in Lexington?"

"His dad," Ed said. "His mother died from cancer. He never mentioned anyone else."

Thad sipped his coffee and wondered what else Ed knew about Josh that he didn't know. He racked his brain, trying to remember anything Josh might have said about friends in Lexington. "I can see who he lists for an emergency contact when the office opens on Monday."

"Good idea, Thad. In the meantime, we need to figure out how to reach Josh's father. Wonder who has the clothes he was wearing?"

"I do," Ed said. "The nurse gave them to me when I got here and asked about him. I threw away the clothes they cut off of him, but his belt, keys, wallet and boots are in my car."

Philip sipped his coffee. "After Josh gets out of surgery, why don't you and Thad drive over to his apartment and see if you can find a number for his father. I'm sure he'd want to know."

Thad saw the police officer Ed had been talking to when they arrived. When the officer saw them, he headed toward their table.

"Mr. Pierson, I just wanted to let you know we've issued a warrant for Adam Gordon's arrest. Nobody was at his apartment—

looks like somebody left in a hurry. He and his partner, Caleb Wilson, have both vanished. Caleb has several outstanding warrants and apparently has quite a temper. You might want to exercise extra caution until we find them."

"Thank you for letting us know," Philip said.

"You're welcome. We've had several bludgeoning deaths in the area recently, but never any witnesses. If we can link the bat to any of the other cases, Adam will spend the rest of his life in prison. Thanks for your assistance."

"Glad I could help," Ed said. "Can we buy you a cup of coffee and maybe a donut?"

The officer smiled. "No, thanks. Never been a fan of donuts myself." He turned and headed back to the cafeteria entrance.

"Wow," Thad said. "Do you think Adam killed those other guys? Wonder where he and Caleb could have gone."

Philip finished his coffee. "I almost feel sorry for them. No telling what happened when they were kids to make them the way they are. Maybe they'll get some help after the police find them. Shall we head back upstairs? Perhaps we can get an update on Josh's condition."

They made their way to the surgical waiting room. Thad noticed it was nearly six o'clock. He grabbed a nine-month-old copy of *People* magazine from a coffee table and took a seat next to Philip. Ed sat on the other side of Philip, leaned back in the chair, and closed his eyes.

Just before seven, a doctor wearing scrubs with a mask pulled up over his forehead came through a door marked Employees Only. "Is anyone here with Mr. Freeman?"

Thad stood up. "Yes, we are."

"I'm Dr. Schwartz. We just finished the procedure to relieve the swelling around his brain and to repair his collapsed lung."

"Is he going to be okay?" Thad asked.

"Frankly, it's too soon to say. We're keeping him in a drug-induced coma which reduces blood flow to the brain and inhibits swelling in hopes of minimizing any damage."

Thad hadn't expected Josh to be in a coma. He had a million things he wanted to say—needed to say and to know had been heard.

"How long will you keep him in the coma?"

The doctor shrugged and turned back toward the door. "We'll monitor the pressure level over the next twenty-four hours. We should know a lot more this time tomorrow."

"Wait!" Thad stopped the doctor before he reached the door. "Can I see him?"

"He's in the intensive care unit. Are you family?"

Philip interrupted before Thad could answer. "Yes, I'm his uncle and these are his cousins. We're the only family he has in town."

"The ICU waiting room is down the hall and to your right. Let the receptionist know you're here with Mr. Freeman. When they get him stabilized, they'll allow you to go back two at a time."

"Thanks, Dr. Schwartz," Philip said. "We appreciate everything you've done for my nephew."

"He's not out of the woods yet. Even if he fully recovers, he's got a long road ahead of him. Be sure to leave your phone numbers with the ICU nurse in case we need to reach you."

After the doctor left, Thad turned to Philip. "Quick thinking, Philip. I was about to say we were just friends."

Philip smiled. "I've run into this situation before and found out the hard way that a friend in the ICU without any family in the area requires a little white lie."

The ICU waiting room reeked of unwashed bodies and stale cigarette smoke. Family members of patients slept in chairs, on the floor, and even under a coffee table covered with empty coffee cups and tattered magazines. Thad, Philip, and Ed tiptoed around the slumbering bodies to an elderly blue-haired woman wearing cat-eye glasses and a pink jacket sitting behind the receptionist's desk. Thad noticed her nametag: Violet Rose, Volunteer.

Philip took charge. "Good morning, ma'am. I'm Josh Freeman's uncle. Would it be possible for me and my nephews to slip in to see him?"

Violet smiled and consulted a card file on her desk. "Certainly. But first, I need an emergency contact for Mr. Freeman." She pulled a page from a drawer and handed it to Philip. "Could you fill this out for me, please?"

Thad took the form and grabbed a pen from a white coffee cup emblazoned with yellow smiley faces to fill it out.

"Thank you, Thad." Philip turned back to the receptionist. "Violet Rose. What a lovely name! Surely you are a gardener?"

"Why, thank you, sir." A coy smile wrinkled her face. "I dabble when I can find the time but would hardly call myself a gardener. My volunteer work keeps me very busy." Violet smoothed her hair, tugged on her pink jacket, and smiled demurely at Philip. "Do you garden?"

"Like you, I merely dabble when I can find the time."

Thad resisted the urge to snort. Philip spent hours and hours every week pulling weeds, cutting back plants that had overgrown their allotted space, and removing spent flowers. He had been after him for years to hire a gardener, but Philip flatly refused.

Philip poured on the charm. "How often do you work?"

"I cover the ICU waiting room every Saturday and Sunday morning for four or five hours and fill in during the week when they need me."

"How very generous of you! I'm sure they really appreciate your help."

Violet beamed. "Last year I was Volunteer of the Year."

"Congratulations! Your dedication is truly remarkable."

Thad handed the completed form back to the receptionist, who now seemed a good ten years younger than before Philip's charm offensive. "When can we go back to see him?"

Violet took the form, looked it over, and filed it away. "Let me check with the nurses." She picked up the phone and dialed a few numbers. "Yes, this is Mrs. Rose in the waiting room. Would it be possible for Mr. Freeman's family to see him?"

Thad heard the crackle of the voice coming from the other end but couldn't make out what was said.

"I see. Yes, I'll let them know. Thank you very much." She hung up the phone and turned to Philip. "Mr. Freeman has only just arrived from surgery. They're checking him in now and when he's more settled, a nurse will come and get you. She said it would be another fifteen minutes or so."

Fifteen minutes turned into an hour. Time seemed to come to a complete stop. Disregarding Philip's admonitions to sit down and be patient, Thad paced the waiting room. Philip browsed through crumpled magazines. Ed leaned back in his chair, eyes closed, snoring softly.

Shortly after eight o'clock, a young nurse in scrubs came through the door from the ICU. She consulted with Violet Rose, who pointed to Philip. Thad stopped pacing as the nurse strode purposefully toward them. Philip poked Ed to wake him up.

"I'm Margie, Mr. Freeman's nurse. Before I take you back to see him, I want to tell you a little about his condition and what you will see."

Thad listened to the nurse explain the care Josh was getting, but had no idea what she was talking about. He tried to prepare himself for the shock of seeing Josh for the first time. He felt Philip's hand on his elbow, guiding him behind the nurse who led them to the door to the ICU.

She stopped before opening the door. "Seeing a loved one hooked up to so much equipment is always a shock. Just remember that everything you see is there to help him. It looks worse than it is. He's not feeling any pain and has no awareness of his surroundings. Are you ready?"

Thad nodded and looked to his Uncle Philip. Philip smiled at him. "Be strong, Thad. Josh needs you to be strong."

The nurse opened the door and they headed down a narrow, dimly lit hallway. Thad's nose filled with a dozen different smells ranging from antiseptic to mildly nauseating. He heard woofing and huffing from several ventilators and the beep of dozens of monitors as they went down the hall toward the nurse's station, surrounded on three sides by about a dozen curtained cubicles. The open side of each cubicle faced the nurse's station. As they continued past several cubicles, Thad heard moaning coming from one, and a nurse calling a patient's name from another.

They turned the corner and there was Josh. Thad gasped. The nurse's explanation had in no way prepared him for what he saw. A skullcap of white bandages covered Josh's head above the ears. A tube hung from his mouth, pumping air into his lungs, making his chest rise and fall in rhythm with the ventilator beside him. A maze of tubes sprouted from the sheet that covered him, snaking in every direction to the machines, bottles, and bags surrounding him.

Philip tightened his grip on Thad's elbow. "You okay, Thad?"

Unable to speak, Thad merely nodded, and wiped the tears from his eyes with the back of his hand. He looked closer. Except for the bandage on his head and the tube coming from his mouth, ashy-white Josh looked the same as ever and appeared to be sleeping.

Thad took a few steps closer, until he stood over Josh's head. He noticed Josh's left arm was free of any tubes and reached down to grasp his warm but unresponsive hand.

"Josh, I'm here."

The nurse returned. "I need you to go back out to the waiting room now." She continued to talk as she directed them down the hall to the waiting room door. "The doctor wants to keep him in a coma for at least the next twenty-four hours. You might as well go home and get some sleep. We'll call you if anything changes, and you can always call the ICU for an update on his condition."

• 34 •

THE police had his bat. Testing would tie the bat to the other murders and they'd be looking for him.

They were probably already looking for him. Josh wouldn't be talking anytime soon, he'd made sure of that. Letting that Pierson bitch get away had been a mistake—a big mistake. He'd tell the police what he saw and who owned the bat. In a matter of hours, they'd have a search warrant for the townhouse.

Adam stepped on the gas. Time was on his side for now. But the clock was ticking, and he needed to make the most of every second or he'd end up on death row in some shithole prison.

He circled the townhouse, but didn't see any sign of the police. He parked two streets over, keeping a wary eye out for anything unusual and sticking to the shadows as he walked back to the townhouse.

Caleb wasn't home. When Adam had suggested they go to the Eagle earlier that evening, he'd acted strange, like he was distracted or preoccupied. Instead of announcing he didn't feel like going out and they would stay home, Caleb had encouraged Adam to go out without him. Something was up. Adam wondered where he might be but had too much to do to worry about it now.

He grabbed two kitchen trash bags and walked quickly through the house, filling them with things he would need to live on the lam for a while. He'd lived on the streets before he met Caleb. With a few tools and accessories, Adam knew how to hide in plain sight. Becoming just another crazy homeless guy made him invisible to most people.

In the bedroom, Adam removed a large abstract painting from the wall and tossed it on the bed. He dialed the combination on the wall safe and smiled when he heard the gentle click of the door unlocking. He pulled the door open.

Shit! Empty! Caleb must have cleaned it out.

Enraged, he slammed the safe closed. He stepped over to the closet, fell to his knees, and began removing boxes and bags from one end. The pile grew until he pulled out a small red toolbox, and he smiled as several crisp stacks of hundred-dollar bills fell to the floor.

Sucking dick for pay made him feel good about himself. Men wanted him bad enough to pay for it. Getting paid meant he wasn't cheating on Caleb—it was a job. So what if they really didn't need the money. Making money made him feel good. Hiding his earnings from Caleb made him feel even better.

Now he had everything he needed. He carried the overstuffed trash bags back to the Jeep, stopping twice to steal out-of-state license plates. He replaced his Virginia tag with one from Florida and stashed the Kentucky tag under the seat for later use. He'd rotate through the three tags as he moved the Jeep around from one public parking lot to another until he could leave town.

He wondered where Caleb had gone and why he'd taken the pistol and all the cash from the safe. He needed to find him before the police did. But first, some unfinished business required his attention. He needed to know if Josh had lived or died and where to find Pierson.

• 35 •

ED DROVE Thad to Josh's apartment building. On the way, Thad went through the bag of personal items Ed had received from the hospital—keys, a wallet, a black leather belt, and Josh's blood-spattered Justin Ropers.

"You sure you don't want me to wait? I don't mind." Ed said as he pulled up to the front entrance of the West Park.

"No, thanks. I don't know how long I'll be." Thad closed the door and leaned down so he could see Ed. "You go on. The walk home will do me good."

Ed yawned. "Okay. Call me if you need anything. I'm going home to sleep for a few hours before I go back to the hospital."

Thad wondered about Ed's relationship with Josh. They had been out on several dates. Thad was reasonably sure they'd even had sex. Was Ed in love with Josh? What if Josh was in love with Ed? Maybe he was interfering in something that wasn't any of his business.

His instincts told him he was doing the right thing. Even if Ed and Josh were now a couple, Josh was his friend. Besides, Ed didn't seem to mind Thad calling Josh's father. Come to think of it, Ed hadn't seemed to mind Thad going back to the intensive care unit to see Josh instead of him, either. He decided not to worry about Ed.

At the door to the West Park, Thad realized he hadn't thought about how to get into the building. He saw the receptionist, an older African-American woman in a bright yellow dress, busily going over papers at a desk just inside the door. When she looked up, Thad waved at her and smiled. She buzzed him in. "Can I help you?"

"Yes, thank you. I'm Thad Parker. My cousin, Josh Freeman, lives in apartment 419. He was assaulted last night and is in George Washington Hospital. I need to go up to his apartment to get a few things for him."

A concerned look replaced the welcoming smile on her face. "Oh my goodness! Is he okay?"

Thad shook his head. "We don't know yet. He's in a coma in the intensive care unit."

"Lord have mercy. Mr. Freeman is such a nice man. Of course you can go up, let me get someone to let you in." She reached for the phone on her desk.

"Thanks, but I have his keys."

"Well, you go right on up, then." She pointed down a short hallway. "The elevators are just through that arch."

Thad took the elevator to the fourth floor and let himself into Josh's apartment. The scent of Quorum cologne greeted him. He noticed the message light blinking on Josh's answering machine and pushed the button.

"Hi, Josh. It's Linda. Glad your dad can join us. Sorry I missed you. Call me!"

Thad cursed when she didn't leave a number. He noticed the list finder beside the phone, slid the tab to "F" and pushed the button. There next to "Dad" was a phone number. Thad wrote it down on the back of his business card. He decided to look for Linda's number. He slid the tab to "A". No luck. He moved through "B" and "C". Still nobody named Linda. He slid the tab to "D", and saw there were only two numbers on the page; one for a Linda Delgado and another for Mrs. Delgado. He wrote both numbers alongside the number for Josh's father.

Thad looked around the apartment. No point in getting clothes for Josh, or anything else for that matter. He checked the refrigerator for perishables and tossed several slices of pizza, some sandwich meat, and an already brown head of lettuce into the trash. He dumped the trash down the chute, replaced the trash bag from a box under the sink, and then, figuring he'd done all he could, he locked the apartment and headed back to the lobby. He stopped at the receptionist's desk.

"Thanks for letting me go up. I'm not sure how long it will be before he gets out. Let me leave my number with you in case something comes up and you need to reach him."

The receptionist took Thad's card. "I'll be praying for your cousin. You be sure to tell Mr. Freeman Vanessa said get well soon."

As Thad walked home, he thought about the phone calls he needed to make. *Hi, you don't know me. I'm a friend of Josh's and just wanted to let you know he was attacked last night and is in a coma.* He thought about asking Philip to make the calls. He was so good with people he'd know what to say, without making a mess of it the way Thad was bound to do.

But no. Calling Josh's dad wasn't Philip's job. Time to man up. As Josh's friend, it was his responsibility.

He found Philip in his favorite chair in the sunroom. He looked up from the magazine he'd been reading. "I called your parents to let them know not to expect us tomorrow. They send their love. Did you find Josh's dad's phone number?"

Thad had completely forgotten about their plans to see his parents. "I did. Thanks for calling Mom and Dad."

"No problem. Would you like for me to call Josh's dad?"

"Yes, but it's something I need to do. Thanks for offering. Any suggestions?"

"Be gentle, stick to the facts, and the less said, the better."

"Josh had a message from someone named Linda. She mentioned his dad. I got the impression they were close. I found a phone number for someone that might be her. I think I'll call her first."

"I'm right here if you need me. Make your calls and get some rest. It's been a long night, and I suspect the week will be long as well."

Thad retreated to his room. The empty, unmade bed beckoned, but he sat at his desk, picked up the phone, and dialed the number for Linda Delgado. He recognized the voice from Josh's machine when she answered. "Hello, Linda. My name is Thad Parker. I'm a friend of Josh's."

"Is something wrong?" Thad heard panic in her voice.

"Yes, I'm afraid so." He fought to control his emotions. Crying wouldn't help. "Josh is in the hospital. He got hit in the head with a baseball bat last night."

Linda's plaintive "no" was followed with several questions. "How bad is he hurt? Is he paralyzed? Will he be okay?"

Thad fought to maintain his composure. "We don't know. Right now he's in a medically induced coma to reduce the swelling around his brain. He had surgery last night."

"A coma? Oh my God!" Thad heard Linda sob.

"Aside from the head injury, he's got some broken ribs and a collapsed lung. Otherwise, as far as we know, that's it. I saw him a few hours ago, and except for the bandage on his head, he looks the same as before."

"Have you talked to his doctor?"

"Yes, but he isn't saying much. He'll know more in twenty-four hours."

"Have you called his father yet?"

"No," Thad replied. "Not yet."

"Don't worry about it, I'll call him tonight. Should I come to DC?" He heard papers shuffling. "I can clear my calendar and be there Tuesday or Wednesday."

Thad paused and thought about how to respond. He understood her desire to run to Josh's side, but doubted her presence would make any difference unless and until Josh woke up. "Why don't you wait another few days to see what happens? There's nothing anyone can do right now. I'll call you every day with an update."

"You're probably right. I hate for him to be alone up there without family or anyone who loves him."

Thad hesitated for just a minute. "I love him."

• 36 •

THAD slept most of Saturday. He'd wanted to go back to the hospital that night, but when he called, the nurse looking after Josh said he was still in a coma and would stay that way for at least the next twelve hours. She promised to call if there was any change in his condition. Having promised to call every day, Thad dialed Linda's number.

"I just called to let you know there hasn't been any change in Josh's condition. The doctor wants to keep him in the coma for at least another twelve hours."

Linda sounded much calmer than she had the day before. "It's sweet of you to call, Thad. We've been worried sick. I talked to his dad yesterday. Like me, he's ready to come to DC any time."

"Honestly, right now there's not much point. Until they bring him out of the coma, he doesn't know if anyone is with him or not."

"I know you're right. I just keep thinking I should be there." Linda paused. "Were you with him when it happened?"

The question surprised Thad. "No, I wasn't. He was with Ed, a friend of ours."

"Yeah, Josh told me all about Ed. He's talked about you too. What do you look like?"

Thad wondered how Josh would have described him to her. "Well, I'm about five nine, wear glasses, have red hair—"

Linda interrupted him. "You helped Josh find an apartment and made his bed for him?"

"Yes, that was me." Thad felt his cheeks grow hot. He couldn't help but smile.

Then Linda lobbed the big one. "Don't you live with an older lover?"

"What?" Thad wasn't sure he'd heard her correctly.

"Your boyfriend—is he an older guy?"

Thad had no idea what she was talking about. He didn't have a boyfriend, and he lived with....

Then it hit him.

"You mean my uncle?"

"You live with your uncle?"

"Yes, I do. We're very close and always have been."

Linda laughed. "That makes perfect sense. Josh said he could tell how much you love each other. He thought he was your lover."

"What?" Thad was stunned.

"He got the impression your uncle was your lover. Glad to hear you're available. I've been thinking you might be the one since he first mentioned you."

Thad couldn't believe the direction the conversation was taking. "Yes, I'm definitely available and have loved him almost from the minute I met him."

"Good. I'm pretty sure he's in love with you too."

Thad didn't know what to say. "I hope you're right."

"I am. He may not know it yet himself—he's slow that way—but I can tell by the way he talks about you that he is."

"You've made my day."

• 37 •

THAD and Philip returned to the hospital Sunday morning. Philip presented a vase to Violet Rose, overfilled with an assortment of roses he'd cut from his garden early that morning.

"I thought you might enjoy these," he said, placing the vase on her desk.

"They're gorgeous!" Violet exclaimed. She leaned in and inhaled deeply. "Oh, and they smell wonderful too! So many roses these days lack any fragrance. And look at all the colors! Thank you so much! Everyone who comes through the waiting room this morning will enjoy them."

Philip smiled. "I tried to put together a bouquet befitting the Volunteer of the Year. I'm so glad you like them."

Violet beamed. She inspected the roses more closely. "You, sir, are far more than a dabbler. These roses are exquisite!"

"You're right, Mrs. Rose," Thad interjected. "My uncle spends every spare moment in his garden and won't let anyone else help. He calls it his therapy."

"I completely understand. When I was able, I was the same way." Violet smiled. "Now, I know you're not here to visit with me." She picked up the phone and punched a few numbers. "Let me see if I can find a nurse to update you on your nephew's condition."

A male nurse in surgical scrubs came through the door from the ICU. "Are you with Mr. Freeman?"

"Yes," replied Thad and Philip in unison.

"I'm Robert Hansen, Josh's nurse since midnight. Unfortunately, I don't have any good news. His condition is still guarded and has not improved. He's running a bit of a temperature and his white count is up, which makes us think he has some kind of infection. Post-surgical infections are not abnormal, and at this point, we're not worried. We've doubled up on antibiotics and continue to monitor him closely for any signs of swelling in his brain. Dr. Schwartz told me this morning that he's going to keep him in the coma for at least another twenty-four hours."

The report was not what Thad wanted to hear. The news that Josh's condition seemed to be deteriorating rather than improving upset him. "Can I go back and see him?"

"Yes, but only for a few minutes."

Thad followed Robert into the ICU and back to Josh's cubicle. Except for the mechanically induced rise and fall of his chest, Josh didn't move. A two-day growth of beard was the only change Thad could see from his last visit.

After a few minutes, Robert returned to the cubicle. "Ready to go back to the waiting room?"

Thad nodded and followed him out of the ICU.

"You're welcome to stay here in the waiting room for as long as you like, but frankly, until the doctor brings him out of the coma, you might as well go home. There's nothing you can do. Get some rest. I promise we'll call you if anything changes."

Philip agreed. "He's going to need us a lot more when he wakes up than he does now."

On their way out, they ran into Ed coming in. "Been here all night?"

"No," Thad replied. "We just got here and we're already going back home. Josh is running a fever, so they're going to keep him in a coma for at least another day. His nurse said he'd call us if anything changed."

Philip gave Ed a hug. "I've got a few errands to run while I'm out. Thad, why don't you go with Ed. Perhaps you two could have brunch somewhere."

"Great idea," said Ed. "Come on, let's get something to eat. I'm starving!"

Thad was hungry too, but a little anxious about Ed's driving. He looked at his watch, saw that it was a little after ten o'clock and, figuring traffic would be light, nodded. "Sure. Let's hit the brunch buffet at one of the big hotels."

Thad and Ed attacked plates mounded high with Belgian waffles, made-to-order omelets, sausage, bacon, fried potatoes, and fruit at the Capital Hilton on Sixteenth Street.

Thad slathered catsup over his fried potatoes. "Josh's friend Linda told me he thought Philip and I were lovers. Can you believe it?"

"Yeah." Ed stabbed a sausage link with his fork. "We talked about it Friday night. He's got the hots for you."

Thad stopped his fork halfway to his mouth and looked at Ed. "What makes you say that?"

"Well," Ed said as he chewed, "his attitude toward me changed the second he found out Philip was your uncle. With you available, he wasn't all that interested in me."

Thad studied Ed's face. "Does that upset you?"

"It bruised my fragile ego a bit, but doesn't upset me. You know me. I'm really not the settling-down type that Josh wants. He'd make me stop seeing Michael and all my married friends. I'd be miserable." Ed shoved a fork overloaded with scrambled eggs into his mouth and then swept a Belgian waffle over his plate, sponging up maple syrup, melted better, and sausage grease. "How do you feel about him?" The dripping Belgian waffle disappeared into his mouth.

Thad paused for a minute to collect his thoughts. That Ed wasn't serious about Josh was a huge relief. He smiled and decided to come clean. "I'm crazy about him. I fell for Josh the first time I laid eyes on him. The more time we spend together, the more I like him."

"Does Philip know?"

Thad nodded. "Of course, and for once, he actually approves. I've complained to him for weeks about Josh's seeming indifference toward me. Philip said to be patient."

"Your uncle is a very wise man. I hope you know how lucky you are to have someone like him in your life."

"I do—and he reminds me every day just to make sure I don't forget. He loves you too, Ed. You're like a son to him."

Ed smiled. "I know. I guess that makes us brothers."

• 38 •

THAD called the hospital several times a day and stopped by every day after work to check on Josh. His condition improved slowly. His temperature had returned to normal and the danger of any swelling dropped with each passing day.

He called Linda daily to update her on Josh's status. By the third call, they were chatting like lifelong friends and had made plans for her Thanksgiving visit to DC. Thad encouraged her to bring Rafael and asked her to invite Josh's father. When Linda asked about hotels, Philip insisted they stay in his guest bedrooms.

Work was busier than usual. Practically everyone at the firm stopped by Thad's office to ask about Josh's condition. Thad nearly fainted when he looked up to find George Walker, the firm's senior partner, at his door.

"Mr. Parker, do you have a moment?"

Thad stood up. "Yes, sir, please come in."

The man walked into Thad's office, unbuttoned the bottom button of his Brooks Brothers suit, and took a seat in the chair across the desk from Thad.

"I just wanted to say that if there's anything Mr. Freeman needs, let me know. He's a valuable member of our team, and we're all praying for his full and rapid recovery."

Thad was touched by the senior partner's sincerity. "Thank you, sir. I'm sure he appreciates your prayers on his behalf."

Mr. Walker cleared his throat and looked across the desk at Thad. "I also want you to know you can have as much time off as you need, with pay, to assist in whatever way may be required with Josh's recovery."

Thad was too shocked to wonder how the senior partner knew about his almost relationship with Josh. "Why, thank you, sir. That's very kind of you."

"We pride ourselves on being progressive here at Walker, Cochran, and Lowe. You're both more than valuable employees to us. You're part of the family."

"Thank you, sir. You've always been very good to me. Working here is a pleasure."

"I'm glad you think so. I'll never forget the kindness your Uncle Philip showed to my nephew when he came out of the closet more than thirty years ago. I'm ashamed to admit that because of our ignorance on the matter, my brother and I turned our backs on him when he needed us most. Your uncle stepped in to fill the void and schooled me on what love is really about. He's a great man."

Thad was speechless. That Mr. Walker knew Philip and that his nephew had apparently been one of Philip's many projects were both news to him.

Mr. Walker rose from his chair, buttoned his coat, and then reached across Thad's desk to shake his hand. "Anything you need, you just let me know. Anything at all."

Thad shook his hand. "Thank you, sir. Thanks for stopping by."

When he got home, Thad found Uncle Philip in his usual spot, admiring the late October sunset from his favorite chair. Philip looked up and smiled when he saw Thad. "Care to join me? I love the way the roses look when the sun sets behind them. How was your day?"

Thad sat on the edge of his chair. "Fine. Old Man Walker stopped by my office this afternoon. I didn't know he even knew who I was. Told me to let him know if Josh needs anything and to take off with pay as needed to help with his recovery."

Philip took a sip of deep red wine from a crystal goblet. "What a pleasant surprise. It's nice to know your employer is so progressive and forward-thinking."

"He also said something about a nephew and how indebted to you he was for helping him after his family turned their back on him."

Philip squirmed in his chair a bit and took another sip of wine.

"Want to tell me what that's about?" Thad folded his arms and glared, waiting for his uncle to answer.

"It was a very long time ago, when you were just a toddler. Very sad. His nephew's name was James."

"What happened?"

"Unfortunately, it's an all too familiar story. James came out of the closet. His family was ashamed, kicked him out of the house, and wouldn't have anything to do with him. He was living on the streets when I met him." Philip seemed to watch a distant point on the horizon.

Curious now, Thad asked, "Another one of your projects?"

"No," he shook his head. "James was never a project, as you call them." He turned and looked at Thad. "We were lovers for nearly five years. One Christmas Eve, after an afternoon of shopping, I came home and found him. He couldn't handle the estrangement from his family and shot himself in the head."

A tear rolled down Philip's cheek. Thad waited.

Philip turned his gaze to the setting sun and continued. "After he killed himself, his father and his uncle—your Mr. Walker—came to see me. They offered me money, as much as I wanted, to keep the story out of the newspapers. They feared the scandal would ruin them professionally and wanted to spare their family the embarrassment of the truth. I don't know if they were more ashamed of our relationship or that he had taken his own life."

Thad thought back to the man in his office that afternoon. "Today Mr. Walker said he took pride in the firm being so progressive."

Philip went on as if he hadn't heard. "I gave the Walker brothers a piece of my mind and made it abundantly clear that their shame was the reason James killed himself. I recounted several occasions when he had reached out to them, only to be rebuffed, and how their refusal to accept him wounded him to the core. When they offered me money to keep things quiet, I threw them out of the house and swore they would pay dearly for turning their backs on a family member."

Philip drank more wine and turned to Thad. "I'm sorry I didn't tell you before. Even these many years later, it's difficult to talk about James."

"I'm so sorry. I had no idea...." Thad thought about everything he'd just learned as Philip sipped his wine in silence. After a long while, Thad cleared his throat. "I just have one question. Did you take the money?"

Philip smiled. "Yes and no. The money is in a trust fund that I draw on to help young men in situations similar to what James faced. The Walkers continue to support the fund, and over the years, their generosity has allowed me to help hundreds of men in ways that wouldn't otherwise have been possible. It's not a requirement, but most of them eventually pay me back. When they do, I put that money back in the fund. George manages the fund, which now has a value in excess of several million dollars. George and I eventually became friends, though we rarely see each other these days unless there's business to discuss about the trust."

A flood of emotions washed over Thad: sadness about the tragic end to Philip's relationship with James; awe at his dedication to lost souls over the years; and anger at just now finding out about such an important part of his uncle's story. That Philip's deep, dark secret involved his employer upset him and gave him something concrete to focus on.

"So my job at the firm is just another payback from the Walkers?"

Philip snapped his head from the fading rays of the sunset to Thad. "Absolutely not! Yes, George told me he had a position and asked me to send likely candidates his way. I did, including you and several others I knew who needed a job. You got that job on your own, with absolutely no intervention from me. George had no idea you were my nephew until you'd been on the job for several months."

Thad knew he was overreacting. Philip would never lie to him, though withholding key facts didn't seem to be a problem.

"I'm sorry, Thad. I wasn't trying to hide anything from you. You never asked and it never came up, so we didn't talk about it."

Thad's anger dissipated like smoke on a windy day. He got up from his chair and walked over to Philip, leaned down, and kissed him on the cheek. "I finally get you. Everything makes sense now. It never occurred to me that your dedication to abandoned gay men was the result of something that happened to you. Knowing the full story just makes me love you that much more."

"Thank you, Thad. I love you too."

• 39 •

FINDING Josh had been easy. Thanks to the local television station, Adam knew Josh Freeman was alive and in a nearby hospital. He just needed to find out which one.

There were only so many hospitals in town. Adam called each one, saying he was a concerned friend looking for his missing friend. When he called George Washington Hospital, he learned that "Mr. Freeman's condition is listed as critical." Bingo.

During the morning visiting hour the next day, Adam entered the hospital with the crowd who'd come to see friends, neighbors, and family members. He stopped at the information desk to get Josh's room number. The stupid bitch informed him that Mr. Freeman was in the intensive care unit. She said his condition was guarded.

Adam smiled and thanked her. If he was lucky, maybe Josh would die from his injuries. That would be good. Dead men couldn't testify, and without witnesses, there couldn't be much of a trial. But Josh kicking the bucket would only solve half his problem. Ed Pierson had to die too. Without them, the DA had no case and no chance of bringing him to trial. Of course, they'd have to catch him first… and that just wasn't going to happen.

Adam pushed a can-filled grocery cart through the parking lot of the hospital. He saw Pierson, and a little later, the redheaded faggot with his big flaming uncle. He'd been watching for patterns for more than a week. The redhead showed up right after five through the week, and as early as ten on Saturday and Sunday. Sometimes the uncle was with him, sometimes not. Finding the fucking castle they lived in had been a piece of cake.

Pierson's patterns were harder to identify and impossible to predict. Finding his Maryland condo had been difficult, but not impossible. The flimsy lock on the front door had been easy to spring with the right tool. He'd gone inside, explored all the drawers, closets, and cabinets, listened to albums on the turntable, and even watched the porn he found in the VCR. He'd dropped by at odd hours several times without ever running into Pierson. He wasn't worried. He still had time. Their paths would cross again, sooner or later.

• 40 •

FIRST thing Saturday morning, Thad and Philip returned to the hospital to check on Josh. Violet Rose summoned Robert Hansen from ICU to update them on his condition.

"We've seen a gradual improvement in his condition over the last week and especially in the last twenty-four hours. His vital signs are good, and there hasn't been any additional swelling around his brain. We started easing him off the medications keeping him in a coma last night and he's showing signs that he's aware of his surroundings. He's still heavily sedated, but breathing on his own. Would you like to go see him?"

"You go, Thad," Philip said. "I'll wait here and share gardening tips with Mrs. Rose."

Thad followed Robert back through the dimly lit hallway to Josh's cubicle. He did look better. Someone had shaved him, and the tube was gone from his mouth. His color had improved, from pale and ashy to something closer to normal.

"He's cried out a few times. When he does, we give him a little Demerol to ease the pain. If you like, I can bring a chair in so you can sit with him for a while."

"I'd like that." Thad stepped closer, reached out, and placed his hand over Josh's fingers, squeezing a little, hoping Josh could feel that he was there.

Robert returned with a chair. "Here ya go. Anything else you need?"

Thad sat down. "Thanks, you've been very kind. Can you send word to Mrs. Rose to let my uncle know I'll be staying here for a while?"

After Robert returned to the nurse's station, Thad held Josh's hand. Being alone with Josh for the first time since the assault was unsettling. He didn't know what to do. He'd heard that people in comas could hear what was going on around them. He didn't know if it was true or not, but decided to give it a try.

"Hello, Josh. It's Thad. I hope you can hear me."

He studied Josh's face. No change. Thad squeezed his hand and continued.

"I took your keys and went to your apartment. Vanessa said to tell you to get well soon. She's praying for you, too. She let me into the building, and if I hadn't had your keys, would have found someone to let me in your apartment."

Thad stopped for a minute to collect his thoughts. He thought Josh's eyebrow twitched, but it might have just been his imagination.

"The message light was blinking on your answering machine. I hope you don't mind, but I listened. It was your friend, Linda. I got her phone number and your dad's phone number from your list finder. Before I left, I also got rid of anything in your refrigerator that might spoil so you wouldn't come home to a stinky apartment."

Thad squeezed Josh's hand again. "When I got back home, I called Linda. She's really something. I can't believe you never told me about her. We talk a couple of times a day now and have become friends."

He looked at Josh, expecting him to laugh or say something about Linda. When he didn't, Thad continued. "She told me the craziest thing. She said you thought Philip and I were lovers. Philip laughed and laughed when I told him what she'd said. Everyone in town knows about us, so we're not really in the habit of mentioning we're family. Isn't that funny?

"Anyway, Linda called your dad to let him know you're in the hospital. They both wanted to come to Washington right away. Philip and I talked them out of it. No point taking off work when there's not anything they could do but sit and wait for you to wake up. Besides, I'm here to take care of you.

"The police are still looking for Adam and Caleb. I talked to one of the partners yesterday morning, Jacob Lowe. He's always liked you and talked with the district attorney's office about throwing the book at Adam. He's already started working on a civil suit for damages and pain and suffering. Phone records make the police think Adam is responsible for the other three murders too. His number turned up among recent calls from all three victims. They won't know for sure until the DNA samples from the bat come back from the lab."

Thad squeezed Josh's hand again. "I don't know if you can hear me or not. It's okay if you can't. Just talking to you makes me feel better." Thad studied Josh's face, watching for the slightest movement that might indicate Josh heard his words.

"Did you know I fell in love with you the first time I saw you? It's true. Blew me away. I'm not the kind of guy that goes around falling in love all the time. I've never really been in love before.

"Oh, sure, I've been interested in guys before. Getting to know them better was usually enough to put an end to things. If not, Philip would casually destroy any remaining illusions in the same quiet, understated way he does everything. Sometimes I try to ignore him, but he's never steered me wrong.

"He loves you too. He told me to be patient and you'll come around. Linda claims you already have. Sure hope she's right. She knows you pretty well, so I'm taking her word for it."

Thad couldn't be sure, but he thought Josh had squeezed his hand. It wasn't a real squeeze so much as a slight increase in pressure. He squeezed Josh's hand again, and this time, felt Josh move his finger against the palm of his hand.

• 41 •

JOSH felt the warm pressure increase again on his left hand. Someone was holding his hand. He tried to squeeze back.

He listened, trying hard to focus on the voice. It was so familiar. In his mind's eye, he saw white eyebrows disappearing behind the black frames of oversized eyeglasses.

He couldn't make out the words. The voice comforted him, but didn't belong to Ben or Linda. He concentrated harder.

The familiar voice continued in a soft, reassuring tone. Josh listened. The image of the black glasses frames and white eyebrows reappeared and grew sharp. Then he saw strawberry-blond bangs and jade-green eyes.

And he knew. The hazy image materialized into a face he recognized. The voice was Thad. The pressure on his left hand was Thad's hand. Josh squeezed his hand so Thad would know that he'd heard him.

Josh tried to open his eyes. He heard Thad's voice again. "Robert! Come quick! I think he's waking up!"

When he opened his eyes, the first thing he saw in the dim light was Thad's green eyes staring into his own. The tears that ran down Thad's cheeks didn't seem to go with the shit-eating grin on his face. Josh croaked out his first words in more than a week.

"What's wrong, Thad?"

"Not a thing, Josh. Not a thing."

• 42 •

JOSH thought he spent several days in intensive care. Because of the pain medication, the details were fuzzy. He remembered the nurses removing the tube from his chest and getting him to sit up in a chair for some chicken broth, strawberry Jell-O, and a Sprite. The broken ribs caused any kind of movement to send a searing pain through his chest. As long as he sat still, except for a dull headache, he almost felt good as new.

Robert, his nurse, moved him to the chair for a breakfast of scrambled eggs, toast, and juice, then got him up for a short walk down the hall. He held onto Robert with one hand and pushed the pole holding his IV fluids with the other as he slowly took first one step and then another. He was vaguely aware of the open back of the hospital gown and his exposed ass, but was too preoccupied with putting one foot in front of the other to worry much about it. Walking was difficult, but didn't hurt. The pain shooting through his chest whenever he stood up or sat down, however, brought tears to his eyes.

Dr. Schwartz said the pain would ease after a few days and gave the okay to move Josh to a private room on the seventh floor. He was glad to get away from the depressing atmosphere of the ICU. In his new room he had a telephone next to his bed, a television to watch, and could have visitors for more than just an hour or two at a time.

Thad visited every day with news from the office, his dad and Linda back in Lexington, and their friends in DC. He told Josh about all the media coverage of his assault and brought in newspapers with articles about it. After DNA evidence connected Adam to two of the three murders and the police discovered a dungeon in the basement of the house he shared with Caleb, the media referred to him as the S&M Killer.

Josh knew he was lucky to be alive. Without Ed, things would have turned out a lot worse. If Adam had hit his head one more time, or if the ambulance had come five minutes later, he might not have been so lucky. Surviving such a close call helped him to keep a positive attitude about the long road he faced to full recovery.

The first person to visit Josh in his new room was Thad, who tossed a newspaper on Josh's lap as he came through the door. Ed's picture was splashed across the front page of the *Washington Blade* under the headline, "Local Hero Leads Police to S&M Killer."

"They caught Adam?" Josh asked.

"No, not yet. They'll find him eventually."

"I hope so. I'd sure hate to run into him again. Knowing he killed those other guys, I don't think I'd be nearly as brave as the night he attacked me. Anything in the *Blade* we didn't already know?"

Thad shook his head. "No. Word on the street is that they had to do a special print run on oversized paper to accommodate Ed's big head."

Josh tried without success not to react. "Ouch! You know it hurts to laugh."

A look of concern crossed Thad's face. "I'm sorry. Do you want me to ring the nurse for a pain pill?"

"No, I'm okay now. Just try not to let it happen again."

Thad sat on the edge of the bed. "Why can I come up with a hundred snappy comebacks when I'm not allowed to make you laugh?"

Josh reached over and put a hand on Thad's leg. "Some crazy kind of karma for letting me think you and Philip were lovers."

Thad smiled. "I think you own that one all by yourself. You could have asked how long we'd been together or something that would have clued me in to what you were thinking."

"You mean you can't read my mind?"

"No, I can't. And you better not forget it, either. I came too close to losing you to let some silly miscommunication mess things up for us again."

Josh looked into Thad's jade eyes. "You're going to have to be patient with me. Talking about my feelings and what I'm thinking is not something I'm used to doing. Just ask Linda."

Thad met his gaze. "I know. She already told me."

Josh's eyes narrowed. "What else did she tell you?"

"She told me I'm a lucky man and that I better take good care of you or she'll hop in her Honda and drive up here to kick my ass."

Josh squeezed a pillow against his chest and tried not to laugh. "She would too. You're bigger than she is but she's feisty, and when provoked, has no qualms about fighting dirty."

"She made that pretty clear. So tell me, boyfriend, why didn't you ever mention this incredible woman to me before?"

"Boyfriend?" Josh looked up at Thad, waiting for an answer.

"Am I jumping the gun?"

"Maybe a little. We haven't even kissed yet!"

"Well, I can remedy that right now." Thad leaned over and kissed Josh lightly on the lips. "That's all you get for now—I wouldn't want to hurt you."

Josh smiled. "Are you that big?"

Thad blushed. "You'll just have to wait and see."

"You know you're the first boyfriend I've ever had who I didn't sleep with first. The suspense is killing me! Couldn't you just whip it out and show me?"

"I think you've been running around with Ed too much."

Josh frowned. "I probably need to deal with Ed."

Thad cleared his throat. "Um, no, you don't. We talked. He likes you a lot but says he's not really the settling-down type. He's got Michael and half a dozen married men he's not ready to give up. Unless you're into sharing...."

Josh shook his head. "I think we've clearly established that sharing is not my thing. I'm not interested in anything but good old-fashioned monogamy. You got any problem with that?"

"Nope." Thad placed a palm against Josh's cheek. "That's what I've always wanted too. You don't have to worry about what I'm doing when you're not around. Linda might be feisty, but Uncle Philip is not one to cross, either. I hate to think of what he'd do if you ever hurt me."

Josh held Thad's hand against his face. "That, boyfriend, is not something you'll ever have to worry about."

"Good," said Philip from the doorway. "I'm getting a little old to do much ass-kicking."

Josh smiled as Philip walked over to the side of the bed. "That's good to know. I'm not sure I could handle another ass-kicking anyway."

Ed followed in Philip's tracks. "Fly right and you won't have to worry about it. Philip might be too old, but I'm not. You hurt my little brother and you'll have me to reckon with."

Josh held up the *Blade* with Ed's picture across the front. "I wouldn't dare mess with a local hero. Can you autograph this for me?"

"I thought you'd never ask." Ed pulled a black Flair marker from his shirt pocket, took the paper from Josh, and scrawled something across the bottom of it before handing it back to him.

Josh picked up the paper to read the autograph.

To Josh. I couldn't have done it without you. Thanks for making me famous. Ed Pierson.

He squeezed the pillow against his chest as he simultaneously laughed and cried out in pain. "Thad?"

"Okay, nurse! We need a pain pill in here!

• 43 •

SPENDING time with Josh was the highlight of Thad's day. He came straight to the hospital from the office, stopping at home just long enough to get the car keys. He loved the way Josh's face lit up when he walked into the room.

"Hey, boyfriend!" Josh beamed. "How do you like my new 'do?"

Thad looked him over. The skull bandage had been removed and someone had trimmed his hair up for him. "I like it a little longer, but it looks pretty good."

"After they removed the bandage this morning, Ed brought Donkey up to even up the hatchet job the nurses gave me before surgery. I thought he did a good job."

Thad sat on the side of the bed and ran a hand through Josh's hair. "I think so too. What do you want to do this afternoon?"

"I need a change of scenery. Other than a few walks up and down the hall, I've been in bed watching television all day." Josh stood up and reached for his tennis shoes. "Let's go for a walk. Is it warm enough to go outside or do we need to take the grand tour again?"

"It's warm enough to go outside. You ready?"

From the edge of the bed, Josh slipped on his shoes and tied the laces. He eased himself out of the bed and reached for Thad, throwing his arms around his neck and kissing him. Thad pushed him away but was glad to see that Josh looked stronger and acted more like his old self every day.

"Let's find a supply closet or someplace where we can fool around," Josh said. "I can't wait to see you naked."

"Just like I told you yesterday and every day this week, that ain't gonna happen while you're in the hospital. I'm aware that dating before sex is not something you're used to, but we're going to wait until the time is right."

"Aww, Thad, come on! Please?"

Thad could easily imagine a much younger Josh using the same tone to talk his mother into giving him more ice cream or letting him stay up to watch television. "Nope. Haven't you ever heard of delayed gratification?"

"Yeah, I've heard of it and so far, I don't like it much. Can we at least go behind those bushes and make out a little?"

"No! You're absolutely incorrigible!" In truth, Josh's constant attempts to consummate their relationship amused him. The idea appealed to Thad too, but he feared showing even the tiniest little bit of weakness would only encourage Josh. He still wore a backless hospital gown but had talked one of the nurses into getting a pair of scrubs for him to wear "so everyone would quit staring at his ass." That a thin layer of cotton fabric was all that stood between him and a naked Josh was something Thad often thought about alone at night in his empty bed.

"The doctor told me today I should be home by next weekend. When I get out of here, we're going to spend a week in bed."

"That's great news! I've been shifting things around at the house to make room for you."

Josh stopped in his tracks and turned to Thad. "That's very sweet of you, but I want to go back to my apartment."

Thad was shocked into silence. "But…."

Josh placed a finger over Thad's lips to shush him. "I've thought about it a lot. Sure, the easy thing would be to go to your place so you and Philip could spoil me rotten. Rushing into things hasn't really worked out all that well for me. I want to do this right, Thad. When we move in together, I want it to be a decision we've made that doesn't have anything to do with me needing you to take care of me."

Thad had never seen Josh so serious. He thought about trying to change his mind, but decided not to waste his breath. He forced a smile. "Whatever you want, Josh."

"Right now, since rolling around naked with you isn't in the cards, I'd like one of those dried-up burgers they have in the cafeteria. You hungry?"

"Starving." Starving and more than a little hurt that Josh wanted to go back to his apartment instead of staying with him at Philip's.

Thad tried to change Josh's mind while they were eating, but Josh had insisted that taking care of himself was something he needed to do if they were ever to be equal partners.

When Thad got home, he talked it over with his uncle. Philip agreed with Josh and pointed out that Josh's seventeen-year relationship had ended less than six months earlier.

"Give him a little time. You won't be sorry if you do, and you might end up regretting it if you don't."

Certain that Josh and Philip were wrong, Thad called Linda. "Don't you think Josh should move in with me and Philip when they release him from the hospital so we can take care of him?"

"No. Bad idea, Thad."

"Why do you say that?" Thad asked, barely able to contain his frustration.

"Except for a few months before the assault, someone has been taking care of Josh his entire life. First it was his mother, then me, and then Ben. We spoiled him rotten. Ben did everything but wipe his ass for him. Being on his own has been good for him, and what's good for him is good for you. Tell him no."

Thad sighed. "I don't have to. He wants to go home to his apartment. Philip agrees with him. I was hoping you'd take my side."

"Aww, poor Thaddy," Linda cooed. "Honestly, Josh saying no surprises me. He's always picked the easy way. Considering this is the first time he's legitimately needed someone to take care of him, that he wants to take care of himself tells me he's grown up even more than I thought."

"But I want to take care of him. Spoiling him would make me happy."

"Maybe now, but eventually you'd resent having to do everything for him and having him take you for granted. The more he does for himself, the more he'll appreciate anything you do for him."

"I just want to make him happy."

"Thad, making Josh happy is not your job. He's responsible for his own happiness, and for the most part, is pretty good at it. Except for a short time after he came out and again after he and Ben split up, he has always been a happy-go-lucky kind of guy."

"I know you're right. Philip has never steered me wrong, either. Guess I'm going to have to concede defeat on this one."

Linda laughed. "You haven't lost anything. Josh is quite a catch. Now that you've cleared up his little misunderstanding about your uncle, he's all yours. I'm the only person he's ever cheated on, and that wouldn't have happened if he could have gone on pretending he was straight."

"Thanks for your advice. This whole relationship thing is new to me and I don't want to mess it up."

"You won't. Because if you do, I meant what I said about kicking your ass."

• 44 •

THAT Josh lived complicated things for Adam. He needed Josh to die, and the sooner the better. He'd already waited a week for Josh to get out of the intensive care unit. Time to wrap things up so he could move on.

Adam walked through the hospital's main entrance at exactly 11:15 p.m. Visiting hours were long over. The dimly lit hallways were empty. Most employees were in unit meetings, with the charge nurse of the second shift updating the third shift on the status and treatment needs of every patient. He wore green surgical scrubs and a paper surgeon's cap on his head, with matching paper booties over his shoes. Although nobody paid him any attention, cameras that monitored the parking lot, elevators, and hospital corridors captured every step.

Thanks to the volunteer who worked at the information desk, he knew Josh was in room 721. The seventh floor waiting area was empty. Adam walked past the empty nurse's station and slipped into the room where Josh slept. He didn't worry about waking him. Like just about every other patient who wasn't in a coma, Josh received a sleeping pill at nine o'clock every night. Smothering him with a pillow would be so easy. He imagined himself slipping the pillow off the bed and placing it over Josh's face, holding him down as he struggled for his last breath.

But he left without harming a hair on his sleeping head. The cameras made him nervous. Besides, he wanted Josh to feel pain. He would have to wait until Josh was released.

Adam called the phone number Josh gave him that night at Omega at random times from pay phones all over DC. Nobody answered. The machine picked up just before the fifth ring. He decided that Josh lived alone and apparently had no family in the area.

Josh would recuperate with either Pierson or the redhead. He'd seen Pierson's place. Even with a lot of rearranging, there really wasn't enough room for Josh. It had to be the castle. Plenty of room and plenty of help.

He'd approached the castle several times, intent on getting in so he could snoop around. There was always someone coming or going who forced him to abandon his mission. He wasn't overly concerned. He only needed to get in once.

• 45 •

JOSH couldn't believe he was finally going home. Dr. Schwartz said he was almost as good as new, and would need to ease back into his normal routine. He'd lost ten pounds during his time in the hospital and still tired easily. Unless he overdid it, the pain in his chest was barely noticeable and the headaches were mostly gone.

He'd also quit smoking—something he'd tried to do for years without success. The first two or three days without cigarettes had always defeated him. Going through the worst part of nicotine withdrawal in a coma had worked. Now Josh had gone long enough without a cigarette to fear picking them up again.

Thad drove the car around to the front entrance of the hospital while the nurse wheeled Josh down to meet him. Josh wanted to walk, but the nurse said the wheelchair ride was hospital policy.

He was glad Thad had finally accepted his decision to go home to his apartment. Besides wanting to take care of himself, the idea of moving in with Philip, even though he had come to love him like a father, didn't appeal to him. He doubted he'd feel differently if Thad lived alone. When they moved in together, it would be into a new place that didn't include the baggage of history—his or Thad's.

Being with Thad felt easy and natural. Josh didn't have to pretend to be something he wasn't. He enjoyed teasing him about it, but was glad Thad hadn't given in to his near constant requests for sex.

He enjoyed every minute of their time together. He could tell Thad felt the same way. The friendship they shared made him wonder how he and Ben had lasted more than a few months, much less seventeen years.

Thad stood beside a beige Lexus with the passenger door open, waiting for him. The expression of pure joy and expectation on his face brought a tear to his eye. Josh pushed it away with his palm as the wheelchair came to a stop a foot or two from the car. Thad moved to his side to help him up. He didn't need the help, but enjoyed Thad's touch too much to say so.

Josh slid into the seat. Thad fussed over him for a few minutes, first fastening his seat belt, then, sliding the seat back to make room for his long legs, and finally reclining the seat a bit to make him more comfortable. "How's that?"

"Perfect. Let's get out of here."

Josh reached over and latched onto Thad's elbow who, as he drove, kept both hands firmly gripped on the wheel. Josh noticed he was being extremely cautious, driving as if he carried rare and valuable cargo. He smiled, remembering Ed's wild driving the last time he'd ridden in a car.

"What are you smiling about, babe?"

"All the reasons I am glad you're taking me home instead of Ed."

"He really wanted to, but I convinced him that it was easier for me to pick you up. You've been through enough. He drives like a bat out of hell."

"True. But we'd be in the backseat making out and probably wouldn't notice."

Thad placed his hand over Josh's and smiled. "Sometimes I wonder if maybe you shouldn't be with Ed. Both of you have sex on the brain."

"He's a lot worse than I am." He dropped his hand to Thad's crotch.

"Could have fooled me." Thad quickly returned Josh's hand to the crook of his elbow. "What am I going to do with you?"

"Anything you want, whenever you want, wherever you want. I'm all yours."

"Finally. Has anyone ever told you you're kind of slow sometimes?"

"Maybe. You got a problem with that?"

"Maybe. I did throw myself at you for several months. I'm still a little bruised." Thad pulled the Lexus into the alley between the bagel shop and the West Park and drove around to the back door to park in the loading zone.

Josh entered his security code, and after hearing the buzz, pushed open the door. Instead of going straight to the elevator, Josh walked over to the receptionist. "Hey, Vanessa. Did you miss me?"

"Mr. Freeman!" She came around the desk and hugged him. "Yes, I certainly did miss your handsome face. You sure are looking good."

"Thanks. I just wanted to thank you for letting my boyfriend in and for all your prayers."

"Boyfriend?" Vanessa smiled. "He told me he was your cousin!"

Josh looked at Thad, who had turned bright red. "I... uh... well... at the time I wasn't really his boyfriend, and I had to get in to the apartment, and I didn't think you'd let me if I told you the truth."

"You didn't fool me for one minute. I remember you coming the day the movers brought Mr. Freeman's things in and telling me you were with his company's relocation office. Was that a lie too?"

Thad smiled. "No, that's true. You don't miss much, do you?"

"Nope. It's my job to keep up with who comes and goes around here. Now y'all get on outta here. I got stuff to do and I'm guessing you do too."

Inside the apartment, Thad set the bag of prescriptions and personal items from the hospital on the kitchen counter. Josh spread his arms wide. "Come here, boyfriend."

Thad walked into Josh's arms and hugged him tight. Josh moaned and sought Thad's mouth with his own. Rather than the desperate and hungry kisses he had envisioned so many times in the past few weeks, they kissed slowly. He lost all sense of time as he savored the feel of Thad's lips on his own, the taste of his mouth, and the sensation of his gently probing tongue. He saw Thad's eyes were open, watching for his reaction the way he watched for Thad's.

Eventually, Thad broke the kiss, put his hand on Josh's chest, and gently pushed him away. "That was even better than I imagined."

"Then why did you stop?" Josh kissed him lightly on the tip of his nose.

"Delayed gratification. I've waited too long for our first real kiss to rush past it. I want to savor it, reflect on it, play it over and over again in my head until every detail is etched in my memory."

Thad's words and the look on his face touched him deeply. Lately Josh had come to see how casual, even cavalier, he'd been about sex and love. Rather than the frustration he expected, acceptance settled over him like a cherished and well-worn security blanket. He smiled.

"Whatever you say, lover."

• 46 •

ADAM saw the nurse wheeling Josh to the beige Lexus as proof he was going to recuperate with the redhead and his nelly uncle. He jumped in his Jeep and parked near the fucking castle they called home and watched for their arrival. When he saw the redhead come home alone, he banged his fist against the steering will and cursed. "Dammit! Where is Josh?"

He drove up P Street toward Dupont Circle. As he waited at the red light, he decided to check out Ed's condo. If Josh wasn't at the castle, then he had to be with Pierson. Good. Now he could kill two birds with one stone.

When the light turned green, Adam hit the gas, then slammed on the brakes to avoid getting hit by a red Oldsmobile Cutlass. He cussed and was about to lay on his horn when he recognized the driver. He couldn't believe his luck. It was that Pierson bitch.

Adam stepped on the gas and fell in behind the Cutlass. He circled the block as Ed parked and walked over to the entrance of the West Park with a skinny, curly-haired guy, both loaded down with groceries. Adam watched them disappear into the building and knew he'd found where Josh was recuperating.

He walked around the building several times, noting the security cameras scattered along the perimeter and the secure entrances. Getting into the building would be difficult, but not impossible. Adam liked a good challenge. Posing as a cable television or telephone serviceman would work, but he suspected his every movement would be captured on one of the security cameras. No, he'd have to do the job someplace else.

Adam wondered where Caleb had gone. As expected, Caleb had been sorry for beating him up so bad. But something had changed. Since the encounter at Annie's, Caleb was different. For several days, he'd just looked at Adam with sad eyes. And then he'd left, without saying good-bye or "kiss my ass" or anything.

Fuck him. Now Adam had more important things to worry about—like killing Josh and Ed without getting caught by the police. The sooner he settled his unfinished business, the better. Then he would drive to Wyoming to join up with a friend of his who ran a compound for like-minded ex-military like him. Nobody would ever find him there, and if they did, they'd never take him alive.

• 47 •

THAD hadn't expected Josh to understand why he didn't want to rush things. That he was so impetuous was endearing, exciting, and sometimes a little frightening. Their first kiss had been all he'd expected and then some. He was pleasantly surprised and more than a little relieved that Josh was now okay about taking things slow.

"You tired?" Thad asked. "This is the longest you've been out of bed for a while now. Want to go lay down?"

"I do feel a little tired. How about we sit on the couch?"

"How about you sit on the couch and watch some television while I run down to the market and pick up a few things. There's nothing to eat around here. Since you won't let me stay with you, I want to make sure you have everything you need before I go. Any requests?"

"I'm a fan of any kind of chicken soup, have never met a cold cut I didn't like, and have been craving some Ritz crackers with peanut butter. Let me get my credit card for you."

"I've got cash. You can pay me back later."

Thad found everything Josh wanted and threw in some fresh fruit, a head of leaf lettuce and some salad dressing, and enough single-serving containers of Jell-O, pudding, and fruit to last a month. He let himself into the apartment with Josh's key. "Josh?" he said, softly. Hearing no response, he assumed Josh had fallen asleep on the sofa and quietly put the groceries up in the kitchen.

When he was finished, Thad walked into the living room and saw the empty sofa. He looked in the bedroom and even checked the bathroom. No Josh. He started to panic, but when he went back to the living room, he saw Josh sitting on the balcony in a chair from the dining room table.

He slid open the door and immediately got a whiff of an acrid, pungent smell. Relief turned to anger. "What in the hell are you doing?"

Josh looked up at him sheepishly. "Smoking a joint."

"Are you kidding me?" Thad stepped out onto the balcony, slamming the door behind him so hard the glass rattled in the frame. Given how little Josh drank, that he would use drugs had never even occurred to him.

"Want some?" Josh smiled and offered Thad the joint.

Thad took the joint from him and threw it off the balcony. "Hell no! And I don't want you smoking it either. You want to get arrested? Think about all you stand to lose."

Josh reached for Thad's hand. "Just relax, Thad. I've smoked pot for years and never even come close to getting busted."

Thad shook his hand loose. "No, I'm not going to relax. Smoking pot is against the law. I really can't believe you do it!"

"It's really not that big of a deal."

"Yes, it is a big deal. Smoking cigarettes was bad enough. Smoking pot is a deal-breaker for me. I won't have it."

Josh stood up and stepped toward Thad, opening his arms as if to hug him. "Come on, Thad. It's really not all that bad. Honestly, it doesn't mess you up nearly as bad as alcohol does. It relaxes me."

Instead of stepping into his open arms, Thad stepped away and pulled the door to the apartment open. "I mean it, Josh. It's me or pot. You can't have both."

Josh crossed his arms and gave Thad a piercing look. "Listen here, Thad. I really don't appreciate your attitude. Us being lovers doesn't give you the right to tell me what I can and can't do."

Thad couldn't believe what he was hearing. "I'm not telling you what to do. I'm telling you that I cannot and will not be involved with someone who uses drugs. You're free to do whatever the hell you want."

Josh lost his temper. "Pot is my only remaining vice, and I have no intention of giving it up. You need to just deal with it."

"Fine. If that's what you want, I'll deal with it." Thad returned to the apartment and headed for the door. "You've obviously made your choice."

"Thad, wait!"

Thad kept walking. He threw open the apartment door, causing it to crash into the wall.

Josh followed five paces behind him. "Come on, Thad. Can't we talk about this?"

"We just did." Thad slammed the apartment door behind him. He ran to the elevator and pushed the button. When the door opened, he stepped in and pushed the button for the ground floor. Josh opened the apartment door just as the elevator closed.

In his anger, Thad went out the front door, forgetting for a minute about the Lexus parked behind the building. Remembering made him even angrier. He stomped through the alley to the car and drove around for thirty minutes to calm down before going home.

He might have overreacted, but he meant what he said about drugs being a deal-breaker. He'd never smoked cigarettes, didn't have his first drink until well after his twenty-first birthday, and had never been tempted by drugs. Life was too short to do things that might make it shorter, or worse, result in time behind bars.

When he reached the house, he let himself in, went straight to his bedroom, and closed the door. He wasn't ready to talk to Philip or anyone else about what had just happened. Doubts about his reaction kept popping into his head. He needed time to think.

He sat on his bed and got angry all over again. He was furious with Josh for ruining what had been, up to the minute he found him smoking pot on the balcony, a perfect day. Instead of reveling in his memories of their first, long-awaited kiss, he fumed. Josh using drugs was bad enough, but it was his attitude that really pushed Thad's buttons.

He heard a gentle tapping on his bedroom door. He lay perfectly still and hoped Philip would think he was asleep.

"Thad… you okay?"

He didn't move. He held his breath and waited for Philip to leave.

"Thad… you haven't been home long enough to fall asleep. What's wrong?"

Thad got up, opened the door, and then flung himself facedown on the bed and buried his face in the pillow. Philip sat on the edge of the bed and ran his fingers through Thad's hair. "Looks like Josh did something to awaken that redheaded temper of yours."

"It's over between me and Josh."

He felt Philip stroking his hair and waited for the arguments he was bound to hear. When none came, he raised his head and looked up at his uncle. "Aren't you going to say something?"

"I learned when you were a child that trying to talk to you when you're this angry rarely produces the desired result. Your mother and I are both convinced you get your temper from somewhere on your father's side of the family. We Potters are an even-tempered lot."

Thad silently agreed. He couldn't recall his mom or Philip ever showing anything he'd describe as anger. For years he had interpreted their calmness in the face of his rage as a lack of caring.

"I ran down to the store so he'd have some food. When I got back, he was out on his balcony smoking pot. I told him doing drugs was a deal-breaker for me and that he'd have to choose."

"Oh dear," Philip said. "Did he tell you he'd rather smoke pot than be with you?"

"Not in so many words. He said he wasn't giving it up and got mad at me for trying to tell him what to do. I told him he could do what he wanted and left."

"I see." Philip sat silently on the edge of the bed, stroking his chin with his thumb and index finger. After a while, he spoke. "You know, Thad, there are far worse things than smoking pot."

Philip's words reignited Thad's rage. "Are you taking his side? After all you've told me about the dangers of drugs—"

"I'm not taking anyone's side. I'm just saying that in the overall scheme of things, smoking pot isn't so bad. Even our president experimented with marijuana. Me too—only I inhaled."

Thad plowed his fist into the pillow. "But it's illegal! We work for a law firm. I don't understand how he could risk getting arrested and losing his job."

"You're absolutely right. You ready for dinner?"

"I'm not hungry. Go ahead and eat without me."

Philip got up and headed toward the door. "I'm downstairs if you need me."

• 48 •

JOSH watched the elevator close in stunned silence. Thad's angry look cut off any words. He walked to the balcony and watched Thad stomping up P Street toward the bagel shop. He could almost see the steam coming off his head.

Talk about a buzzkill. Thad's temper tantrum had come out of nowhere. He reached for his jewelry box to roll another joint, but stopped. If Thad changed his mind and came back, he'd see Josh smoking on the balcony and get angry all over again. He called Linda.

"Hey. Josh! Did you get home okay?"

"Yeah, I suppose."

"What's wrong? You sound down in the dumps."

"Thad and I just had a huge fight. I fucked up. It's over between us." Josh longed for a cigarette. Instead, he picked up a pencil and twirled it with his fingers.

"What did you do?" The accusation in her voice startled him.

"Hey, whose side are you on?"

"Josh, you know I'm on your side and that makes me want things to work out with Thad. Besides, there's a mani-pedi in it for me. What did you do?"

"Thad got pissed when he came back from the store and found me smoking a joint on the balcony. You should have seen him. His face turned bright red and his nostrils flared like some kind of raging bull. I've never seen him mad before."

"Well, I personally believe every couple should see each other mad as hell before they settle down together. This is probably a good thing."

"I don't think so. He gave me an ultimatum—said it was him or the pot."

"Josh, if you told him you'd rather smoke pot than be with him, I'm gassing up the Honda and coming up there to beat some sense into your thick skull."

"No, I never said that. All I said was that I didn't appreciate him telling me what I could and couldn't do. He stormed out like the place was on fire. I tried to talk to him, but he just kept walking."

"So what are you going to do?"

"I don't know. That's why I called you."

"Are you willing to quit smoking pot?"

Josh looked at the jewelry chest, and his prolonged silence made Linda ask, "Josh?"

"Yeah. Yeah, I'm here. I had lots of time to think while I was in the hospital. Seeing Thad was the best part of every day. Thinking about his last visit and looking forward to the next one kept me going. I feel horrible about our fight, especially after all he's done for me."

"But are you willing to give up pot for him?"

"I suppose. I mean, I started smoking while I was with Ben because our relationship was really... more than a little boring." Josh laughed bitterly. "Stable, but boring. I think the pot dulled the edge or filled some kind of void I didn't know I had.

"Who are you, and what have you done with Josh?"

"Have I changed that much?"

"Yes, you have, and it's about time. I'm proud of you, Josh."

"So what do I do about Thad?"

"First you let him cool off. Then you tell him what you told me about why you smoked pot, and that because of him, you no longer have a void to fill. If he really loves you, and I'm sure he does, he'll forgive you."

"I sure hope you're right."

Josh felt a little better. Except for getting angry about Thad trying to tell him what to do, he really hadn't said anything that couldn't be unsaid, or done anything he couldn't undo.

The buzzer startled him. He pushed the intercom button. "Who is it?"

"Your knight in shining armor and his sidekick, bearing gifts."

Josh buzzed them in and waited with the door open for the elevator to arrive. The doors slid apart to reveal Ed and Greg, loaded down with bags of groceries. They pushed past him into the kitchen and proceeded to move the contents of the bags to the refrigerator and cabinets.

"I sure am glad to see the two of you."

"Are you hungry?" Greg asked. "I'd be happy to fix you something to eat."

Josh hadn't eaten since he left the hospital. "That would be great. Now that you mention it, I'm starving."

Ed gave Josh a gentle hug, careful not to squeeze him. "Me too!"

"How does homemade potato soup with grilled cheese sandwiches sound?" Greg asked.

"That's what Mom used to make for me when I was a kid and under the weather," Josh replied. "I'd love some."

Ed said, "Me too!"

"Good." Greg nodded as he quickly emptied the bags of groceries. "I'll whip that up for you in no time. This kitchen isn't big enough for the three of us. You two go talk in the living room or something."

Ed walked into the living room and sat down. "Where's Thad? I thought he'd be here."

"He was until we had a fight." Josh sat down next to Ed, wringing his hands nervously as he talked.

"Uh-oh. What did you do?"

Josh looked at Ed. "Why does everyone automatically assume I did something?"

"If Thad had done something, you'd be all outraged or indignant instead of looking like a whipped puppy. So what happened?"

Josh told him about Thad finding him smoking a joint on the balcony and the fight they'd had.

"Ooops. I probably should have warned you. Thad's always had a zero-tolerance policy for drugs."

"So I gather." Josh sighed. The smell of onions sautéing with bacon wafting from the kitchen made his stomach growl.

"How mad was he?" Ed asked.

"Furious. I've never seen him so mad. In fact, I've never seen him angry at all. Let me tell you, Thad pissed is downright scary."

"Yeah. It's his red hair. He doesn't get mad often, but when he does, look out. So what are you going to do?"

"Well, I'm going to flush all my pot down the toilet and wait for him to cool down."

"You'll ruin the plumbing. Why don't you let Greg and me take it off your hands?"

Josh smiled. "That works too. I just want it out of here." He opened the jewelry box and handed Ed a nearly empty bag.

"Is that all you have left?" Ed asked, disappointed.

"No, there are two more ounces in the freezer. I didn't know if I'd be able to find a connection here, so I brought a quarter pound with me from Lexington."

"Flushing all that pot down the toilet would definitely mess up the plumbing. Glad we got here in time."

After Ed and Greg left, Josh called Thad. Philip answered. "Hi, Philip, is Thad around?"

"He's been in his room with the door closed all day. He told me what happened."

"The pot's gone." He almost told him Greg and Ed had taken it, but caught himself. No point getting them in trouble too.

"I'm glad to hear that and know Thad will be too."

"Can I talk to him?"

"You could, but I suggest you wait. Let him sleep on it. He rarely explodes, but once he does, it's wise to give him plenty of space."

"I hate the thought of him going to bed still mad at me or thinking I'm mad at him."

"He's not mad at you. After he refused to come down for dinner, I took him a tray and visited with him for a while. He's mad at himself now for overreacting and afraid he's messed things up with you. Stewing in regret overnight might help him to think twice before allowing his anger to get the better of him. Do you need anything?"

"No. Thanks for asking. Greg and Ed came over with a bunch of groceries and made a pot of potato soup and grilled cheese sandwiches. I've got everything I need but Thad."

"Don't worry about Thad. He'll be fine in the morning, I'm sure. I'll tell him you called. Now get some rest. Sounds like you've had a long day."

• 49 •

SATURDAY morning, Thad got up early and went to the gym. His anger at Josh had dissipated the night before, only to be replaced by anger at himself for the way he had reacted to seeing Josh smoking pot. After a grueling workout in the weight room and forty-five minutes on the treadmill, he felt a lot better.

He headed for the shower. Philip was right. In the overall scheme of things, smoking pot wasn't so bad. He knew most of his friends smoked it at least occasionally, and he'd never held it against them. Why should he treat Josh any differently? Josh had said it was his only remaining vice. It wasn't like he was smoking crack or shooting up heroin.

As the steaming hot water washed away his remaining anger, regret settled in. Thad realized his own actions were quite a bit worse than Josh's. He wished he could take back saying that smoking pot was a deal-breaker.

No, he didn't approve. He couldn't stand the smell of burning marijuana. But more than that was his concern that Josh could be arrested and lose his job. Just because the firm had not conducted random drug tests didn't mean they couldn't start. And if that wasn't enough, inhaling all that smoke was surely hazardous to Josh's health.

Still, relationships are about negotiations, not ultimatums. Not for the first time, his temper had crowded out reason and caused him to say things he otherwise would never have said. Issuing the ultimatum was wrong. And walking out during an argument had just made things worse.

The blowup had given Thad a new appreciation for Josh's decision to go home to his apartment. Josh wanted them to be equal partners, even if it meant doing something the hard way. Thad realized he was going to have to make a few changes of his own.

Although the fact that Josh smoked pot still upset him, in no way did it change his feelings for him. He loved him. No ifs, ands, or buts about it. Loving Josh meant accepting him just the way he was. Trying to change him implied he was somehow better than Josh—that he knew more or was superior to him. So much for equal partners.

If their relationship was going to work, Thad knew he'd have to relax and be more open to change. Instead of walking back home, he headed for Josh's apartment. He wanted to apologize—for losing his temper, for the ultimatum, and for running away instead of talking things out.

He reached the West Park and pushed the button for Josh to buzz him in. He waited and pushed the button again. Still no answer. He waved when Vanessa looked up at him and watched her push the button to buzz him in.

"If you're looking for Mr. Freeman, he's not here. He left about thirty minutes ago."

Thad couldn't imagine where he'd gone. "Was anybody with him?"

"No, he was by himself. Acted like he was in a big hurry—he barely spoke as he walked by, which isn't at all like him. Is everything okay?"

"Yes, yes, everything is fine," Thad lied. "If you're here when he comes back, let him know I stopped by."

Sick with worry, Thad exited the West Park. Thinking maybe Josh had been hungry for breakfast, he walked over to the bagel shop and looked inside. No sign of Josh. He wasn't in the market either.

Thad walked slowly toward Dupont Circle. He looked in every open business, going inside if necessary while keeping a wary eye on the street in case Josh walked by. Where could he have gone? Why was he in such a hurry? The closer he got to the traffic circle, the wilder his imagined answers to those questions became.

He must have wanted a Croissan'wich for breakfast. But no, he wasn't at Burger King.

Perhaps he needed something from the pharmacy? No, no sign of him in CVS.

Maybe the police had called and needed him to come down to the station. Or maybe he'd found someone through one of those 900-numbers Thad saw advertised in the *Washington Blade*.

Maybe Adam had lured him into a trap. According to the police, Caleb and Adam had vanished. Both of them had plenty of reasons to go after Josh.

Thad crossed the traffic circle. He saw men playing chess on the concrete boards. He scanned the blankets that dotted the shade of the grassy area, checked all the people sitting on benches, and scoped out those sitting on the edge of the fountain enjoying the sun. No Josh.

He sat down on an empty bench and put his head in his hands. He thought back over his fight with Josh, recalling his ultimatum and Josh's words that he would do what he wanted to do. He'd blown it and chased away the only man he'd ever really cared about.

Was he really sitting on a bench in the middle of Dupont Circle, crying? He tried to pull himself together before someone noticed.

Too late. The wood beneath him shifted as someone sat down beside him. Thad squeezed his eyes shut. He choked back a sob and hoped that the roar of the fountain prevented his benchmate from hearing him. Barely audible above the roar he heard a voice.

"You okay?"

Embarrassed, Thad lifted his head up, wiped his eyes, and focused his attention on the fountain. "Yeah, I'm okay. Thanks."

"That's good. Wish I could say the same."

"Josh!"

"I've got something I need to say."

"No," Thad exclaimed. "I've got something I need to say, first."

"Mine can't wait. I've waited too long as it is. It's been on my mind since I woke up this morning. I went to your house to tell you, but Philip said you weren't home and he didn't know where you were. I was on my way back to the apartment when I saw you."

"I've been looking for you too, and driving myself crazy imagining where you might be."

Josh got up, stood before Thad, and then dropped to one knee. "I'm right here with you, and if you'll have me, that's where I'd like to stay. The pot is gone. With you in my life, I don't need it anymore."

Thad looked into Josh's eyes. "Hell yes, I'll have you, and it doesn't matter to me if you smoke pot or not. I love you, Josh. I overreacted. It was wrong of me to try to tell you what to do. I'm so sorry."

"I love you too, Thad." Josh leaned in and kissed him. Thad was too happy to be embarrassed by the applause of the people around them.

• 50 •

JOSH paced back and forth outside the gate, waiting for the flight from Lexington to arrive. He'd made Thad stay at the house with Philip, and had declined their offer to let him use their car to pick everyone up from the airport. He didn't know what Rafael or his dad would think, but he knew Linda would love riding the Metro.

When they came through the Jetway door, it was all Josh could do to keep from jumping up and down so they would see him. Except for the handsome, aristocratic man on her arm, Linda looked the same. His father followed a few steps behind them, looking quite a lot older than the last time Josh had seen him.

When she saw Josh, Linda ran to him and threw her arms around his neck. Josh lifted her off her feet and spun around a couple of times. He ignored the discomfort from Linda's weight pressing against his still tender ribs and kissed her on the cheek.

"It's so good to see you again!" she gushed. Then she stepped back and looked him over. "I'd be lying if I said you haven't changed. You look a little thin. Love the short hair and the mustache. Is that what makes you look so much more grown up?"

"Probably." Josh smiled and offered his hand to Rafael. "You must be Rafael. I'm glad to finally meet you."

Rafael grasped his hand firmly and shook it. "No, sir, the pleasure is mine. If you weren't gay, I'd be jealous. As it is, I must thank you for keeping Linda unattached until I found her."

Josh laughed, relieved to discover that Rafael seemed likeable enough. He'd worried about how they would get along. If, for some reason, he didn't like Rafael, he wouldn't have been able to hide his dislike from Linda, which would have caused all kinds of problems.

Tom Freeman stood awkwardly behind Linda and Rafael. Josh hesitated for just a second before walking over and hugging him. "I'm so glad you could join us, Dad. Did you enjoy the flight?"

"I sure did. Never flown first class before. Sure was nice of Philip to use his frequent-flyer miles for our tickets. Of course, now that I see how the other half lives, I'm not sure I want to go back to coach."

Josh laughed. "I didn't know you'd be flying first class. That's so Philip. I can't wait for you to meet him."

"I'm looking forward to meeting him too," Linda chimed in, "but it's that redheaded boyfriend of yours I'm really anxious to meet. Where is he?"

"Philip and Thad are back at the house. They wanted to come, but I made them stay home. Since you're staying at their house, you'll probably see more of them than you will me. And this way, I get to show you a few things before I turn the touring over to the experts."

Tom said, "You're not living with them?"

"No," Josh replied. "I still have my apartment. Thad and I are trying to take things slow."

Linda whistled. "I can't believe how much you've changed. The Josh I know wanted to move in together at the drop of a pair of jeans."

Josh felt his face flush and decided to change the subject. "Y'all ready to retrieve your luggage? Hope you took my advice and got bags with wheels. We've got some walking to do. "

"Sure did," Linda replied. "And believe it or not, I only brought one bag."

FROM two gates away, Adam watched the happy reunion. A long wig, dark glasses, and oversized clothes made him look overweight and out of shape. Since hitting the streets, he changed his appearance regularly, and after years of wanting to stand out in a crowd, he'd mastered blending in.

Following Josh to the airport had been easy. The man was oblivious and had no idea Adam was behind him. With his friends in tow, Adam had stopped worrying about Josh noticing him and had watched from the very next car on the Metro ride to Dupont Circle.

Expecting Josh to take his friends home to his apartment, Adam had positioned himself at the top of the escalator so he could fall in behind them. But instead of heading toward the West Park, they headed in the opposite direction. *Shit!* As the group walked past him, Adam kept his back to them, turning around like he was trying to get his bearings.

He sat on a bench in the park and watched as Josh and his friends headed down P Street. Now he knew where they were going. The castle.

• 51 •

THAD paced from the sunroom to the front door and back again. Josh and their guests from Lexington should have been here by now. He should have gone with Josh to the airport to meet them. Sure, Josh had been back at work for more than a week, and was more or less back to his old self. But taking the Metro to the airport involved a lot of walking, and he still tired easily. Thad would have worried less if he had taken the car.

That Adam was still on the loose made him nervous. Sometimes, when he and Josh went for a walk, he couldn't shake the feeling they were being watched. He knew he was just being paranoid—people who looked like Adam could hardly blend into a crowd. Still, he'd rest a lot easier with Adam off the streets and in jail where he belonged.

"Nephew, sit down before you wear a path in my beautiful floors. They'll be here soon enough. Come sit with me and watch the squirrels rooting through my flower beds."

Thad walked over and dropped into the chair next to Philip. "They should have been here by now. I hope nothing has happened."

"Relax, Thad. Perhaps the flight was delayed a few minutes, or it took longer than usual to unload all the baggage, or they had to wait for a train. Or maybe they went to Josh's apartment first or decided to do a little sightseeing."

"They didn't go to Josh's apartment. He promised they'd come here before doing anything else—it was the only way I'd let him go without me."

Philip shook his head and smiled when Thad got up and started pacing the floor again.

When the doorbell rang, Thad took off like a sprinter responding to the starter's gun. Philip was right behind him. By the time they made it to the entryway, Josh had already used his key to unlock the door and was herding everyone into the foyer.

"Wow," Linda said, looking around, "this place is gorgeous!"

"Thank you, my dear. You must be Linda." Philip offered his hand, but Linda brushed past it to hug his neck.

"And you must be Uncle Philip. Thanks so much for inviting us to your beautiful home."

"You're quite welcome. We're so glad you could join us."

"And you must be Thad." Before he could respond, Linda threw her arms around Thad and kissed him on the cheek. "Thanks for taking such good care of Josh. He looks great, and you're even better-looking than he described." She turned to the two men standing awkwardly just inside the front door. "This is my boyfriend, Rafael Maccado, and Josh's father, Tom Freeman."

After everyone had shaken hands, Philip took control. "Josh, Thad, grab that luggage and show our guests to their rooms. Linda, Tom, Rafael, please, make yourselves at home, then come down to the sunroom for cocktails and light refreshments so we can get better acquainted."

Thad grabbed Linda's bag. "Follow me. You too, Rafael. Philip put you in the same room—hope that's not a problem."

Linda smiled and followed Thad up the stairs. "Only if you've arranged for a chaperone."

"Are you suggesting I'd take advantage of you?" Rafael asked as he dropped in behind them.

"I certainly hope so! I didn't go to Victoria's Secret for Josh."

Tom picked up his bag and looked at Josh, who turned and headed up the stairs.

At the top, Thad directed Linda and Rafael down the hall to the right while Josh and his dad headed to the left.

"Here you go. You have your own bathroom too, just off to the right."

"Thanks, Josh. Geez, how much money does Philip have? First-class plane tickets. A swanky place filled with museum-quality pieces in the heart of DC. This place is even nicer than a four-star hotel."

"I have no idea, and you better not ask, either."

Tom smiled. "Aw, come on, Josh. Surely you don't think I'd be that rude."

Josh looked at him. "Honestly, Dad, I don't know. It's not like we've spent much time together. I barely even know you."

"I guess I deserve that. I know I was never around when you needed me. Your mother was such a strong woman—I felt like I was just in the way. She always had everything under control."

Josh slid into one of two wing-backed chairs on either side of a large window overlooking Philip's garden. "I still needed you, Dad. I needed to know that you loved me and cared about what I was doing."

Tom sunk into the other chair, rested his elbows on his knees, and put his head in his hands. "Oh, Josh. If you only knew...."

"Knew what?"

Tom looked at him. "I have always loved you more than anything in the world. I know, I have a shitty way of showing it, but I do care. Always have. I'm so proud of you and the man you've become."

Josh felt his dad was holding something back. "Why am I just now finding this out?"

Tom got up and looked out the window. "I was angry at your mother and you got caught in the crossfire."

"Angry? Why? You're the one who cheated and ripped our family apart."

Tom didn't answer. He kept looking out the window. Josh saw a tear slide down his cheek. Finally he sighed, took a deep breath, and turned to Josh.

"I loved your mother. I know you've always thought I cheated on her. I did, but not until after she had an affair with an old high school boyfriend."

"So now that she's not here to defend herself, you want to blame her?" Josh snapped.

"Her affair was short-lived, barely more than a one-night stand. I was so angry I hooked up with my secretary because I wanted to hurt her—to get back at her for hurting me. It sounds so silly now."

Josh sat in stunned silence. His mind was reeling. How could he have been so wrong for all these years? He tried to recall anything his mother might have said that would support or refute his father's claim that she had cheated on him first.

His father continued. "The affair with my secretary was the single biggest mistake, among many colossal mistakes, that I've made in my life. I never stopped loving your mother. I tried to replace her, but no one ever came close."

Josh looked at his dad. "Why haven't you told me this before?"

"At first, you were too young to understand. Then I put it off because I didn't want to rock the boat and dredge it all up again. Once she got sick, it was too late."

"Then why tell me now?"

"When you hit sixty, your perspective changes. The women I married have moved on. Since we never had children together, I have no reason to stay involved with them. My parents are long gone. I was never close to my brother, and even if I wanted to be, it's too late now. He died last year. You're all I have left.

"I've thought a lot about our relationship and the mistakes I've made. You deserved better. I'm not blaming your mother—for the divorce or for keeping you away from me. I have in the past, but not anymore. I did what I did and can't blame anyone else. If I had it to do over, I'd make different choices. But life doesn't give you any do-overs."

Josh needed to think. He stood up and headed toward the door. "I'm glad you told me. Philip and Thad are expecting you downstairs. I need to go help them with the hors d'oeuvres."

Instead of going downstairs, Josh walked down the hall and knocked on the door to the room where Linda and Rafael were staying. Linda opened the door and smiled. The look on his face must have startled her.

"Are you okay?"

"Not really. You up for a walk?"

Linda looked back at Rafael. "Sure, can you give me three minutes?"

"Yeah, meet me downstairs."

Josh ran down the steps and headed to the back of the house. He found Thad arranging little quiches on a tray half filled with stuffed mushrooms.

"Everything okay?" Thad asked.

"Linda and I are going for a walk. We'll be back within the hour, okay?"

"You want me to go with you?"

"No, stay here. We'll be back soon, I promise." Josh knew Thad was concerned, but there wasn't time right now to fill him in. Besides, he still needed to process what his father had told him. Talking it over with Linda would speed that up.

Linda was coming down the stairs when Josh returned to the entryway. "Where are we going?" she asked.

"No place in particular. I just need to talk."

• 52 •

AFTER stopping at Starbucks for coffee, Josh and Linda sat down on one of the benches surrounding the fountain at Dupont Circle.

"Isn't this where you were attacked?" Linda asked.

Josh pointed to a grouping of evergreens on the other side of the fountain. "Yeah, over there. He came out of those bushes."

"Have they caught him yet?"

Josh shook his head. "Not that I know of. Last I heard, both he and his lover had vanished. They're probably hundreds of miles from here by now."

"I hope you're right." Linda shivered and wiggled closer to Josh. "What's up? Why the sudden need for a walk?"

Josh took a sip of his coffee before responding. "Dad said Mom had an affair before he did, and that he hooked up with his secretary to get back at her."

"So now you know the whole story," Linda said. Josh stared at her. "My mom told me about it years ago and made me promise never to tell you."

"Are you shitting me?"

"We fought about it. Mom was as loyal to her as I was to you. She said it wasn't our place to tell you. After we talked about it, I had to agree with her. Keeping that kind of secret isn't easy. Why do you think I've kept after you to stay involved with your dad? I kept hoping he would tell you."

"So it's true?"

Linda took Josh's hand in hers. "Yes, it's true. My mom said the affair was brief and that your mom knew it was a mistake as soon as it happened."

"But she led me to believe—"

"No, she didn't. You just assumed that since your dad married his secretary he was the one who busted up the marriage. She should have told you. I don't know why she didn't. Mom said she was afraid you wouldn't be able to forgive her. Was she right?"

Josh sipped his coffee before answering. After a long silence, he finally spoke. "If she'd told me the truth while she was still alive, I definitely would have been pissed, and I might not have forgiven her until it was too late." He took another drink of coffee and sighed. "Getting mad at her about it now serves no purpose."

Linda squeezed his hand. "Good answer, and I didn't even have to tell you what to say. Now, what about your dad?"

"Honestly, I'm amazed he never told me before now. I would have. He's suffered enough. Now that I know the truth, I kind of feel bad about the way I've treated him all these years."

Linda smiled. "You're batting a thousand today. Sounds like maybe you need to start making up for lost time. You ready to head back?"

"Yeah. It's getting dark. Thad's probably beside himself worrying about what's going on with me."

"He's quite a catch, and Uncle Philip is a sweetheart."

"They're both pretty amazing. Rafael seems like a really nice guy too. I'm glad you've found someone special."

They headed back up P Street toward Philip's house, arm in arm. Being early in the evening on the day before Thanksgiving, the street was nearly deserted. Josh shivered as the wind picked up and wished he'd worn a heavier coat.

Halfway home, Josh noticed a shabby-looking character walking toward them. Though he normally ignored the homeless people who haunted Dupont Circle, since it was Thanksgiving, he reached for his wallet for some cash to give the guy.

As the homeless man approached, Josh noticed he held something in his hand. It looked like a cane. Funny, he didn't walk like he needed a cane. Josh looked closer and realized the cane was, in fact, a tire iron. His eyes jumped to the man's face. He recognized the smile, and his heart flew into his throat.

Josh pushed Linda toward the nearest door. "Run!"

Linda stopped and turned to Josh. "Why? What's going on?"

Josh grabbed Linda's hand and started running, pulling her along behind him. "It's Adam!"

"Oh my God!" Linda picked up the pace and in seconds was dragging Josh behind her.

"My chest is killing me," Josh wheezed and slowed. He let go of Linda's hand. "Get help."

Linda bolted for the nearest door and when she reached it, began pounding furiously with both fists and screaming for help.

Josh gasped for air as Adam approached. He darted quick looks up and down the sidewalk to see if anyone was around. The street was deserted. Even if someone answered the door that Linda continued to pound, he knew it would be too late for him.

The smile on Adam's face grew. Josh took in the blond wig and the oversized coat that had made him think Adam was just another homeless person. From ten paces away, he noticed the gleam in Adam's eye. He looked over and saw Linda had darted to the next doorway and was again furiously pounding on the door. Josh scanned the ground around him for something to use as a weapon. Nothing.

Josh took off running again. Pain seared through his chest with every step. His pace slowed. He tried to ignore the pain and focused all his energy on putting one foot in front of the other as fast as he could. The sound of boots steadily hitting the sidewalk drew closer. Adam's much quicker pace rapidly devoured the space between them.

Adrenaline kicked in. Josh picked up his pace to a slow jog. Adam's steps changed from slow and steady to rapid and purposeful as he closed the distance between them. Josh set his eyes on the street ahead and hoped someone would be walking on it and come to his aid.

As he neared the corner, a dark figure stepped onto the sidewalk. Josh called out to him. "Help me!"

He felt rather than saw Adam closing the distance between them and knew he was almost in range of the tire iron. Ahead of him, the dark figure raised his arm. Josh saw a glint of steel and realized the man was aiming a gun in his direction. He heard a male voice.

"Stop!"

Josh stopped in his tracks. He looked back. Adam, too, had stopped and turned his attention to the man with the gun who now walked rapidly toward them. As he approached, the beam of a streetlight struck his face, and Josh gasped. It was Caleb. Josh was trapped between them with nowhere to run.

Caleb stopped and raised his arm, leveling the barrel of the pistol. Josh raised his hands over his head and darted glances toward both men. Adam stepped closer, brandishing the tire iron.

Josh faced Adam and braced himself. Adam raised the tire iron over his head and took another step toward him. Then Josh heard a loud pop, like a firecracker exploding, and knew that Caleb had fired the gun. Josh dropped to the ground and covered his head with his arms.

The sound of the tire iron hitting the sidewalk drew Josh's attention back to Adam. He watched as Adam's expression changed from triumph to confusion. Josh heard another pop. Adam lurched hard to the right before falling to one knee and slipping to the ground.

Caleb took a step closer. Josh rolled into a fetal position, covered his head with his arms, and waited for the gunshot that would end his life. As Caleb walked past him, Josh realized the pistol was aimed at Adam.

Caleb walked over to where Adam lay sprawled on the sidewalk. He stood over Adam and pointed the gun at his head. "I told you what would happen if you ever cheated on me. If I can't have you, nobody can."

Josh sat up, his eyes on Caleb as he slowly rose to his feet and started backing away. Before he had taken two steps, Adam jerked one last time from the bullet Caleb fired at his head from point-blank range.

Linda screamed. Caleb turned toward Josh and smiled. Josh backed away slowly with his hands up in front of him, as if they could deflect any bullet shot in his direction. Josh watched the scene play out in slow motion: Caleb raised the gun, stuck the barrel of the still smoking pistol into his mouth, and pulled the trigger.

• 53 •

THE sound of sirens wasn't all that unusual, but the quantity and persistence—not to mention his concern about Josh—brought Thad to the front porch. He looked up the street and saw a conglomeration of police cruisers and an ambulance about a block away. Without even getting a coat, Thad ran to the scene, certain something had happened to Josh.

His heart jumped into his throat when he saw two sheet-covered bodies on the ground beneath the steady flash of a camera as detectives photographed the scene. He knew that one was Josh and the other was Linda. He headed toward a policeman cordoning off the area with bright yellow crime-scene tape.

"Excuse me, Officer." Thad waited for the policeman to acknowledge his presence. "Could you tell me what happened here? My best friend, Josh Freeman, and his friend Linda Delgado went out for a walk earlier and haven't returned."

"Two guys got shot. Your friends may have been witnesses." The officer pointed to a small group gathered between two police cars. "Is that them talking to the detective?"

Thad looked where the officer pointed. The flickering lights from the police cars reminded him of strobe lights on a dance floor. The way the distant figures lurched and jerked between flashes made it hard to recognize anyone.

Then Thad saw Linda and yelled her name. She must have heard him, because she turned and said something to the detective, who was apparently questioning her about what had happened. He looked over and motioned for Thad to join them.

As he approached Linda, Thad saw Josh being interviewed by another detective. Relief washed over him. Linda nodded at the detective and headed toward Thad.

"I'm so glad you're both okay," Thad said as Linda hugged him. "What happened?"

Linda filled him in on the near assault that had turned into a murder-suicide. Though stunned by the turn of events, he was relieved that Josh and Linda were alive and that Adam wouldn't be bothering them any longer.

Thirty minutes later, the detective interviewing Josh finally ran out of questions. Thad saw Josh take the detective's business card, shake his hand, and then head to where he and Linda waited. Josh's face lit up and his pace quickened when he realized Thad was with Linda.

Thad closed the distance between them in four steps and threw himself into Josh's open arms. They held each other close. Josh murmured in Thad's ear, "I thought for a minute tonight that I would never see you again. As Adam was closing in on me, all I could think about was you—the great times we haven't had yet and everything we would never get to do together."

Thad met Josh's eyes. "We've been given a second chance."

Josh smiled. "More like a third chance, and this time around, I don't want to waste a minute. How do you feel about sleeping together tonight?"

"There's nothing I want more." Thad pulled Josh's head down and kissed him.

Josh pulled Thad closer and returned the kiss. He whispered in Thad's ear, "Your place or mine?"

"My place is kind of crowded. With all our guests, we'd have to be quiet. I'd be embarrassed if your dad heard us going at it."

"True. No point keeping everyone awake all night. My place is totally deserted. And since I've never met any of them, I don't care if my neighbors hear us."

"Then it's settled. Your place it is."

Linda stood with her hands on her hips. "Hey, what about me?"

Josh let go of Thad and turned to Linda. "Well, you could join us if you want, but I assumed you'd want to sleep with that sexy Latin man you brought with you."

"No offense, you're both very sexy men, but I'm thinking I'd get a lot more attention from Rafael. Are you going to escort me back to Philip's? Or should I just walk back by myself."

Philip and Rafael waved from the other side of the police line. Thad, Josh, and Linda practically ran to them, talking at the same time in an attempt to explain what had happened.

Philip finally got everyone's attention. "It's over now. Let's all go back to the house for some hot chocolate and peppermint brownies."

Josh grabbed Thad's hand and walked over to Philip. "I hope you don't mind, but we're going to have to get a rain check for those peppermint brownies. Thad's coming over to my place to tuck me in. Don't wait up!"

Josh held Thad's hand as they walked through Dupont Circle and down P Street to the West Park. He ignored the whistles and catcalls from passing cars. He didn't care what anyone else thought. He was just happy to be with Thad.

They held hands through the lobby, and when the elevator door closed, they stood face to face, holding hands and gazing into one another's eyes. When the doors opened on the fourth floor, they laughed and ran across the hall, working together to get the key in the lock and the door open. They fell into the apartment, giggling like schoolboys as they rolled around on the floor and tickled each other until they finally collapsed in a heap, laughing too hard to get up.

The next kiss was almost an accident. As they laughed, they pressed their noses together and the energy changed from wildly playful to intensely serious. Like they were just now aware of how close together they were, their kisses intensified as they explored each other with hungry eyes and trembling hands.

Josh held Thad's face in his hands and kissed his nose. "We are not going to do this on the floor inside the front door. I don't care if we move to the sofa, the bed, the balcony, or the shower, but we're not staying here."

Thad jumped up. "I agree." He ripped off his shirt, threw it at Josh, and ran. Josh chased him into the living room and had no trouble catching him on the sofa. Thad yanked Josh's shirt off and pulled him close, pressing his chest up against Josh's and kissing his chin. He reached up and kissed Josh's lips as he slid his hand down Josh's chest, pinching each nipple gently, savoring the feel of the silky hair against his fingers.

Josh moaned. Thad broke away and dared Josh to chase him as he ran into the bedroom. Seconds later, the jeans he'd been wearing came flying out the door, followed by a pair of tighty-whities. Josh jumped off the sofa, stripping off his clothes as he made his way to the bedroom.

He gasped. Thad was sprawled across the bed in all his naked glory. Josh admired the sculpted body and ran his hands through the dense, tight curls of reddish-blond hair that covered his chest and disappeared beneath the sheet wrapped around his waist. Josh stepped back, taking in the sight, studying every curve and memorizing every nook and cranny.

Thad motioned for Josh to join him. Josh stepped closer. Thad reached out, grabbed his hand and pulled him into the bed. The first thing Josh noticed was the warmth. The heat coming from Thad's body drew Josh in like a moth to a flame. Then he noticed the hardness of Thad's body, and felt the tightly curled hair that covered him brushing against his arms, chest, and thighs.

They settled into each other's arms, pulling each other close, exploring the lover's dance they'd waited so long to enjoy together with rabid curiosity and lusty demands. There was no top or bottom, no dominant versus submissive, or passive. They were both totally aggressive, taking in turns whatever they wanted, as happy to give as to receive.

Josh took Thad on the sofa and the kitchen table. Thad took Josh in the shower—twice—on the living room floor, and toward morning, again in the bed. In between, they kissed and cuddled, told each other deep, dark secrets, and tried to get some sleep.

THAD woke up the next morning with his head on Josh's chest and Josh's arm over his shoulder. Though the circumstances were less than ideal, his first night sleeping with Josh had been everything he had hoped for and more. In truth, there hadn't been a lot of sleeping. Thad smiled and wondered if any of Josh's neighbors had heard the noise they'd made.

"You awake?" Josh whispered.

Thad rolled over so his chin was on Josh's chest. "Yeah. Have I ever told you that you have the dreamiest brown eyes I've ever seen?"

Josh smiled. "I don't think so. Have I ever told you how much I love you?"

Thad rolled his eyes in an exaggerated way. "That's all I ever hear from you. Can't you come up with anything else?"

Josh laughed and kissed him on the forehead. "Last night was sensational. I'm really glad we waited. Having sex for the first time with someone I'm in love with tops anything I've ever experienced."

"Same here. Did I hurt you?"

"Yes, and remembering how makes me hard. Wanna go again?"

Thad reached under the sheet. "We really need to get up so we can help Philip get ready for dinner. I'm sure he's already up to his chin in holiday meal preparations."

Josh stuck out his lower lip. "Please?"

"No, we really can't. There's too much work to do."

"Then you better quit stroking my dick."

Thad tightened his grip. "I can't. How about a compromise?"

"I'm all about compromise. What's your offer?"

"Meet me in the shower?"

Josh groaned. "Let's go!"

• 54 •

JOSH looked over the sumptuous feast Philip had prepared for the guests sitting around the Thanksgiving table. The aroma of cinnamon, roasted turkey, and fresh yeast rolls filled the air, causing Josh's stomach to growl. Thad took a seat to the right of Philip, who sat at the head of the table, resplendent in a purple paisley smoking jacket and black turtleneck.

Thad patted the chair next to him. "Sit here, Josh." Linda and Rafael rounded out his side of the table. Ed sat at the foot of the table with Greg to his right, then Tom Freeman and Thad's parents, Alex and Mary Parker.

Philip cleared his throat. "Thanks, all of you, for joining us. I'm thankful you're all here. Whether connected to me by blood or some other bond, you're my family and I love you all. Before we eat, if you don't mind, I'd like to ask everyone to share something they are thankful for this holiday season. Mary, could you start us off?"

Everyone turned toward Mary. She had Thad's green eyes, and except for her chestnut hair, could almost have passed for his twin. "Oh dear, where do I start? I'm thankful for so much we could be here all day." She smiled and looked around the table. "I'm grateful for my kind and loving husband, for my sweet, generous, and fabulous brother, and the gift Philip's presence in this family has been to my son, and for the fine man Thad has become."

Alex ran a hand through his wavy black hair, then wiped both hands across the top of his lap. "Let me see. I'm thankful for nearly forty years of marriage to the most wonderful woman I know, for our son, who makes me more proud with each passing day, and that he has finally found someone to share his life with."

"My turn." Thad turned to Philip and then to his parents. "I'm grateful for my family and the unconditional way you have always loved me." He nodded to Ed and Greg. "I'm thankful for my friends— those I've had for years and those I've only just met." He turned to Josh. "And I'm grateful that Linda talked you into moving to DC, that you finally figured out Philip was not my lover, that you survived being the target of a serial killer, and that we'll have the rest of our lives to sort it all out."

Thad sat back down in his chair. Josh felt Thad grab his hand beneath the table and squeeze. Tom Freeman cleared his throat. Josh wondered what his father would say and hoped he wouldn't be embarrassed. Like everyone else at the table, he looked at Tom expectantly.

Tom glanced up and down the table before settling his gaze on Josh. "I'm thankful for a son who has always been there for me, despite the fact I wasn't always there for him. I love you, Josh."

"Thanks, Dad." Josh felt the emotion in his throat. "I love you too."

"I'm thankful to be part of this celebration," said Greg. "I'm also thankful for good friends like Ed, Thad, and Josh, and for my mentor, Philip, whose rock-steady support and constant encouragement give me hope that I can one day do half as good a job as curator as he does."

Thad squeezed Josh's hand again. He knew why—no telling what Ed would say. They both turned to Ed.

"I guess it's my turn," Ed said. He looked around the table and smiled. "I'm thankful for Philip and all he's done for me over the years. He's like a father to me, and I wouldn't be here without him. I'm also thankful for my friends, and am happy that Josh and Thad have ended up together. Finally I'm grateful to Josh for making me a local hero and for the impact celebrity has had on my love life."

After the laughter died down, Rafael stood. "I'm thankful that last night, this beautiful woman agreed to be my wife." Applause and exclamations erupted around the table.

Linda flashed the ring she now wore on her left hand. "I'm thankful that Rafael finally asked me to marry him, and that he's okay with Josh being my maid of honor." Everyone laughed. "I can't imagine asking anyone else. Will you do it, Josh?"

Josh stroked his chin as he considered the question. "As long as I don't have to wear one of those ugly bridesmaid dresses, I'd be honored."

She put a hand on his shoulder. "I'm thankful that my best friend in the world has finally grown up, and along the way, found himself the perfect partner. I'm so proud of you. And I'm so grateful that Thad took such good care of you when you were recovering, and for Philip's generosity in hosting us this weekend."

Josh looked around and realized this was his family. The people he loved most in the world were in this room, sitting around this table. He stood up and remained silent for a moment as he took it all in. An expectant silence filled the room as everyone focused their attention on Josh.

"Before moving here, I really thought the best years of my life were behind me. I was sure I would never find love again and felt like I had nothing to live for." He looked at Thad and smiled, then turned to Linda.

"I'm thankful for Linda, my adopted sister. She's seen me do a lot of stupid things over the years and has never been shy about letting me know when she thinks I've made a mistake. It's because of her that I had the courage to move here. Take good care of her, Rafael."

Rafael nodded solemnly and reached his arm protectively across her shoulder. "I will."

"I'm thankful for my father. For a lot of different reasons, we've never had an especially close relationship. That's changed now, and I'm grateful. I love you, Dad.

"I'm thankful for Ed and Greg. Next to Linda and Thad, you're the best friends I've ever had. I can't imagine how different things would have been here without you.

"I'm thankful that Mr. and Mrs. Parker did such a good job raising Thad. He's the finest man I've ever met, and in just the past few months, he's made me a better man too. Thank you for welcoming me into your family like a long-lost son.

"Philip, I'm thankful to be part of your family. You are, beyond a doubt, the most incredible man I've ever met. Thad told me about James and the trust fund, and all you've done over the years for so many abandoned young men. I'm especially grateful for the way you took Thad under your wing when he came out."

Josh looked at Thad. "Finally I'm thankful to have found Thad. He's shown me that there's a lot more to loving someone than sharing a bed. Thanks for all you've done for me over the past few weeks. Because of you, I feel alive like I never have before. I love you."

Ohs and aws erupted around the table when Josh fell to one knee in front of Thad. "Thad Parker, I would be honored if you'd marry me."

Green eyes gazed back at him above a smile that lit up the room. "I can't imagine my life without you. I'm yours for as long as you'll have me."

Everyone applauded as Josh took his seat. "I love you all. And I'm thankful there's nobody else at this table. I'm starving! Now can we eat?"

For as long as he can remember, MICHAEL RUPURED has loved to write. Before he learned the alphabet, he filled page after page with rows of tiny little circles he now believes were his first novels and has been writing ever since. He grew up in Lexington, Kentucky, where he came out as a gay man at the age of twenty-one in the late 1970s. He considers it a miracle that he survived his wild and reckless twenties.

By day, Michael is an academic. He develops and evaluates financial literacy programs for youth and adult audiences at the University of Georgia and is Assistant to the Dean for Family and Consumer Sciences Education. He's received numerous awards and honors over the years and is a Distinguished Fellow of the Association for Financial Counseling and Planning Education. Michael is also an avid gardener, a runner, and because he loves it and rarely misses a class, is known locally as the Zumba King.

In 2010, he joined the Athens Writers Workshop, which he credits for helping him transition from writing nonfiction to writing fiction. Michael writes gay romance thrillers that, in addition to entertaining the reader, highlight how far the gay rights movement has come in the last fifty years. A serial monogamist who is currently between relationships, Michael writes with his longhaired Chihuahua, Toodles, in his lap from his home in Athens, Georgia.

To find out what Michael's up to now, visit his blog: http://rupured.com, follow him on Twitter: @crotchetyman, or send an e-mail to mrupured@gmail.com.

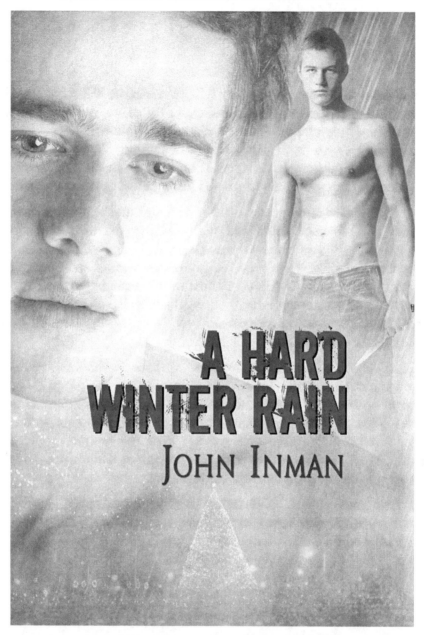

A HARD WINTER RAIN

JOHN INMAN

CPSIA information can be obtained at www.ICGtesting.com
Printed in the USA
LVOW070911081212

310698LV00002B/75/P